The Fauna and the Flora

Book 1: Return To Chenoa City

Ali Cattail

The Fauna and the Flora

Book 1: Return to Chenoa City

© 2025 Ali Cattail

ISBN 979-8-90046-156-4

Published by Restless Forest Books

An imprint of Puckmedia

RestlessForest.com

Printed in the United States of America

This book is dedicated to soap opera fans:

The most loyal people on Earth...

Prologue: The Outer Forest

Trees tower like skyscrapers over the forest floor. At just three inches tall, Victor Newmouse towers... over a dead body.

It's uncanny.

The dead mouse looks exactly like him: the same walnut brown fur, the same muscular tail. Even his mouse 'stache looks the same.

Victor kneels in the dirt beside his dead doppelgänger. His ears twitch, sensing for any witness to the scene.

No. Only the wind knows his secret—and it dares not breathe a word. This creature's cruel fate has just become Victor's strange fortune.

The best-laid plans of mice go oft' awry...

Standing too fast, the tangled underbrush swirls beneath him. He touches the back of his head, and his paw returns a dizzy vision of blood.

A surge of urgency floods him. He does not belong here. The Outer Forest is unfamiliar—but its inhabitants are infamous.

In the distance, the hollow hum of water suggests he's near The Great River.

Follow the riverbank out of the forest and disappear into the prairie.

He rolls up the sleeves of his favorite black satin button-up, reaches into his black trouser pocket, and retrieves an antique brass watch.

The sun will be setting in a few hours.

"I'll be dammed. I've got to get out of here."

THE FAUNA AND THE FLORA
STARRING...

VICTOR NEWMOUSE

A single green leaf sweeps across the ground, skimming over the top of worn boots. Victor kneels down to pick it up, examines it, twirls it between his fingers, then flicks it over his shoulder.

The leaf catches a breeze, moving swiftly through the air and landing into soft ivory fur.

GRACE ATOMS

Grace turns her head, feeling the leaf flutter down her back. She gently sways her hips and swats it away with her long tail.

The leaf sails away on a gust of wind before suddenly lodging in a nest of honey blonde curls.

MIKKI NEWMOUSE

Mikki plucks the leaf from her hair, holding it delicately in her palm, then takes a quiet breath and blows it into the air.

The leaf dances away, swirling between two long ears. A paw reaches up to catch it mid-flight.

JACKRABBITT ABBITT

JackRabbitt grins, clutching it tightly, then flings it high into the air.

The leaf soars to the treetops, then drifts lazily onto a silver-feathered shoulder.

KATHRA CHANSOAR

Kathra raises an eyebrow, casts a downward glance, then brushes it away with her wing.

The leaf

tumbles

down

and dissolves into script:

Chapter One

From Forest To Farm

The forest and the prairie are the yin and yang of the world—distinctly different, yet harmoniously connected by The Great River. For some creatures, stepping off the edge of either side means stepping off the edge of the universe. For Victor Newmouse, however, it's all just another place to set up shop. He earned his first million scraps while most mice his age were still being fed by their mothers. Now is simply an opportunity to do it again.

As the cool darkness of woodland gives way to the increasing light and heat of the prairie, he stops for a cleansing drink of rainwater that has collected on a fern. He wipes the dripping liquid from his snout and glares back once more toward Chenoa City.

With a defiant flick of his tail, he growls, "To hell with you all," then slips through the final branches that separate the life he's leaving from... whatever lies ahead.

Grass.

Nothing but grass.

Can't see through it. Can't see over it.

Continuing south along the forest edge, he—w*hack*—walks straight into a burr bush, ripping the finely woven fibers of his satin shirt.

His fur is instantly invaded by little green burrs.

Sharp. Sticky. Unrelenting.

"This must be my lucky day," he quips, plucking a few burrs from his fur.

Gradually, the grass becomes thinner until it becomes… beans!

A bean field.

There must be a farm nearby.

He scurries along the planted path toward higher ground and climbs atop a mound of dirt. The brightness of the prairie sun is blinding to a creature who is used to living in the shadows, but he can mostly make out the terrain. Fields of sky-high corn and wheat sit alongside sprawling plots of lettuce and squash. The river continues south beyond the prairie, but here, it spills into a lively little brook. Near the water, a mill wheel spins and splashes beside a shipping port.

A community has settled here.

Victor has bought and sold enough real estate to recognize the distinct architectural styles of different animal families. This appears to be a mixed community—mostly mice, squirrels, and rabbits—but the commercial farming operation is definitely of mouse-proportion.

A big barrel barn, a tall log silo, and a leafy picnic pavilion stand clustered together. Further in the distance, a red roof catches his eye. The peculiar roof sits atop a stately old tree stump farmhouse, settled deep in a meadow.

Refuge.

The tree stump farmhouse is backed up to the woods. If he's stealth, he can reach it without running afoul of the field mice. The farm workday will provide enough distraction for him to sneak through the back door, scrounge a few medical supplies, and perhaps grab dinner to-go.

With sun-blind determination, Victor sets his path toward the red-roofed farmhouse. The sheer heat of the day is exhausting. He unbuttons another button on his torn black satin shirt. As he passes an old windmill, the breeze ripples through his burr-infested fur.

He slips easily under a broken fence post and crouches underneath a weathered old swing, half-buried in grass and wildflowers.

He watches.

He waits.

No light is shining through the windows—or beneath the door.

The owner doesn't appear to be around.

Staying low to the ground, he scrambles down a cobblestone pathway and creeps up the steps to the home's back entrance.

But then—

He stumbles. He misses a step. He crashes onto the stone with a hard *smack*!

He freezes.

Crouching.

Waiting for the commotion to stir the attention of somemouse inside—

But nothing happens.

With a round, cupped ear to the ground, he listens for activity.

No voices.

No vibrations.

The house is empty.

He taps the door lightly with his knuckles, twists the wooden knob, and pulls it open confidently, like a magician revealing a trick. He slips through the arched doorway, gently clicking the door behind him.

It's dark inside this unlit house on a blazing summer afternoon.

He scans the walls for a light switch.

No electricity.

Charming.

Slowly, his eyes adjust enough to make out his surroundings.

He's in a kitchen.

A large picture window sits above a sink, its curtains drawn, leaving the room in shadow. He separates the curtains just enough to let in a few beams of light... but not enough to attract attention.

In the center of the room sits a modest dining table. Along the walls, an elaborate set of carved-wood cabinetry and countertops stretch into the darkness. To his right, an old-world-style icebox—and to his left, a wood-burning stove with an iron pot hanging above the cooktop.

A small fire smolders.

He grabs a pitcher of water, pours it into the pot, and waits for it to boil.

Somemouse has been here recently.

But for now, it's silent.

It's safe.

Not a creature is stirring, not even a—

Suddenly—

From the shadows, a scream pierces his ears.

His head swells with a throbbing ache.

He spins around, searching for the direction of the ear-splitting shriek.

As he struggles to focus his eyes, a female voice shouts.

"Out my house, varmint. Now!"

Blame it on instinct or blame it on the head injury—

He lunges.

In a flash, he's wrestling the shrieking figure into his arms, one paw clamped tightly over her mouth.

"Sorry, doe. I can't have you screaming and bringing the field mice in here."

She tries to cry out, but her sound is smothered beneath his paw.

"*Shh! Shh!* Quiet now. I won't hurt you."

She thrashes in his arms.

"I'm just looking for some hot water and help. I was injured in the forest!"

She's a small mouse, barely half his size, but she's putting up a fight.

Flashes of her ivory fur streak through the dim light as his paws sink deeper into her downy texture, clasping onto her slender bones.

Guilt grabs hold of him.

He would never lay harsh paws on a womouse.

He just needs a pot of hot water!

"Okay, okay. I'm going to let you go, doe. But promise me you'll stop screaming. I've... got a bit of a headache."

She nods her head, and he releases his paws.

She steps back from his reach.

Slowly.

Cautiously.

Then—

She dashes to the wooden countertop, reemerging with a pair of —salad tongs?!—and she's thrusting at him, as if she had a sword.

"For heaven's sake." He chuckles. "Salad tongs?! What are you going to do with those? Toss me out of here?"

She is not amused.

She charges toward him, snapping the tongs wildly around his head with a *snip* and a *snap* until—

"Yeowww!"

She rips the tip of his ear.

The thin skin tears in two.

She returns to parrying position, poised for counterattack.

Victor can hear the pain in his ear—a cruel trick of the senses— as the blood pulses, dripping onto the floor.

"That is going to leave a mark."

A wry smile snaps across his face.

"Well, doe, I suppose I deserve it."

"Consider it a warning," she hisses, snapping the tongs—*snip, snap*—sharp as a blade.

"And stop calling me 'doe'... or these tongs will find *more* tender bits of yours to snip!"

So much tenacity for a womouse who won't even look me in the eye!

He lets out a breathy chuckle, wincing as the blood pools in his paw.

"Well, now we're getting somewhere, at least."

He scans the room for a towel.

"Tell me your name, and we can get down to business."

She allows for a long silence that only seems to magnify the sound of his throbbing pain.

"I... am Grace Atoms, and *you*... are a trespasser."

"There now. Names are a good start to any negotiation! My name is Victor Newm..."

He pauses.

"My name is Victor Miller. You may call me Victor."

She lifts her chin defiantly.

"Very well... Mr. Miller. Now, since you seem to have an injury of the ear, perhaps you didn't hear me the first time. Get out of my house, or I'll make more than salad of you!"

"I'm inclined to believe you... Grace."

He lets the name settle.

"But now I have *two* wounds to tend to."

She taps the salad tongs against the countertop with a slow, rhythmic beat.

A reminder.

"I'd wager a bet you had the first one coming to you, too."

"Well, that's a bet you'd lose."

His body wobbles, weakening.

"Listen, I was attacked and robbed on my way out of the forest, and... can't you see I'm bleeding here?"

The question somehow stuns her into silence.

Only the sound of the boiling water fills the air.

"Fetch your hot pot then," she insists, softening somewhat. "I have sycamore leaves in the cabinet. We'll get you fixed up, and then you can be on your way."

Breathing a sigh of relief, Victor allows himself the feeling that he's averted one crisis. Now, he's ready to resolve the original one. He turns his attention to the stove and reaches for the hot hanging pot.

Then—

A wave of dizziness crashes over him.

"Ah, I think I'm going to..."

He staggers. He stumbles. He reaches out to steady himself.

There's nowhere to go but down.

He collapses—and the hot water pot follows, splashing and crashing to the kitchen floor.

Burned.

Wet.

Bleeding.

Covered in burrs.

His gaze drifts upward, searching for Grace.

She's standing above him.

Holding a carving knife.

He sighs.

"Put down the knife, Grace. You can't kill a mouse who's already dead."

Chapter Two

The Deal

Slowly...

blink

his eyes...

blink

open.

An old clock pendulum swings back and forth.

Victor lies comfortably in bed, legs and arms tucked under a thin blanket. Daylight filters through the flowing curtains of an open window, spilling soft beams into the room. His black satin shirt, once torn, has been mended and draped neatly over the back of a quilt rack.

In the corner of the room, Grace is poised in a rocking chair, lost in thought, slowly swaying with the motion.

"No salad on the menu today?"

Victor nods toward the tray of food sitting next to him on the bedside table.

Grace shifts upright, preparing for another round of words with the mysterious stranger.

"It would have wilted. You've been asleep for a full day."

His eyes dart around the room as he processes his surroundings. He pushes himself upright, his mind and body simultaneously switching on.

He lifts a paw to his head—

Bandages. Neatly wrapped.

He kicks the thin blanket aside and glances down.

His fur is clean. No burrs.

Grace hadn't killed him.

She had cared for him.

Tock.

Tock.

Tock.

Tock.

"Quite a timepiece you have here."

For once, Victor doesn't know what to say.

"Yes," she replies curtly. "My father collected them."

"Your father? Will he be here soon?"

Her shoulders stiffen visibly.

"No, sir. You are in my house, in my spare room, and you are alive because of me... but I can change that at any time."

"You drive a hard bargain," he sighs, absorbing the emptiness, the lifelessness of the room.

"You've paid the price with a piece of your ear, I'm afraid."

Damn it.

He hadn't forgotten, but hearing it aloud makes it real all over again. His ear twitches involuntarily at the reminder, and pain lances through the raw wound. He resists the urge to touch it.

"Let that serve as a reminder for you to not enter a mouse's premises without her permission."

"I had no intention of—"

She holds out her paw to stop him right there.

"You could have chosen to knock on the front door. And I would have helped you then, as I have helped you now."

His lips press together in a fleeting moment of remorse. The strange emotional mixture of guilt and gratefulness is unsettling to him.

She continues. "Is there somemouse I can contact for you?"

His whiskers twitch as he takes a moment to consider how best to answer this delicate question. Then, he settles on a reply that sounds like an answer yet gives nothing away.

"There is no one looking for me. And... there is no one I wish to see."

She pauses, curious enough.

"Surely, you have colleagues, or a wife, or children who are wondering where you are."

"My *ex*-wife is likely gallivanting around Chenoa City with a wild hare right now." His expression curdles—half a grimace, half a smirk. "I suppose I should have kept the pictures of their little affair for my photo album."

His gaze drifts toward the curtains dancing in the breeze, mildly entertained and relaxed by their performance.

"I thought she and I were reconciling, rebuilding our family. I guess I was mistaken." He shakes his head dismissively. "Our two children will be well-provided for."

Without realizing it, Victor suddenly becomes very clear to Grace. When she found him in her kitchen, she had first assumed he was a forest varmint, drifting in from the woods to prey, pilfer, and disappear back into the shadows.

But now, with time to think, she sees him differently.

This... Victor. He's confident. Well-spoken. His shirt feels... expensive. Foreign. He doesn't have the grainy scent of a field mouse—and his fur feels groomed and polished.

She decides to press.

"You're a long way from Chenoa City. So, what are you running from?"

He grips the edge of the bed.

"I'm not running from anything! I'm a mouse of action. An adventure-seeker."

His voice strikes sharp against the air, like a clock cranked one notch too far, on the verge of snapping.

He exhales, forcing himself to loosen, to let the tension unwind —

Tock by measured tock.

"There's simply nothing for me in Chenoa City any longer. Now it is time for a new adventure."

Victor settles stiffly against the pillows, regaining composure. He runs a paw over his bandages absent-mindedly.

"Funny thing about this particular adventure: It started with me on the wrong end of a hijacking!

And then, led to our *memorable* introduction."

"The pleasure is all mine, I'm sure," she says, a tiny smile on her face.

Her smile eases him.

He stretches his legs out to claim the bed space, then continues, "I'm a businessmouse by trade, but I have also been an aviator for many years now."

"An aviator?"

"Ah, yes." He waves a paw casually. "Very few mice know the practice of aviation."

Shifting toward the bedside table, he pours a cup of water from the familiar pitcher.

"I have a variety of feathered friends who are happy to provide flight services in exchange for payment."

Grace tilts her head, puzzled.

The idea of a mouse flying on a bird is completely perplexing.

"The Colonel—one of the most steadfast crows I've ever known— agreed to carry me from the forest to the prairie. It had been a long journey, and we needed a break."

He takes a long, ravenous drink, not realizing how thirsty he actually was.

"We landed in The Outer Forest only briefly."

He pours another cup of water and gulps it down, quenching his long thirst.

"It was quiet and calm... or so I thought."

Thunk!

He slams the cup down on the table.

"There I was, resting on a mossy log, having a drink from my canteen... when, from somewhere behind, I felt a crushing weight come down upon my head. By the time I regained consciousness, a wild mouse had run off with my satchel... and my favorite leaf-leather jacket! He had robbed me!"

Grace leans forward, unconsciously drawn into Victor's tale.

"Did he get away?"

"In a sense, I suppose."

He lets out a slow, measured breath.

"By the time I could focus my eyes, I could see that the mouse was wearing my jacket and my satchel... and he was trying to hijack my best friend!"

He pauses, reflecting on the scene.

"There must have been some great confusion.

The Colonel took off, and the mouse plummeted to the ground.

You see, flying a crow—flying any bird—takes practice. It takes skill. It takes partnership. One mistake can be fatal. The thief learned that lesson the hard way."

She gasps, lifting a paw to her mouth.

"How awful!"

"Awful, yes. But let's not forget: before he fell, he gave me quite a crack to the skull. I was dazed. Disoriented. Bloody. I was certainly in no condition to hold vigil. I must have been a hundred feet away."

He refills his cup of water and takes a long, purposeful drink.

"When I finally came to my senses, that's when I saw it."

"Saw what?" she blurts, now aware of her own investment in the story.

"I saw The Colonel.

Cradling the dead body.

His wings wrapped around it, trembling.

And then—a low, broken caw.

He was weeping.

For me."

Grace's whiskers quiver—just for a second.

But then she catches herself, clearing her throat and stiffening slightly.

"Well, why didn't you just call out to the bird?"

"No, Grace.

Not just a bird.

The Colonel.

My closest confidant."

Victor lowers his ears momentarily.

"If The Colonel could believe that I was the mouse lying dead on the forest floor, well... I knew everyone was capable of believing it."

"So, you said nothing?"

"So, I said absolutely nothing."

He takes a deep inhale, grounding himself.

"The Colonel must have injured his talon in the struggle. He tried in vain to grab hold of the body and fly off, but ultimately, he had to leave it behind.

Once he was gone, I approached the thief, lying there.

And as I looked into his dead eyes, I realized he had given me a strange gift.

By now, I'm sure the whole forest believes I'm dead."

"But why? Why would you want everyone to think you are dead?" she asks, now clenching her tail in her paws.

"Well, Grace. I suppose the opportunity was simply... too perfect to ignore."

His gaze drifts downward to the plain white sheets, where his secret has just been spilled.

"I left Chenoa City in search of new life.

Eventually, someone would have come looking for me.

But...

No one would come looking for a dead mouse.

Now, would they?"

He looks up and realizes that Grace is once again avoiding his eye contact. For the first time since the incident in the forest, he feels a twinge of shame.

She folds her paws neatly in her lap, settling deeper into her chair as the weight of his story settles over her.

"You see, Grace, regrets are only useful if they spur you into action. For me, the action is a new life... in a new place. Who knows? Maybe here."

"You? You want to live in Southbrook?"

The idea of this mouse adventurer settling into a farm community like Southbrook is amusing to her. She tries to suppress a chuckle... but is unsuccessful.

"What's so funny about that?" he asks in earnest.

"Nothing. Oh, sure! You could live in Southbrook. You could work in the field or stock the grocery store, or you could... sell oatcakes at the church bake sale!"

"You laugh," he says, "but I could sell oatcakes to a lion."

Grace laughs in spite of herself—

And her laugh has a cleansing effect on Victor Newmouse.

Perhaps Southbrook could be a place to wash away the foul taste of the forest and begin life anew as Victor Miller.

In this moment, in this place, he's comfortable. Even the silence following the final breath of Grace's laugh is comfortable—and comfort is a feeling he hasn't known in a long time.

"Tell me more about Southbrook," he politely demands. "Tell me more about your farm here. Well, how am I to choose a job unless I know the lay of the land? Also, I... think I'd appreciate the company."

Unwilling to admit that she is warming up to her houseguest, Grace rocks slowly in her chair, then chooses a noncommittal response.

"You need to eat."

"I will eat... but only if you tell me about Southbrook while I do it.

And please, call me Victor.”

Stubbornly, she replies, “Okay, Mr. Miller.”

Victor sees the crooked smile on her lips but notices again how she hangs her head low.

Shifting his concentration to the tray of food beside him, he takes in the mouthwatering array of fresh farm delicacies, far less common in the forest: sweetgrass slaw, roasted potatoes, juicy tomatoes, a colorful bowl of mixed wildflowers, and barley biscuits with a small jar of honey on the side.

Greedily, he attacks the tray as if he’s afraid it might run away.

Grace is pleased to see her patient enjoying his meal.

“Southbrook...” she says with quiet pride, “is the Glowstone of the Great River. I’ve lived here all my life. My father and mother built most of the town while living right here on this farm.”

She continues to rock lightly in her chair.

“It started as a homestead, then grew into a small commercial operation... and then into a larger one. My father and his team worked the fields, and my mother opened the grocery store.”

Her paws unclasp in her lap, fingers spreading slightly.

“They believed in building a better life for themselves and for our family. I learned everything I know from what they taught me.”

Her breath deepens, syncing with the rhythm of her rocking.

“My family, the Atoms family, founded the church, the community center, and contributed to the opening of the first schoolhouse in Southbrook. The town came to rely on their ingenuity.”

Her rocking slows, then stops altogether.

"Now, it's all my responsibility."

Tilting an ear to the ever-present ticking of the clock her father patiently restored—one of many—she continues.

"When my father got sick, my mother became his caretaker.

She barely ate. She barely slept.

She died twelve days after him."

Her tail slowly coils around the base of the chair leg.

"It became my job to run the farm, to manage the store—and, most importantly, to continue their legacy of service to the community. Atoms Farm and Grocery is the largest food supplier in Southbrook. We provide resources to the town and share profits with over three hundred employees."

"Remarkable," he whispers... but he isn't commenting on the business operation. The sentiment is reserved for Grace herself.

In all the haze of the past few days, with all his focus on his own predicament, he realizes now he's been so thoughtless.

How could he not see it before?

She's blind.

Suddenly unable to sit still—or to sit at all—he returns his empty food tray to the bedside table and drops his feet to the floor.

His lungs are void of air.

He springs toward the open window, desperately pulling the dancing curtains aside to catch a breath.

She senses the change in him but doesn't know why.

Have I said too much?

She stands, moving to occupy the empty space beside him at the window, choosing to shift back into a more professional tone.

"What do you see when you look through this window, Mr. Miller?"

Flustered by the realization that she *can't* see—and rattled by his own reaction to it—he stammers, "Uhm. Fields? Crops? Looks like a pumpkin patch in the distance?"

"What you see," she smiles, "is a pumpkin patch. What I see," he flinches, "is future community housing."

"I've been working for years on a project that will convert each of those individual pumpkins into a single-family home on a spacious plot of land. And I've been investing in the latest innovations for sustainable housing, too. We've already built a dozen prototypes. Now, we just need to secure the remaining supplies to begin the final stages of development."

She brushes away the ivory fur bangs that have fallen in front of her face.

"It's the continuation of my parents' mission for Southbrook. Pumpkin Acres will be a place where generations of creatures can live, raise their families, and be free."

Who is this womouse?

He turns his head, seeing her—truly seeing her—for the first time.

The doe who sliced his ear, then saved his life.

Blind. Alone.

A creature who gives of herself yet takes so little in return.

Look at her.

She weighs next to nothing.

She's barefoot.

She wears none of the fads and fashions of the forest females.

Instead, she dons a long, loose sundress that was once white, patterned with tiny, faded bluebells.

If anyone deserves to taste the sweetness of success...

It's her.

Victor gives his mouse 'stache a tug, as if drawing from its strength.

"Grace, I'd like to propose a deal. I will join the Pumpkin Acres construction crew in exchange for room and board. You need labor to help build your community, and I need a place to recover. It's a small town, and I assume there is no hotel..."

Grace is usually much more cautious than the proposal she's considering. But something in her trusts Victor... or wants to.

His help would be beneficial to the project, but that's not why she's about to agree to it.

The truth is, he's the most exciting thing to happen to my life in a long time... or ever.

Allowing a few *tocks* of the clock to fill the silence between them, she holds out her paw formally to shake his.

"Alright, Mr. Miller. You have yourself a deal."

Chapter Three

Outhouses

Victor Newmouse knows all about organic housing construction...

But Victor Miller stays quiet and listens as Grace explains the process.

"Timing is everything. We have only a small window of time at the end of each growing season to preserve the pumpkin at its peak size and shape."

It's been two days since Victor woke up... in more ways than one.

And in that time, he has observed the way Grace navigates her world.

Inside the tree stump farmhouse, she commands every corner with confidence, her paws gliding effortlessly along familiar surfaces while her tail sweeps ahead, detecting anything out of place.

Outside, on the farm ground where she now stands, a carved hickory wood cane scouts each step before she takes it. Her tail moves with instinctive precision—sweeping lightly ahead to test for obstacles, then trailing behind, tracing the ground in a silent map of where she's been.

"The key ingredient to our success here is a pine sap compound called Stickum."

She taps her cane on the dry dirt, stirring a cloud of dust.

"Come with me," she tells him. "I'll show you the prototype we completed last year."

Walking side by side toward the patch, she continues to school Victor on the construction process he knows full well.

"When the pumpkin is ripe, we remove the strands and seeds to create a hollow. Then, we wash and smooth the interior and apply three full coats of Stickum to preserve the vegetable structure from deteriorating. It's a labor-intensive process, and raw materials are crucial. Stickum is harvested from pine trees, of course, so we can only import it from Chenoa City."

His mouth runs dry as a look of delight washes over her face.

"Well now, you must know all about Stickum, Mr. Miller, being from Chenoa City. It's my understanding the Stickum manufacturing operation is a large part of the local economy."

"Yes, I've been privy to the Stickum production process," he says quickly and curtly.

He does not want to lie... but he also does not want to reveal the extent of his knowledge—or give away any clues about his identity.

He's on the cusp of reincarnation here!

Grace notes his tart response and shifts the conversation forward.

"Yes. Once the structure has been stabilized, we are ready to begin construction. We hang the doors and windows, install the chimney and stove, and depending on the size and shape of the natural pumpkin, we also build a staircase to the second, or even third, floors."

Perking her ear toward the clanging sound of an approaching tool belt, she chimes, "Ah! I hear our construction crew chief coming now. Mr. Miller, meet my assistant, Biff Milson. He is the craftiest squirrel in all of Southbrook. There's no job he can't do."

Squirrel?!

Victor looks up and sees a tall, muscular squirrel laboring upright toward them. He's two full heads above Victor and Grace, carrying a full load of lumber in his arms. He's wearing a torn overshirt and cutoff work pants. His tool belt sags below his hefty hips, and his long tail thrashes mightily behind him.

As Biff drops the load of lumber to the ground, the earth shakes, sending a few field mice scurrying.

He removes the half-shell hard nut hat that sits atop his head and runs his fingers through his sun-bleached fur.

Beaming at Grace, he announces, "It's gonna be a hot one today. We better get down to work, or we'll be eatin' pumpkin all winter long."

A toothy smile plants itself on his broad face.

Grace returns his smile, giving a polite giggle of delight at his enthusiasm for the project.

"Well then, it's a good thing we have two extra paws," she exclaims. "Biff, I would like you to meet Victor Miller. He will be joining our construction team."

Victor has never seen a smile disappear from a face so quickly.

In Chenoa City, there are a hundred creatures with a hundred different reasons not to like him, but Biff dislikes Victor's mere introductory presence.

The feeling is mutual.

Squirrels are better at hiding things than building them.

Biff scratches at the dirt with his toenails. "Ahh, geez, Grace. The beavers are done chuckin' supplies from the river, the gophers are busy diggin' fence posts, and we've got a full crew of rabbits chewin' today. No need for any extra help."

"Nonsense, Biff," she retorts. "There's always a need for more help. Mr. Miller will be contributing through the end of the season."

"Yes, ma'am," Biff responds promptly.

"Put him to good use... and don't go easy on him." Grace smirks, then raps her cane against the ground.

Swiftly, she strides down the path leading to Atoms Grocery, where the day's work awaits her.

Victor is now alone with Biff... and ready to show this squirrel how to manage a construction site.

"Well now, Biff, old boy. I see you have a total of four houses being gutted here today. We can optimize our workday by dividing the—"

"Uhm, I take care of the worksite and the crew around here, George."

Biff may not be the smartest squirrel on the farm, but he knows he's the boss.

"I've got a crew of six rabbits who can gut these pumpkins faster than sixty mice. But, oh... I'm sure I can find a job for you, pip-squeak."

Victor lets out an indignant snort as Biff's face begins to show signs of hard thinking.

"Ya know what? We've got some, uh... outhouses that need to be dug in the back. Yeah. Why don't you grab a shovel over there, start diggin', and... try to stay outta the way."

Outhouses?!

Victor Newmouse has engineered dozens of large-scale construction projects, managed thousands of employees, and earned a billion scraps in the process.

He wickedly imagines himself stuffing Biff into one of the gutted pumpkins.

I'll feed him the seeds and then gut him too!

Victor arches himself upward, takes a step toward Biff, then pauses, remembering Grace.

She deserves to succeed.

So, if outhouses are what Pumpkin Acres needs...

Then Pumpkin Acres will have the best damn outhouses in all of Southbrook!

"I'll do it!" he shouts.

...and I'll do it for Grace.

Victor has been dealing with bullies like Biff his entire life. He refuses to be intimidated by squirrels, rabbits, birds, or anything else on Earth.

They work for him!

Out of nothing, he built a powerful business empire—

From the ground up.

Just days ago, this 'pip-squeak' held a view of the entire forest from his office high atop the tallest tree in Chenoa City.

He was a tycoon—

A titan of industry—

A force to be reckoned with.

But now—

He's dead.

VICTOR NEWMOUSE DEAD

Chenoa City reels in shock today as news spreads of the untimely death of Victor Newmouse, the billionaire engineer, real estate magnate, and architect of the modern forest economy.

Newmouse, founder and CEO of Newmouse Enterprises, perished late last evening when his flight operative, Colonel Austin Douglas, went down over The Outer Forest. "The Colonel," a retired military tactician, survived the crash with only minor injuries. Newmouse's body was recovered and declared dead at the scene.

Authorities have launched an investigation into the crash, but with no clear cause, questions remain about what went wrong.

A Legacy Built From The Ground Up
The loss of Victor Newmouse marks a seismic shift in the landscape of commerce and power across Chenoa City. Known for his daring vision and unapologetic ambition, Newmouse was more than just a business mogul. He was a force of nature.

From his earliest days as CEO of Chansoar Industries to the founding of Newmouse Enterprises, he carved a legacy into the very roots of the forest. His empire was built on aggressive land acquisitions, resource extraction, and an unparalleled ability to turn the natural world into profit.

His company, the largest and most powerful commercial entity in the region, has stakes in mining, real estate, manufacturing, and energy. From upscale treehouses to city-wide development, his work transformed the forest into a thriving metropolis.

Newmouse Tree Tower: A Monument to Power

Of all his achievements, none stands taller—literally or figuratively—than the iconic Newmouse Tree Tower. Once an ancient Black Walnut tree, it was transformed into the corporate headquarters of Newmouse Enterprises, seamlessly blending natural grandeur with modern innovation.

The project carried a price tag of half a billion scraps and took six years to complete, making it the most ambitious corporate expansion in the city's history.

The Tower's winding corridors and graceful suspension bridges rise to its crowning jewel: The Sky Chamber. Built on a reinforced platform, this executive penthouse, wrapped in floor-to-ceiling glass, offers an unmatched panoramic view of the forest, sky, and river—an experience few have been privileged to witness.

Throughout its structure, Newmouse Coal quietly powers a variety of modern amenities: running water, electricity, and Chenoa City's first tree-trunk elevator, ushering visitors in comfort and style.

For those arriving by air, a blazing airstrip crowns The Tower, a bold testament to Victor Newmouse's unwavering vision—a vision that, even in passing, leaves an indelible mark on the skyline of Chenoa City.

The Uncertain Future of an Empire

With Newmouse's unexpected passing, all eyes now turn to the future of Newmouse Enterprises. In an emergency vote, the company's board of directors has elected JackRabbitt Abbitt to step into the role of Chief Executive Officer.

Abbitt, currently CEO of Shabó Cosmetics, is known for his sharp business acumen and unflappable demeanor, and has long been a fixture in the city's corporate scene. However, many question whether he possesses the sheer force of will that defined Newmouse's reign.

Can Abbitt maintain the empire Newmouse built, or will the cracks in the foundation begin to show?

One thing is certain: Chenoa City will never be the same.

For ongoing coverage of Victor Newmouse's legacy and the future of Newmouse Enterprises, stay with The Chenoa City Chronicle— your trusted source for forest commerce, politics, and culture.

Chapter Four

Welcome To Chenoa City

"As the newly appointed Chairmaster and CEO of Newmouse Enterprises, it is my honor to present you with a new vision for the future of this company—a future that encompasses not only Chenoa City... but the entire world."

JackRabbitt Abbitt stands at the head of the grand oak boardroom table in the center of The Sky Chamber, high atop Newmouse Tower.

He glances at the portrait of Victor Newmouse hanging on the far wall, then sharpens his showroom smile.

"Our current business plan is built around Chenoa City real estate expansion." He snaps his fingers. "We need to change course. We need to capitalize on... the export market."

All eyes follow as JackRabbitt strides toward his presentation piece: a custom-built 3D model of the forest. Every territory is represented: Chenoa City's towering structures, the sprawling suburbs, the untamed Outer Forest, and the endless prairielands.

"Why focus on Chenoa City alone when we can sell our resources worldwide?"

He presses a switch on the model's edge.

A soft metallic *click*.

Hidden lights flicker to life, sending ripples across the miniature landscape like water in motion.

"Imagine it. Newmouse coal, lumber, and pine sap—sailing

downriver to The Outer Forest, and flooding back to us as profits well beyond what our local market could yield."

He pauses for a standing ovation.

But instead—

"Let's not hop too far ahead, J.R."

The Ten Gallon Mouse.

He's the biggest mouse in the room—but he's still just a mouse.

"You wanna scrap the urban expansion to do business with those brutes in The Outer Forest?"

He plunges his pen onto the table.

To him, it is a bold, decisive act. To JackRabbitt, it lands like a discarded toothpick, rolling a pitiful distance before coming to an unimpressive stop.

The room, just moments ago alive with corporate theater, now collectively observes... a pen.

Across from him, a crow tilts his head. He extends a broad feather and nudges the pen, testing whether it's even worth acknowledging.

The Ten Gallon Mouse shadows his eyes beneath the brim of his hat, then continues on as if nothing had happened. "Victor's real estate vision put us on the map, plain and simple."

His eyes flick to his lost pen.

Oh, he wants it.

His paw twitches, like a gunslinger itching for the draw.

But he holds.

Ain't worth it.

Not yet.

A throat clears, cutting through the awkward silence.

A nerdy mouse with speckled fur adjusts his red bow tie. "Yes. Well. Real estate development has put my kits through college."

"...and I just bought a third treehouse!" exclaims Olive, a petite mouse with a feather in her hair.

Murmurs and chuckles ripple through the room, paired with a few uncertain glances.

"Look, J.R., you give a hell of a pitch, but I ain't buyin' it." The Ten Gallon Mouse leans back. "Our local markets are turnin' a real nice profit. I don't see no reason to stir up the pot. Hell, I like my toys."

Five mouse heads bob without hesitation, all following the Ten Gallon Mouse's lead—his own personal fan club, forever nodding on cue.

But JackRabbitt has anticipated this response.

He straightens his stance, tightens his tie, and brings both paws to a folded prayer position.

"Our venerable founder, Victor Newmouse—may he rest in peace—had a brilliant but short-sighted vision. Our Ecosystem is thriving! And it can produce enough resources to sustain our local demand while increasing trade."

He walks around his model of the forest, tapping key locations.

"Morel Ground, Acorn Alley, Southbrook. These areas are underdeveloped... and desperate for the resources we can provide."

Without breaking stride, he glides around the table, sliding a presentation packet in front of each board member.

"We're already selling to The Outer Forest—but not efficiently, not at scale. Better trade routes mean bigger profits."

He pauses, running his manicured claws through his trademark bouncy bangs.

"My strategy will make Newmouse Enterprises more than just the dominant force in Chenoa City. We'll be the dominant force… everywhere."

He smacks his own packet down on the table and flips it open.

"On the final page of the proposal, you'll see that I have negotiated tentative deals at 150% above the local price. The Outer Forest has the demand… and they are willing to pay."

For a moment, the air in the room holds still.

The Ten Gallon Mouse wiggles in his seat with capitalistic anticipation.

"Well, now. That's a whole different pot of gravy. You're tellin' me you got verbal agreements with a faction in The Outer Forest?"

JackRabbitt leans in close.

The scent of upscale hare gel lingers on his caramel-colored fur.

"I've got verbal agreements with *four* factions in The Outer Forest."

The Ten Gallon Mouse's eyes glimmer wide.

The five mice who opposed the proposal just moments ago now nod along in approval.

A satisfied grin spreads over JackRabbitt's lips.

He casually tugs at the sleeves of his double-breasted navy jacket.

"Victor ruled the skies. But I command the currents. I've been able to negotiate deals all the way up and down the river."

A few veiled nods and muffled murmurs ripple around the table. Some sit up, intrigued. Others shift uncomfortably in their seats.

At the far end of the table, Kathra Chansoar, a silver-feathered owl, remains still.

Unlike the others, she neither nods nor murmurs.

She just watches.

A saucy rabbit doe leans forward, her eyes sparkling with interest. "Sounds exciting," she says, giving JackRabbitt a wink of approval.

"Yes, it is!" JackRabbitt's long ears lift with the rising energy. "Chenoa City is entering a new era, my friends!"

A voice chimes in from across the table, a portly mole with gray-streaked fur. "The demand for pine sap is high... and we're the leading supplier."

His twin brother jumps in. "There's less competition in exports. We'd own the whole market."

An aristocratic crow shakes his head, the glint of his silver moon pendant catching the light. "No, no. The Outer Forest has no treaties. A few shipments, a few backdoor deals—that's not a trade network."

He tilts his head toward the abandoned pen.

"That pen was more stable than their economy."

The Ten Gallon Mouse's gaze lingers to his pen, stranded in the middle of the table.

His whiskers twitch.

A second crow, adorned with a golden sun pendant, gives his companion a wing-tap. "I'd rather fly over The Outer Forest than into it."

JackRabbitt's tail flicks once, as if striking a match.

"This isn't about flying over The Outer Forest. It's about stabilizing the trade routes. No treaties mean no competition. But hey—if we're not in the mood to make money, I can slow down."

His grin sharpens as the crows exchange thoughtful looks.

Kathra exhales loudly, then straightens a fold in her silk shawl.

The Ten Gallon Mouse nudges his hat up with a slow tap of his paw. "You got vision, J.R.—we all saw that when we put you in the chair. But this idea? It's a gamble. The investors want a sure thing."

The five mice exchange glances and nod along. Where Ten Gallon leads, five mice follow. Always.

A jet-black bat slides off his sunglasses and leans in. "Newmouse Enterprises wasn't built by playing it safe. We don't have to gamble everything at once, but if we don't capitalize, some other company will."

The saucy doe taps her manicured claws against the table. "What if we establish the trade lines first? Secure the contracts, get the groundwork laid. If we succeed, we'd hold the keys to an entire sector of the economy."

JackRabbitt knocks once on the wood. "Now we're talking! If I can just get board approval on these preliminary contracts, I—"

Suddenly—

A voice slices through the room, sharp as a talon.

"Let's end the performance, shall we?"

The debate fizzles out instantly as Kathra leans forward, her silver feathers fluffing in a slow, deliberate wave.

"I appreciate your vision, JackRabbitt. Truly. But the creatures of Chenoa City deserve our..." She searches for the words. "Undivided attention."

She settles onto the table, bringing the tip of her wing to rest under her chin.

"Darling, nobody cares about foreign trade. They care about having homes where they can raise their families. And stores where they can spend their scraps."

"Kathra, I had a feeling you'd—"

She cuts him off, eyes scanning the table.

"Tell me—who here is eager to risk their fortunes on verbal agreements with some creatures we've never met?"

She raises her neck, fixing her wide eyes directly onto JackRabbitt.

"The Outer Forest is *not* our priority. Chenoa City is."

Across the table, a black mouse in a pinstripe suit looks up from his fedora. "Kathra's right. The Federation is keeping a close eye on us. If we start funneling resources outside city limits, it could make us look suspicious. We're already walking a fine line with The UFF."

Silence—

A rare and beautiful moment of corporate unity, built entirely on the shared desire... to not get arrested.

The Ten Gallon Mouse interjects. "Well, maybe it's time we pulled the Everwood Condominium project off the shelf. When Victor pitched it last spring, folks were talkin'. If he were still here, he woulda broke ground by now."

Kathra leans back, as if delivering the final word. "The domestic real estate projects keep everyone happy."

"I agree. Domestic infrastructure keeps the economy thriving," says the nerdy mouse.

The Ten Gallon Mouse nods.

The others do, too.

Kathra looks up to Victor's portrait on the wall. "The Everwood Condominiums were Victor's last great vision. This is, after all, his company. We owe it to him to see it through."

She sweeps her wing across the presentation packet, closing it with a *fwip*.

"Enough posturing. Let's vote."

A flicker of irritation crosses JackRabbitt's face, then vanishes.

"Fine. All in favor of *my* proposal?"

Two mole paws shoot up immediately, joining him with enthusiasm.

The saucy doe effortlessly glides her paw into the air too.

Across the table, the crows shake their heads in disapproval.

The bat raises a wing confidently.

Then, a shy paw lifts halfway—

But the pinstripe mouse clears his throat, and the shy paw drifts back to the table.

The remaining mice—the Ten Gallon fan club—hover in uncertainty.

Their eyes flick to their leader, waiting for a signal.

And then—

JackRabbitt sees it.

The Ten Gallon Mouse nudges his hat up just enough, then shoots a look—too quickly—at Kathra.

Not at his mice. Not at the board.

At Kathra.

Turns out, the Ten Gallon was only half full.

Kathra owns the well.

Without a word, she extends one wing and—*swipe!*—snatches the pen from the center of the table.

Everyone sees it. No one stops her.

She settles back, smoothing the feathers around her face.

The sides of her beak curl slightly.

Not quite a smile—but close.

The Ten Gallon Mouse exhales, his head swaying like a fence post caught in a hard wind.

Then, he tips his hat down a notch. "Sorry, J.R. Now just ain't the time."

Not a single paw twitches. When Ten Gallon decides, so do the rest of the mice.

Kathra scans the room, unsurprised. "It seems you have five votes. But seven is the majority."

JackRabbitt nods. Slow and thoughtful.

Five votes.

Not bad.

Better than I expected.

"Ah, well. Timing is everything, isn't it?"

He returns to his 3D model of the forest and gives it a tap for a job well done.

The Ten Gallon Mouse picks up his briefcase from the floor and sets it on the table in front of him. "Well, that settles it. Dust off them Everwood plans, and we'll give 'em a look next week."

His eyes dart to where his pen once was... then to Kathra.

In his mind, the saloon doors swing open and he challenges her to a duel at high noon.

But he knows better.

He holsters the thought and looks away.

The pen is gone. The point has been made.

And he exits... smaller than he came in.

JackRabbitt moves toward the door, offering reassurances as the board members shuffle out. Some avoid his gaze. Others offer silent sympathy.

The saucy doe thumps in front of him, tugging at the breast of his blazer. "It was a strong idea... but apparently, fear is stronger."

"Well. Fear's a hell of a thing," he muses. "Good thing I don't have any."

She softly touches his chin, then leans in and whispers, "Call me."

He gives her a slow, naughty smile, his lower lip caught gently between his ample incisors.

But then—

Kathra slices her wing between them like a blade, cutting the moment cleanly in two.

With a single dismissive swoop, she brushes the saucy doe toward the door as if shooing away a nuisance.

JackRabbitt straightens, his playful grin now deflated.

"I'll warn you, JackRabbitt, you have your work cut out for you here. Your family has done a beautiful job over at Shabó Cosmetics. But Newmouse Enterprises is a very different animal. It's not the same as selling pine soap."

He raises a brow, but says nothing.

"Darling, you have to adjust your thinking. With a company like this, the goal isn't to sell the most products. The goal is to ensure that everyone keeps buying." She gives him a pat on his shoulder. "I have a lot of faith in you, my dear... but don't get too far ahead of yourself."

JackRabbitt produces an easy smile. "You're right, Kathra. No sense in rushing. After all, patience is a virtue."

He fastens his jacket, his fingers lingering on the final button.

Fact is: He didn't need a win. He needed a list of names.

Now, he knows who will bend and who won't.

Who has power and who only *thinks* they do.

And that... is more useful than a victory.

Chapter Five

Taking Out The Trash

JackRabbitt closes the door behind the final board member.

He flops into his chair, folds his paws behind his head, and kicks his leaf-leather loafers onto the boardroom table.

He tilts his head back, gaze drifting to the massive oil portrait of Victor Newmouse looming large on the far wall.

He gives the portrait a slow, knowing wink.

"Checkmate."

Just then—

The door bursts open.

JackRabbitt's younger half-brother, William, strolls into the room without knocking—a crisp newspaper clutched in one paw. He waves it high, unfolding it with a dramatic flick of his wrist.

He begins to read:

"Can Abbitt maintain the empire Victor built, or will the cracks in the foundation begin to show?"

He crumples the paper between his fingers.

"Who writes this garbage?"

With an effortless toss, the newspaper arcs through the air and lands squarely in the trash.

"Well, how did it go?" William asks, grinning. "Are we celebrating or not?"

JackRabbitt springs forward in his chair, paws dropping to the table. "Five votes. Two more is all I need."

"Well done, brother." William motions to Victor's picture. "One day, your smug face will be up there on the wall."

William gives the portrait a long, unimpressed stare. "Who did Victor think he was anyway—walking around in his stupid silk shirts with that ridiculous mouse 'stache? One good punch and that thing would've flown off like a toupee."

JackRabbitt studies the scattered presentation papers in front of him, then draws them in with a single swipe. "Remind me to have that picture removed."

He spins around in his chair.

"Also, remind me to have this place redecorated—and get rid of that ugly, old Grandfather Clock. Even in death, Victor's still ticking in my ears."

"Ah! Now that you mention it..."

William strolls toward the clock, motioning for JackRabbitt to follow.

He grips the edge and pulls the casement door open with slow flourish—*creeaaak*—revealing a hollow passage and hidden staircase inside.

"The staircase leads up to the landing strip on top of The Tree. It's kind of cool in a magician sort of way." He lifts his paws and wiggles his fingers. "Now you see me... now you don't."

JackRabbitt rolls his eyes. "Are you kidding me? That megalomaniac had a secret entrance installed? Why doesn't that surprise me?" He scans the room. "This whole place reeks of Victor Newmouse. Fortunately, we're one step closer to exterminating all traces of him."

William closes the clock door, mildly disappointed that his brother doesn't share his enthusiasm for the amenity. Oh well. If JackRabbitt won't appreciate a secret passage... he'll save it for his own adventures.

William shifts his focus to the nearest trash can, eager to start the redecorating project.

First up: a portrait of a black crow, encased in a heavy, ornate picture frame.

Upon closer inspection, the crow in the picture is wearing a gleaming gold crown—and in fact, the frame itself is forged from gold.

It's an expensive and enigmatic piece.

William studies it intently—

Then tosses it into the trash.

JackRabbitt gives a sly smile. "Now that I'm on the inside, I can control the day-to-day operations. I just have to dazzle the board long enough to keep my job while I work on buying up majority shares."

He taps his papers into a neat stack, then stands.

"Victor Newmouse was a leech. Someday, Chenoa City will thank me for getting rid of him."

Slowly, he drifts toward the windows, watching the glow beyond the glass.

"I knew that mouse was a crook from the moment he bought the pine sap rights. I see exactly how he operated, William. Look at what he did to the poor fools in Morel Ground.

It was always the same formula: He buys the natural resource rights, mines out the town, sells the product back to them at a higher price, then moves on somewhere else after he's emptied it all dry.

Eventually, he would have done the same thing here.

Chenoa City would have become a wasteland—and he'd be long gone, sucking the blood of another unsuspecting host."

William patiently endures another one of his brother's Victor Newmouse rants. No need to engage in this particular conversation. He's heard it all before.

That leaves him free to scan the room for more treasure to trash.

An hourglass? Trash.

A feather in a display case? Trash.

An ancient-looking mouse head statue made of stone? Definitely trash.

The talking has stopped.

William bets his brother hasn't noticed his absence. So, he interjects a pre-recorded response. "I couldn't agree with you more, JackRabbitt."

"So, why doesn't our father see it that way? He and Kathra are both stuck in the old way of thinking." JackRabbitt quickly unbuttons the collar of his white dress shirt. "When Victor bought up the pine sap rights, do you know what Dad said? *'Go work it out, son. Victor's reasonable.'*"

He laughs.

"Reasonable? That plague-rat wouldn't even hear me out. He just sat there, smiling like he already owned the whole damn forest."

He casts a glance toward his 3D model, still alive and humming with potential.

"Pine sap wasn't just some ingredient. It was the main ingredient in *Fluff Soap*.

Our best seller. Our name brand.

And Victor knew it.

He bought the rights, jacked up the price, and left us with two options: pay him, or start from scratch."

The faint sound of William's latest donation to the trash can reminds JackRabbitt that he's not alone.

"Victor Newmouse could have put Shabó Cosmetics out of business. Our father worked his whole life to build that company."

Suddenly, JackRabbitt catches his own reflection in the glass.

"Taking control of Newmouse was the only way I could right the ship."

William yanks open a drawer, tosses a fistful of papers into the trash, then pauses.

"You sure you can handle running Newmouse while still holding the helm at Shabó?"

JackRabbitt's reflection disappears from the glass as he pivots back to the board table.

"Our family business is a well-oiled machine. But I'm counting on you to do some heavy lifting."

William grunts once. The trash has some weight to it—and he's not about to break a sweat.

He swings open The Sky Chamber door and gives the can a half-hearted shove into the hallway.

"I do the heavy lifting wherever I go."

The can barely hits the floor before Victor's secretary appears at the door.

Bonnie.

A petite, brown mouse.

Very polite. Very accommodating.

The Abbitts would've fired her after Victor's death, but they decided to keep her around for now—just to keep up appearances.

"Another round of trash, Bonnie!" William announces triumphantly, motioning to the full can at her feet.

"Trash?" she repeats, her eyes scanning through the belongings of her beloved former employer. "Victor's photo of Prince Obsidian is... trash?"

William taps the can with his foot. "Nothing sentimental... unless you're sentimental."

"Uh, Bonnie?" JackRabbitt interrupts, sensing the need to do damage control. "I've asked William to gather these things, and I was hoping you could box them up and send them to Mikki."

He grabs Bonnie's tiny paw, sandwiching it between his own.

"I'm sure she will want to preserve these... mementos... for the family."

"Yes, Mr. Abbitt," she responds wearily.

JackRabbitt holds the door open as she steps out, straining to lift the can.

"You're a gem," William murmurs as she disappears down the hall.

JackRabbitt stays behind, eyes locked on the nameplate bolted to the door.

Victor Newmouse, CEO

William drops into the nearest chair and raises his arms into a relaxing stretch. "We've earned a few hours on the boat, don't you think?"

From his sky-high vantage point, JackRabbitt can see the majestic river stretching far beyond the forest. How he wishes he were gliding on the water instead of being perched in a tree. He can imagine the sound of the waves and the smell of the sea air. Truth is, he can even imagine being free enough to set sail from Chenoa City forever—leaving his anchor of obligation behind.

He bolts to the credenza, flinging open drawers in search of something sharp.

His paw settles on a letter opener—sleek, silver, just sturdy enough.

He wedges it beneath the nameplate on the door, prying it free with a satisfying *snap*.

He turns the nameplate over in his paw, reading the engraving one final time.

Then, without ceremony, he tosses it onto table with a hollow *clack*.

"There's no time to rest now, William. We've got work to do... and I'm going to see Mikki tonight."

"Ohhh!"

William twists his lips, as if he's holding back a secret...

And he is.

"Planning to enjoy the biggest catch of the day?"

JackRabbitt's attention shifts abruptly toward his brother's remark. "Don't make jokes about that."

"Why? There's no rose bushes in here." William pushes away from the table, pretending to search underneath it. "No photographers either."

In an instant, JackRabbitt materializes as a dark shadow lurching over William.

"I don't want to hear you ever breathe a word about that again. Do you understand? Only you and I know that secret."

William throws up both paws in surrender.

"Alright, alright."

Mr. Uptight.

Sensing he has made his point, JackRabbitt relaxes his shoulders and glides toward the built-in wet bar.

He pops open a cabinet and surveys the selection.

Pulling out a bottle, he looks toward William.

"Victor's private stash. The good stuff."

He retrieves two glasses and pours two drinks.

"Have you seen Mikki since the funeral?" William asks.

"No. She locked herself away at The Ranch, and she's not been taking house calls.

Tonight, that changes. I'm going to see her... even if I have to scale a wall to do it."

He gives the treequila a thoughtful swirl.

"Mikki's grief is the only part of this whole thing that I regret. Victor needed to believe that something was going on between us."

He pauses, eyes fixed on the slow turn of his drink.

"I wanted him out of Chenoa City... but I didn't want him dead."

He lifts the rim to his nose, breathing in the aged aroma.

"But now that he *is* dead..."

JackRabbitt raises his glass.

"Cheers."

Chapter Six

The Ranch

Knock Knock Knock Knock

"Delivery for Ms. Newmouse. Ms. Mikki Newmouse."

Mikki glances up from her magazine.

She briefly considers the rudeness of the interruption—but chooses to ignore it.

She brushes her honey-blonde curls to the side, then flips the page and continues reading.

The knock comes again—more forceful this time.

Her peachy ears twitch with irritation at the persistent pounding on the door.

She sighs, tosses the magazine to the floor, and pushes herself up from her chaise lounge.

In a flash of black satin pajamas, she flies across the room and flings open the door to investigate the offense.

"Oh, for heaven's sake. JackRabbitt? Is that you?"

Two long, lean ears poke out from beneath the collar of a rain-soaked coat.

JackRabbitt shakes the water from his shoulders, runs his fingers through his bangs, and leans into the doorway.

"You haven't returned any of my messages."

Mikki's paw floats to her hip.

"How on earth did you get past security?"

He looks at her—partly offended, partly amused.

"Come on, Mikki. There isn't a gate in this town I haven't slipped through at least once."

The Newmouse Ranch is located on the secluded northern side of Chenoa City. The property is situated among sprawling acres of farm grounds, flower gardens... and heavily guarded forest.

Mikki and JackRabbitt both know it was a feat for him to get past Victor's goons.

"Mikki, you can't keep hiding away out here. I'm worried about you. Can I come in? Just for a few minutes."

He gives her 'the look'—

The one that usually gets him anything he wants.

Mikki returns 'the look' with a sternly lifted eyebrow.

"I'm very busy. I have a lot going on right now."

She spins around, her tail sweeping the door closed behind her—

But JackRabbitt slips his foot into the frame, catching it just in time.

Defeat is not an option.

"Come on, Mikki. It's raining. I'm shivering here!"

He coughs, sniffles, and gives his best effort to look pathetic.

"I've come all the way from Newmouse Tower to see you."

She hesitates—but finds herself drawn in by the face she's trusted more times than she can count.

"It's a relief that you've taken over my proxy at Newmouse. That's one less thing I have to be concerned about. I owe you for acting on behalf of the children."

She swings the door open and waves him inside.

"Can I get you a drink?"

"Brownberry bourbon. Neat."

A victory drink.

She turns her back and disappears down the long hallway.

He closes the door and prepares to glide along behind her.

But suddenly—

A lump of guilt festers in his stomach as he takes in the quiet chaos cluttering the foyer.

Unpaired shoes are strewn across the floor.

Greeting cards, paperwork, and daily mail have accumulated into a precarious pile on the desk.

Dry pots of dead funeral plants are crammed into every spare nook.

Junk has grown like a jungle around this once-grand entrance.

Victor had built The Main House as a wedding gift to Mikki, promising to make all of her dreams come true.

It was carved from a hollowed fallen tree—low and wide—nothing like the sky-high design of Newmouse Tower.

She'd insisted on the shape—round, cozy, perfect for raising a family.

But of course, Victor got his way on a few things: the arched foyer, the grand staircase, and the second-story suites that now echo with too much silence.

"How are the kits?" he shouts down the hallway with growing concern.

Mikki drifts toward the bar in the living room, massaging her furry forehead with her fingers in a vain attempt to rub away a headache.

She raises her voice to respond.

"Mick is such a sweet, energetic young buck. He went back to Walnut Grove yesterday. Of course, I'd rather him be at boarding school than mourning here with me. Victoria, on the other paw..."

She unscrews the cap of a half-empty bottle.

"She and I are constantly at odds. She challenges me on everything. She finally graduated high school but has no direction. I thought maybe you could offer her a job at Newmouse? Maybe something in the mailroom?"

Her voice echoes down the long hall.

JackRabbitt moves cautiously toward the living room, navigating the sea of junk at his feet.

But then—

He stops.

Dead in his tracks.

Behold:

A sight of unspeakable horror.

The entire living room has been painted...

PINK.

"You redecorated?!"

"It's mauve," she sighs, sweet as ever.

"No," he says flatly. "It's pink."

Her shaky paw pours a generous amount of bourbon into a glass, then—*clang*—sets the bottle back down onto the bar.

"I painted this place the least-Victor-like color I could think of. I changed the carpet and the furniture too."

She leans forward, bracing herself on the bar top.

She catches her reflection in the mirrored backsplash, then erupts into tears.

"No matter what I do, he's still here!"

"Mikki!"

He rushes in close behind her, gently grasping her petite shoulders.

He can smell the Shabó Cosmetics on her fur.

With soft affection, he whispers his nickname for her:

"Mikki Mouse."

She spins around in his arms, looking up at him.

"Oh, JackRabbitt. Why would Victor leave Chenoa City without telling me? Without even considering me?! The Colonel said he was furious that night!"

Her body goes limp.

"I thought we were getting back together. I thought we could be a family again!"

He pulls her in tightly for a deeper embrace—but she breaks free, spins back around, reaches for the bar, then swallows the brownberry bourbon she had just poured for him.

Woozy, she dashes toward her pink chaise lounge, crumpling onto the plush throne like a beautiful rag doll.

He rushes to sit beside her, noting that the pink chaise is a new addition to the room—and it is clearly where she's been spending most of her time.

The white carpet around the chair is littered with tissues, empty bottles, and boxes of the same chocolate bonbons.

A sick swell of guilt rises through him, pressing against his throat until he can barely breathe.

I did this to her.

"There were times when I thought nothing could touch us. Like our love was invincible! And we tested that love. Oh, how we tested it. The breakups, the makeups, the endless cycle of riot and romance."

"I'm... sorry."

These are the only words he can muster, and he nearly chokes on them.

With sudden awareness, she pulls herself together.

"My dear JackRabbitt, you've been so good to me. I know I must look a mess, but I want you to know that I love how much you care. Even before Victor's death, you always made time to come visit. Our afternoon rose garden walks had become so important to me."

He winces, remembering the trap he so carefully set.

"Victor was at work or traveling so often. I was almost as lonely then as I am now."

Her voice trails off.

Her attention slides away into the distance.

"Mikki!" he shouts. "You have to know... you did nothing wrong! You were a wonderful wife. You're everything that a husband could ask for... and more!"

Her mind returns from wherever it wandered—straight into a skeptical look.

"Ex-wife, need I remind you? I was no angel. Neither was Victor."

She half-laughs and wipes away a tear.

"I realize now, he was never going to be the world's greatest husband. Not after what his mother did to him."

She sniffles.

"Who could believe he had any decency in him at all after that? It's amazing what he went on to accomplish with his life. Whoever would have thought that a mouse could become King of the Forest?!"

For a flicker of a moment, JackRabbitt's disdain for Victor overrides his own shame.

"Yeah, he was something else."

Her eyes flash with defiance.

"I know what you thought of him. Everyone in the world saw him as... ruthless... but he was different with me. He was the love of my life, the father of my children."

A wadded white paw-kerchief materializes from her black satin pajama sleeve.

"I was an exotic dancer when I met him," she muses. "He changed my life forever. He taught me how to be a lady. He used to call me... his ruby in the rubble!"

Her talking turns to sobbing.

She buries her face in his blazer, smearing makeup all over the lapel.

But JackRabbitt doesn't care about his jacket.

He pulls her tiny body in close.

She surrenders weakly to his embrace.

Mikki's agony is his penance.

Guilt is his burden to forever bear for ridding the city of that pest.

Victor Newmouse would have destroyed her too, eventually.

She's a fool for loving him—

and I'm a fool for loving her.

Chapter Seven

The Crow House

The best and worst years of Mikki's life have been spent on The Ranch. Her home represents the security she had to fight for, the stability that wasn't given to her, and the proof that she is worthy of it all.

But it hasn't always been happy.

Passion is a wildfire that can burn everything in its path.

Eventually, she learned to love the flame.

When times were good, Mr. and Mrs. Newmouse spent their spare time tending to the details of their vast estate, little Victoria and Mickolas in tow. The children splashed in the fountains, played hide-and-seek in the gardens, and peeped curiously into the guest houses.

On the west side of the property, Victor built The Crow House—the official headquarters for his side venture, Newmouse Air. While his days were spent maintaining a corporate empire, The Crow House was his passion project. The business relies on a highly trained network of skilled crows who manage deliveries, carry secure messages, and gather intelligence from across the forest. Even now, it remains active—part business, part clubhouse—the fleet still loyal to the Newmouse family.

Just as Victor managed The Crow House, Mikki meticulously maintained her prize-winning rose garden. Each precious bush bore a piece of her heart. She spent countless hours overseeing its care and cultivation—all while never digging a single nail into the dirt.

Tonight, Mikki sits alone in the rose garden, her feet gently swinging from a painted white iron bench. She sighs a heavy sigh as the evening sun orchestrates a symphony of blooms, marking the day's grand finale.

Seemingly on cue, a voice spills down from the treetops.

"Sounds like you could use a wise old owl."

Mikki's face quickly shifts from solemn to saved.

She looks up to the silver birch tree above, instantly knowing who's calling.

"Oh, Kathra! How do you always know right when I need you?"

Kathra and Mikki's relationship has withstood the test of time. Kathra is both a friend and mother figure to Mikki, but not just because of the age between them. Kathra has felt a protectiveness over Mikki ever since Victor first introduced her as his new doefriend. In her more reflective moments, she realizes she always knew the bouncy blonde mouse was in over her head inside Victor's world.

She cranes her neck downward, and a magnificent pearl necklace spills into view—each pearl like a mini moon, strung in delicate orbit around her neck.

Kathra never leaves The Chansoar Mansion without her gems and jewels, be it day or night. She's often seen with a ring on every toe, each one twinkling like a well-timed remark.

"I've come to rescue you from your sugar coma," Kathra hoots. "I'll have you know—I visited The Chenoa Chocolatiere yesterday, and he told me he was all out of bonbons—because you bought the last of the case."

"I was hoping chocolate might help fill the hole in my heart..." Mikki sneers. "Turns out, it's only filling out my hips!"

She stands up, wiggles her hips, and adjusts the belt on her one-piece summer romper.

"It's wonderful to see you, it really is! I'll have Mugel make us a pot of tumble tea up at the main house, but oh... it's a bit of a mess."

Mikki thinks twice about the invitation.

"Actually, come with me to The Crow House instead. It's late. I should check on Victoria. I know she'll be glad to see you too!"

Kathra swoops to the ground in a glittering flash, her talons striking onto the stone path next to Mikki.

As they make the journey to The Crow House, Kathra glides just above the ground, her wings occasionally fluffing as she adjusts to keep pace with her petite friend.

Mikki's paws shuffle hurriedly, her thoughts already drifting ahead of her.

"Victoria's been at The Crow House all day and night, ever since her father's death."

"Yes, well. We all deal with grief in our own ways, don't we? Victoria escapes to The Crow House. And you... escape into a bottle?"

Mikki looks up, expecting to meet her best friend's knowing gaze —but Kathra keeps her eyes straight ahead, as if nothing was said. Mikki turns her focus to the beauty of the setting sun and lets out a relenting sigh.

"Victor and I used to dance in the garden in the evenings—when he wasn't busy running the world, of course."

She laughs uncomfortably.

"He would arrange a magnificent meal of grilled melt mushrooms and dandelion wine."

She twirls a lock of her hair.

"Oh, we'd twirl on the garden stone, right there in front of the fountain.

Sometimes it seemed like the whole world just... disappeared around us."

"I know," Kathra replies softly, her large eyes filled with compassion. "He loved to watch you dance."

Mikki brushes an errant blond curl from her face.

"Now I can barely remember how to move at all."

"That's because you're still holding onto the shadow of what was."

Kathra's voice is filled with an honesty that only a true friend could muster.

"Mikki, you have got to honor his memory—but you can't let it keep you from living."

"I don't even know how to live anymore! My house is a disaster. My head is a disaster. My heart... is a disaster."

She bites her lip to suppress the flood of tears.

"I'm not the mouse I used to be, Kathra. There was a time when I was a dancer and a pianist—and then, I became a mother. But the best part of me was being Mrs. Victor Newmouse. Without him... I don't know who I am."

Kathra tilts her head, her feathers softly rustling as the wind picks up.

"I know exactly who you are. You are Mikkole Reid Fester Manecroft Newmouse—and we are going to get your life back!"

The sun dips below the horizon as Mikki and Kathra reach their destination.

Tonight, The Crow House is alive with a cacophony of caws.

No doubt, there are many tales of daring escapes, lost treasures, and gossip from lands near and far.

The frame of the open-air aviary is constructed from robust wooden posts, but Victor commissioned a specialized team of crows to add nesting elements to the design. Beneath the entwined branches of the roof, there are braided willow nooks for perching, a stone basin washroom, and a communal kitchen for preparing and sharing meals.

A sunken auditorium sits in the belly of the open space—a stage surrounded by 360-degree seating, where Victor held meetings.

As we speak, some captivating creature is on that very stage, capturing the fleet's attention.

Mischievous laughter echoes off the walls as Mikki strains her eyes to see what could be so entertaining.

Just then—

A sea of glossy black feathers begins to part—

and she can see—

that the captivating creature holding court—

is her daughter.

Victoria Newmouse possesses a powerful cocktail of Mikki's beauty and Victor's intensity. As she speaks to the group, she uses her claws to comb through her light chocolate brown fur, smoothing and bouncing the natural waves into a variety of shapes.

Her hair never looks the same for more than a few moments. Every flip and fluff reveals a different style, each somehow more intriguing than the last.

Suddenly, she looks up and sees her mother.

What was once a salacious smile now turns to a scowl.

"Mother?" she says, stomping away from the circle of crows. "What are you doing here? You don't need to check on me. I'm perfectly capable of taking care of myself."

"Well, I know that, Victoria. It's just that I—"

The impatient mousetress interrupts and turns her attention to Kathra.

"Oh! Hello, Kathra." She adjusts her tone dramatically. "Are you here on business, or just to check in on Mother? If the answer is both, you're too late. JackRabbitt beat you to it." She smirks, looking pleased with herself. "He was here late last night!"

Kathra turns to Mikki, who is genuinely shocked by what seems to be an accusation.

"Yes, he was here... and we should be grateful that he has been taking care of business at Newmouse." Gathering her indignation, Mikki adds, "You know, Victoria, one day that company will belong to you and your brother. JackRabbitt is protecting your interests."

"JackRabbitt is protecting his own interests," Victoria responds, echoing her father's unfavorable opinion of the Abbitt.

In an effort to shift attention away from the developing family squabble, Kathra moves in to give her gawd-daughter a hug.

"Victoria, my dear? How are you doing?"

Victoria looks up at Kathra with suddenly innocent eyes.

"Daddy is gone. And Mother is... not here."

She shifts a judgmental eye toward Mikki.

"Mick has gone to summer school, and I graduated free and clear —but I'm not allowed to take a break. I'm being told I should get a job in the mailroom at Newmouse. So... I'm doing just peachy! Thanks for asking."

Mikki sighs. "Victoria, please. Can we give it a rest for just one day?"

"Fine. You know what?" she says dismissively. "Kathra, it's always a pleasure seeing you, but if you'll excuse me... Blade needs a bath."

With that as her final word, the heiress quickly disappears behind an impenetrable wall of wings.

"Blade can bathe himself," Mikki mutters under her breath. "What can I do? She's old enough to make her own decisions now."

She leans her weary body against a wooden post, looking for some form of support.

"When Victoria was a little pup, I used to bathe her every morning." She laughs lightly. "She loved to play with the bottle of *Fluff Soap*, sailing it around in the water as if it were a boat."

A happy memory turns to sadness.

"She used to trust me. We were so close. Now, I feel like I'm on the outside looking in at her."

"Mikki, you have got to move forward. You have got to rediscover who you are. Darling, I have a grand idea. Now, just... listen to me before you say no."

Kathra straightens her neck, raises an brow, and looks Mikki in the eye.

"Let's host a charity event. It will be wonderful. It will be grand. It will be..." She searches for the words. "Something to look forward to."

"A party?" Mikki considers the idea, her blonde brow furrowing. "Kathra, I can't just throw a party and pretend everything is fine."

"Not pretending, my dear.

Planning.

It's something tangible, something concrete you can hold onto... something besides a bottle."

Kathra ignores Mikki's look of skepticism.

"Come on. You are a brilliant hostess. You have a style and a charm that are, quite frankly, going to waste. Perhaps if you surround yourself with others... you will find yourself again."

"A party won't bring back the love of my life," Mikki mumbles as the shadows of despair creep in.

"It's not about bringing Victor back, for heaven's sake. It's about allowing yourself to move forward. You cannot let your memories of him keep you trapped in the past. Mikki, my dear, look at me.

Look. At. Me."

Kathra stretches out her wings and straightens her friend's weary body into an upright position.

"Promise me you'll at least consider it. And let me take you to an Animal Alcoholics meeting. You've got to get ahold of yourself."

Leaning in closely, she makes her final, and most convincing, argument.

"It's time for a fresh start.

You owe it to Victor...

But more importantly, you owe it to yourself."

Mikki looks into the eyes of her dearest friend, knowing her heart is in the right place.

"Maybe.

Maybe I can try.

I just feel so alone."

"You are not alone," Kathra says reassuringly.

"You have me."

And for the first time in a long time, a bud of hope blooms in Mikki's heart.

Chapter Eight

Atoms Grocery

Atoms Grocery is every bit the country general store you'd imagine, carved into the side of a grassy hill. Its wooden beams and stone foundation blend seamlessly into the landscape.

A small bell, fashioned from an old brass acorn, jingles cheerfully when the door swings open, announcing each visitor with a soft, tinkling chime.

Inside, the space is warm and inviting, scented with pine shavings, dried herbs, and fresh bread. Lanterns cast a soft golden light over the wooden shelves, packed tight with essentials—flour, preserves, and paw-made soaps.

It's a place where time moves slow, where nothing much changes.

Except for tonight.

The bell jingles.

Grace doesn't lift her head, but she doesn't have to. She can feel the ripple in the room. A shift in posture. A breath held a little too long. The rustle of aprons being straightened and smoothed.

The handsome stranger has arrived.

His boots hit the floor—sharp, confident steps, but not rushed. He carries the scent of something faintly smoky, like he's been near a fire.

"Evening, ladies," he says, his voice low, rich, easy.

A chorus of mice reply, overlapping one another in their eagerness.

"Oh, evening, Victor," Lila all but sings, tail flicking.

"Need help finding anything?" Willow asks, smoothing her apron, ears perked too high.

Even Poppy, who has a mate and is pushing a shopping cart full of pups, murmurs, "Well, well," with a little too much interest.

Victor chuckles, warm, good-natured. "As a matter of fact, yes. I could use a little help."

He pauses near the shelves, scanning. "You wouldn't happen to carry a tin of *Whisker Wax*, would you?"

Old Ruth clears her throat—pointedly. The coolness in her voice lands like a bucket of cold water on the hot does. She jerks her chin toward the grooming section near the back.

"Middle shelf, left side."

"Appreciate it."

He ambles over, taking his time, his presence somehow filling the space without demanding it.

On his way, he passes the floral section, where Grace is inventorying the latest delivery, fingers gliding over petals, breathing in each bundle to ensure its freshness.

A few faded bluebells sit among the brighter blooms—soft, delicate, easy to miss.

He slows just enough.

"Grace," he says, a simple acknowledgment, smooth and unassuming.

She doesn't turn.

"Mr. Miller."

A pause. Nothing more.

He lingers, waiting for something—an opening, a shift.

She gives him nothing.

He exhales, almost a laugh under his breath, then moves on.

Grace steadies a sprig of lavender, pressing it a little too hard into place.

Her ears feel warm.

She lifts a paw, brushing them absently, as if there were a logical explanation for the sensation.

Victor finds his tin of *Whisker Wax* and carries it to the counter.

Old Ruth squints at the tin, her paws rough from years of work.

She taps the counter with a no-nonsense rhythm. "Four scraps."

Victor touches his whiskers, giving them a thoughtful stroke. "Worth it."

He reaches into his pocket, pulling out three clay bits and a drift coin.

But as he moves to give them over, the drift coin... vanishes!

Willow gasps.

Lila's ears twitch.

Old Ruth narrows her eyes. "Now, where'd that go?"

Victor's expression is all innocence.

He waves his paw over Old Ruth's ear, and suddenly, the missing drift coin is back, pinched between his fingers.

Poppy lets out a delighted squeak, her pups giggling in wide-eyed wonder.

Old Ruth snorts, unimpressed but amused.

"You're a slick one."

Victor grins, sliding the proper scraps across the counter. No more games. Just the exact amount owed.

"City mouse trick," he says easily.

As he turns to leave, Old Ruth calls after him, the usual gruffness in her voice softened. "Don't be a stranger now."

The bell jingles again. And he's gone.

Then—

"Oh, Grace," Willow sighs, practically melting against the counter. "How can you be so cold to him?"

Lila's tail flicks. "He's so charming! You'd have to be blind not to notice—" She stops short, wincing. "I mean... you know what I mean."

Grace presses her lips together, adjusting a bundle of rosemary. "So. He's charming. And?"

"And handsome," Poppy chimes in, hoisting a wiggling pup onto her hip while another tugs at her dress. "And strong. And confident. And that accent?"

Lila groans dramatically. "And he's staying in your house! You're living with a stud, and you won't even crack a smile at him. That's just cruel."

Grace continues with her herbal inventory. "I don't really know him."

"You don't have to know him to be nice to him," Willow argues.

"She's just shy," Poppy teases. "She wouldn't even know he was flirting unless he submitted it in writing."

Grace scoffs. "Please."

Old Ruth jumps in to put a stop to the nonsense. "Will you all stop pesterin' Grace? She's liable to fire you!"

But the truth sits there, unspoken. They're not wrong. Lila, Willow, Poppy—they all had plenty of suitors growing up. Grace was always more focused on her education than on socializing. She was behind the scenes at town dances—working, not waltzing.

Then, Victor waltzes into her life. And for the first time, she realizes—he unsettles her.

Not because of what he does. But because of what he makes her feel.

Excited. Curious. Alive.

She has no frame of reference for these feelings, no past experience to measure them against.

She understands hard work, structure, responsibility.

But this? She doesn't even know where to put it.

So, she puts a bundle of rosemary neatly into its place, tucking it in tightly—right where it belongs.

But maybe the mousy matchmakers have a point.

Maybe she played it *too cool*.

What's the harm in being just a little more friendly?

And besides...

If he's staying, I may as well figure out what to do with him.

Chapter Nine

Lunchtime

Workdays on the farm are hot and grueling. Biff continues to reserve the most tedious tasks especially for Victor... but it doesn't matter. He no longer feels the need to control or resist anything. The only thing that matters is the hole that must be dug or the post that must be hammered.

Letting go of his own single-minded ambition, working toward some other creature's goal—it's completely freeing. When he closes his eyes in Grace's spare room at night, he feels only pride and contentment in an honest day's work.

The sun surges high in the sky. He reaches for his pocket watch and flips it open. Noon. Grace always cooks lunch for herself at noon, and today, she's offered to fix him a plate.

He scurries to the house, anxious to replenish his energy.

In the daylight, the tree stump farmhouse kitchen looks far more welcoming than it did weeks ago when he first snuck through the back door. Now, it's charming and homey. The picture window offers a magnificent view of the farm, illuminating the carved wood details of the stump's impressive construction.

To his surprise, Grace has already set the table, but she is nowhere in sight.

His nose twitches as he sniffs the air.

A loud grumble bursts from his belly as he imagines what fresh farm harvest must be on the kitchen menu today.

He approaches the dining table, and suddenly—

A deep laugh erupts from him.

An oversized salad bowl sits on his place mat...

With the notorious salad tongs balanced over the top.

Grace snickers as she shuffles into the kitchen, leaning her cane against the wall. "I thought I'd make a salad for you."

"You almost made a salad *of me*," he reminds her. "Is my missing ear one of the ingredients?" He tugs at his scar, then glides past her toward the sink to wash up.

"It was just a little piece of your ear, Mr. Miller. You'll hardly miss it!" she teases.

She whisks away the salad bowl and replaces it with a heartily stuffed vegetable sandwich.

If only the grocery store mice could see her now—lighthearted, teasing, just friendly enough.

But Victor senses there's more to her motivation.

"Grace, don't you ever feel guilty for defending yourself. You did right, and you know it. Let's consider it a draw, shall we?"

He wrings a cotton towel in his paws.

"As a sign of our truce, perhaps you might start calling me by my first name? Are we not friends?"

She takes a moment to consider what exactly it would mean to be this mouse's friend. She doesn't have much experience with friends—or males—or friends who are males.

However, if what's happening here is indeed friendship, she knows one thing for certain—she wants to keep it.

"Yes... Victor. You and I are friends," she says reluctantly. "Now eat your sandwich!"

He takes his place at one end of the table and surrenders to the sandwich.

Hearing Grace say his name for the first time produces an unforeseen thrill in him.

He savors the feeling, as with every bite of the farm-fresh food she's prepared.

"You stuff me like a pepper!" he teases.

"Oh, Mr. Mil—" She corrects herself. "Victor."

She shuffles from the counter to the table, transferring her lunch plate and two glasses of iced dandelion tea.

"It's true!" he insists. "You've been more than generous with me. Why don't you let me cook for you tomorrow night?"

She pulls a chair from the opposite end of the dining table and sits down to join him. "That's really not necessary."

Feeling embarrassed now and fidgety, she arranges the lunch plate and tea glass in front of her, but then pauses with amusement.

"Do you even know how to cook?"

"Do I know how to cook?" he chuckles. "My dear, I will make you a melt mushroom filet that will curl your tail."

Slowly, her tail begins to curl.

Quickly, she reigns herself back from an unexpected reverie and returns to the reality that she has just spilled the tea on the table in front of her.

"Ahm. Melt mushroom?" she flusters, sopping up the liquid with her napkin.

"Melts in your mouth!" he replies. "Hence the name."

Jumping up from his seat, he finishes the mop job with his own napkin, then clears the evidence from the table. He returns to the kitchen sink to wash the sticky liquid from his paws.

Gazing through the window, he absorbs the view of the wide-open prairie sky. He exhales longingly and announces, "Yes. With a bit of stealth, I should be able to fly into the forest, pick a quick bouquet of mushrooms, and prepare dinner for you tomorrow night. I promise!"

"Fly into the forest. You're going to… fly into the forest? Just like that?"

Truly, she is intrigued, but she's also grateful to shift the attention away from her little spill.

Taking his seat again at the table, he elaborates. "Well, I will call for the crows, of course. It should only be a half-day's trip. I could go in the morning and be back in time for—" He pauses as a grand idea takes flight in his mind. "You should fly with me!"

"Fly with you?" she asks, stunned by the ridiculousness of the notion.

"Yes!"

"On a bird…"

"Yes! You will love it! There is nothing more thrilling than defying the laws of nature. The wind is in your fur, the feathers are in your fingers. The world belongs to you! From that height, there's so much to see—"

A painful pause fills the sky as his flight of fancy crashes to the ground.

"Grace, I apologize. I didn't mean to—I don't know what to—"

"Please, don't be uncomfortable," she says uncomfortably. "There's nothing to apologize for. I detest the idea that anyone feels sorry for me. I'm not sorry at all.

I was born blind. It's not as if I've lost something. I can't very well miss what I've never had."

She lifts her nose, twitches her whiskers, and begins to talk nervously with her paws.

"Yes, I have certain limitations, but I have other extraordinary advantages. Sight is only one sense, you see, and I have more sense than most."

She's given this speech before—even if only in her own mind.

"The evidence of my accomplishment is planted all over Southbrook. A few months from now, Pumpkin Acres will be just one of my many successes. I've accomplished everything I've ever set my mind to here.

I'd say my vision more than makes up for my lack of eyesight."

She smacks her paw to the table, picks up her fork, and dips it into a plate of roasted vegetables, sliding the pieces around but making no attempt to eat them.

She's a mouse with something to prove.

Victor recognizes the determination all too well. When the world treats you as small, there becomes no forest too deep, no tree too tall. Only the boundlessness of the sky can hold you.

Victor pushes his chair back from the table and springs to the pads of his feet.

"Well then, you, my dear, are up for a challenge. Come fly with me!"

Her fork drops to the plate with a triple *clang*.

"Are you serious? Victor, but I have no experience. I didn't even know a mouse could fly until I met you. You've told me it takes years to learn the skill. There's a dead mouse in the forest wearing your jacket who can attest to that."

"We'll take extreme caution. Don't you worry about a thing. You'll be in good paws."

She has no doubt about that. But the idea is both terrific... and terrifying.

Risky adventures are not allowed into her well-designed world. Yet, flying with Victor is no more of a risk than letting him stay in her home. It's no more of a risk than calling him friend.

For as long as she can remember, her life has been full of better-not's and supposed-to's.

For years now, she's imagined breaking free of these things that protect but imprison her.

Perhaps now is a chance to soar.

"Okay!" she cries out, almost surprised by her own response.

"Okay?" he asks. "You're absolutely sure?" He shifts his weight to the tips of his toes, then drives his feet to the ground.

"Yes!" she exclaims.

"Yes, Victor.

Let's fly!"

Chapter Ten

The View

Dashing out the back door, Victor leads Grace toward the forest. She is holding her trusty cane in one paw and Victor's paw in the other. Together, they reverse the steps he traveled on the day of his death: down the stone steps and the cobblestone pathway; past the windmill and the watermill beside the brook; through the empty rows of the bean field; and back to the grass at the edge of the forest.

He clasps his paws together, takes a deep breath, and blows a whistle into the wilderness—

One long note, followed by three sharp bursts.

The call echoes up throughout the open prairie, then vanishes into silence.

He whistles again with a faster tempo, then waits.

Nothing.

Grace's quiet anticipation has bloomed like a morning glory, now fading with the onset of afternoon.

"I don't think they're coming," she sighs.

Victor forgives her for doubting him and whistles again.

Suddenly—

The silence erupts into a raucous, and a throng of black wings spill like ink onto the sky. With flawless convergence, an army of a hundred crows descends into the field surrounding them.

With trembling arms and legs, Grace begins to fear... this was all a mistake.

Wild crows have a warrior culture. They've been known to share an occasional wartime partnership with ground dwellers, but Grace now realizes she has acted on trust with no evidence to believe that a single mouse has the power to command this army. Instinct tells her to dart backward toward the bean field, but she can hear—they are surrounded.

"We're outnumbered!" she gasps, thrusting her ears in all directions to the sound of the unnerving symphony.

"Grace. You have to trust me. They will abide by my call."

The air falls sharply silent.

From the black mass, a single crow emerges and sways toward them.

"Who calls in the name of Prince Obsidian?"

These are Outer Forest crows.

Victor doesn't know them, and they... don't know him.

"I am Victor!" he responds, lifting his chest toward the sky and raising both arms to form a 'V'. He sweeps his arms slowly downward, as if carried by the wind, letting the weight of his presence settle over the gathered crows.

"Through honor, I am bound to Prince Obsidian. Through trust, I call to you." He bows his head just enough to acknowledge their authority, yet holds his stance firm, yielding nothing of his own.

"Do me the honor of a special request." He straightens and motions to Grace. Twitching his whiskers and smiling at her, he announces, "This mouse was born to fly."

The crow leader turns his head to the side and examines Grace.

He is massive, and she can feel him studying her. She plants her feet on the ground and holds her head high, determined not to flinch.

The crow lowers his head and stretches his neck downward.

She can feel his breath.

His beak is within striking distance.

He opens his razor mouth slightly and clamps it around her cane.

My cane!

Grace's cane has always been her guide. It has always been her guardian... and now it's the only thing standing between her and a really big bird.

Grace. You have to trust me.

She loosens her grip. The crow slowly draws the cane away, securing it safely in his beak. He then bows his head and crouches his full body to the ground.

"You didn't believe me?" Victor gloats, the old thrill of command settling back into his bones.

For a moment, he feels like himself again.

She exhales a sigh of relief. "I'll never doubt you again."

Victor again takes Grace's paw and guides her smoothly toward her awaiting chariot. He boosts her little body onto the back of the crow, then reminds her of the most important instructions:

"Move with the wind, not against it. Grip the feathers near the base—they're sturdier there. You'll need to stay low. Tuck your tail beneath you. Do not let it slip! If you start slipping, tap twice on his back—he'll level out. Use your whole body to hang on tight. Here we go."

He scoots into position behind her, lays his body weight over her back, and pins her down protectively using his arms.

Victor turns his attention to the crow. "Alright, old boy. Just a quick joyride. Are we ready? In three, two, one... Ascend!"

On his command, into the air ascends not just one crow—but one hundred crows!

Victor and Grace and a storm of crows soar skyward together. The wind ripples rhythmically through fur and feathers. As they rise higher, flapping wings form a safety net below.

Grace tightly caresses the silken feathers of her crow and merges her body with its inhales and exhales.

Swooping up lifts her out of her mind.

Diving down pulls her down through her belly.

The ground is becoming a distant memory.

She hears the whirring of the world pass away.

Leaning left into fear, leaning right into passion, she embraces both power and powerlessness—with utter surrender to it all.

Victor squeezes his arms into a tighter embrace and leans closely into her ear.

"Hold on, Grace. We're gonna catch wind!"

Whoosh!

At once, they are pulled into an airstream that propels them faster, yet more effortlessly than before. The exhilaration sends her tail flipping and flopping wildly beneath her. She clings tighter in vain to control her own excitement, and just when she thinks she can't hold on any longer—

They are ejected from the airstream with a forward jolt.

All is calm and drifting down.

There is nothing to see or not see.

There is only this moment of blind bliss.

It is everything and nothing at all.

The *thud* of the landing barely registers to her. She's still in the clouds.

Hell, she is the clouds!

Victor releases his weight from behind her and slides off the back of the crow. "Jump down! I'll catch you."

So, with the same trust and abandon that brought her here, she falls off into Victor's waiting arms.

She can barely stand. Her body is weightless. She feels the breath of the beast returning the cane into her paw... but she is too weak to accept it.

The cane drops to the ground, and soon, so will she.

"Catch me again," she whispers breathlessly.

On the edge of the restless forest, Grace falls into Victor's arms... and into a kiss that makes flying feel like an afterthought.

THE FAUNA AND THE FLORA IS BROUGHT TO YOU BY...

ANNOUNCER
"Mothers trust *Fluff Soap* for their little ones."

CUT TO: A mother rabbit washing her kit.

ANNOUNCER
"Tough on dirt. Gentle on fur, feathers, and scales."

CUT TO: Mr. Otter is slicking back his freshly washed fur.

Mrs. Cardinal is fluffing her spotless feathers.

Mr. Lizard is drying his spotless scales in the sun.

CUT TO: A bottle of *Fluff Soap*.

A bubble floats up and pops.

JINGLE PLAYS
"Soft and clean, fresh and bright,
Morning, noon, and through the night,
Fluff Soap!"

ANNOUNCER
"*Fluff Soap* by Shabó Cosmetics. From our family to yours."

FADE OUT.

Chapter Eleven

Shabó Cosmetics

In the wispy Willow tree office of Shabó Cosmetics, the aromas of fresh berry juices, herbal extracts, and seed butters swirl through the air.

JackRabbitt sits behind the expansive CEO desk, diligently attending to the family business.

His sister, Ashlyn Abbitt, sits across from him—tall and poised, her platinum blonde rabbit fur catching the light like brushed silk.

On the desk in front of her, she guards a sleek black case with both paws, the tips of her manicured claws resting possessively on the latch.

"For the Fall season, my lab team has developed six new colors of *Berry Cherry Lip Stains.*"

William straightens from his leaned-back position in the chair beside her.

He cranes his neck to see what's inside the case—but Ashlyn's tall, statuesque ears sway along with him, blocking every attempt.

"Aw, come on, Ash. Just show us the goods!"

Ashlyn grins with satisfaction.

She opens the latch with a tiny *click*, revealing the harvest of her hard work.

Beneath the glow of the office lights, six glass pots gleam with rich berry hues—deep crimsons, playful pinks, sultry mauves.

The colors are warm, cozy, radiant. A stark contrast to Ashlyn herself, her steely elegance wrapped in a blue metallic dress that clings to her like liquid cobalt.

"William, do you have our marketing layout ready to go?" she asks.

Always willing to do half the work, William waves in the Shabó executive assistant to swiftly drop the proofs in front of her.

"Good work, Zip," he cheers. "Why don't you take a lunch break? Ooh! Let's order a pizza. Beet sauce? Radishes? Who's in?"

Ashlyn's glare lands sharply upon her younger half-brother. A lesser rabbit would wither under the cold burn of her icy blue eyes.

"There's that higher education our father paid for."

William grins, unfazed.

"Technically, I have a bachelor's degree in... Strategic Leisure."

Ashlyn pinches the bridge of her nose, visibly restraining herself.

"Remind me again how I share a last name with you?"

William wiggles his eyebrows.

"Because fate is cruel... and my mother slept with your father."

Ashlyn shivers lightly at the idea, then shifts the conversation back to business.

"That'll be all, Zippy. You can go now."

A quick-footed rabbit twitches at the mention of his name, then zips toward the door and clicks it shut.

Without missing a beat, Ashlyn reaches for William's ad copy, her claws tapping lightly against the paper as she lifts it.

She leans back, crossing her long legs with effortless poise, skimming the page with a single, discerning glance. Even in a moment of stillness, she exudes the polished control of a sculpture brought to life.

She begins to read the ad copy aloud, unimpressed.

"Try our classic potted lip color in a variety of new Fall colors—Uh huh—Made using this year's harvest of berry juices—Okay."

Suddenly, she stops.

"Well, now here's something worth my time: Dip your lips and make a kiss!"

Ashlyn looks up at William.

He's giving her a kissy face.

He puffs his lips dramatically, making an obnoxious puckering sound. His eyes flutter, paw to chest—as though he's a romantic poet rather than the slacker son at their father's top-tier cosmetics company.

Ashlyn ignores him.

"Dip your lips and make a kiss," she repeats. "Hmmm... You know, I actually do love that. But I wouldn't seal it with a kiss just yet. JackRabbitt, what do you think?"

JackRabbitt doesn't respond.

His eyes are vacant. His ears are limp.

His weight sinks into his father's wood desk like he might fuse with it.

"Uh. Jacky?" she presses, raising her voice to jolt him back to the present. "Are you still with us?"

JackRabbitt's eyes snap open, his large ears flicking upward in surprise.

"Seal it with a kiss. I love it!" he blurts, his voice just a tad too eager.

Ashlyn and William share a glance, silently agreeing that JackRabbitt had only caught bits and pieces of the conversation.

Growing tired of the inefficiency of this meeting, Ashlyn announces, "I really should get back underground to the lab. Somerabbit needs to do the work around here. I have three new *Furfume* scents to finalize today, and I'll have them to you by the end of the week for approval. Oh, and JackRabbitt? I need you to talk to Brack about those sales figures for my *Fur-ever* anti-aging line."

He shakes his head, widens his eyes, then flashes a desperate look toward William.

"Yessss, ma'am," William interjects, responding on JackRabbitt's behalf with a mock salute.

Ashlyn raises an eyebrow but chooses to let it slide.

"Forget it. I'll talk to Brack myself. I guess I'll just leave you two to do..." She waves a paw. "Whatever it is you do... while I make all the magic happen."

Ashlyn pushes back her chair and rises, the metallic fabric of her dress catching the light as it clings to every curve.

She snaps her magic case shut with precision, adjusting the drape of her lab coat—an amusing contradiction over such a show-stopping ensemble.

Without so much as a backward glance, she flows out of the

office.

Her tall ears are the last thing to disappear beyond the doorframe before the *click* of the door seals the room behind her.

William calls through the closed door in his most annoying little brother voice. "Bye-bye, big sister!"

JackRabbitt lets out a sigh of relief.

"Thanks for backing me up."

"Always! I've always got your back. I know you've got your paws full, running Newmouse and Shabó at the same time."

William scooches his chair closer to the desk and leans in for an inspection. "You look tired."

"I am tired," JackRabbitt admits, slumping further back into the CEO chair.

"Well, how's the takeover tour going?"

"As a matter of fact..." he says, suddenly coming back to life, "that is where my work is finally paying off."

A sly grin creeps onto JackRabbitt's face.

"Watership Inc. bought a few more shares of Newmouse this week—quietly, of course."

"A shell corporation? Nice touch."

"Well, here's the twist: I think I've really got some allies on the board. I wasn't expecting that. The mole brothers seem to trust me. And the bat wants to play widget at The Country Club next week. And the saucy doe... Well. Let's just say our negotiations have been... productive."

William's long ears shoot upright, his tail giving an involuntary twitch.

"You hound dog! No. Wait. Wrong species."

He leans in, grinning like an idiot.

"Damn, Jacky. Business and pleasure? That's some next-level work-life balance right there."

JackRabbitt bites his lower lip, his head bouncing in humble affirmation.

"Alright, alright, playbunny."

William rolls his eyes, pretending to gag.

"Let's get back to the plot, shall we? What about the mice? They've all got a serious case of hero worship when it comes to Victor."

William throws a paw to his forehead.

"Oh, what will the world do without Victor Newmouse?"

JackRabbitt raises a brow.

"The mice aren't the problem.

Kathra is.

She's not just an obstacle. She's an iceberg."

William drops his paw and narrows his eyes.

"Well, how are you gonna get around her?"

JackRabbitt leans back in his chair, tapping a thoughtful rhythm against the desk.

"Well, that's where you come in, brother. I think the best way to deal with Kathra… is to create a Gillian-shaped distraction.”

William groans, throwing his head back dramatically.

“Oh no. Not my mother! Don’t make me deal with her. Please, Jacky. I’m begging you!”

JackRabbitt smirks. “Hear me out! All we have to do is force a couple of mice to vacate their board seats.

Another round of salacious photos, perhaps?”

William groans again—the kind of groan that always comes right before he says yes.

“I’m listening…”

“We just need two empty board seats that you and Gillian can fill. Then we’ve got the majority vote. Do you think she’ll go along with it?”

“A chance to do boardroom battle with Kathra? Oh, hell yeah. But I’m warning you now—have the cleaning crew on call. Feathers and fur will fly.”

JackRabbitt chuckles, arms crossing as he leans back.

“I do have a great sense of drama, don’t I?”

William crosses his arms too, smirking.

“But… do you really think my mother is just going to fall in line with whatever you want to do?”

JackRabbitt hesitates for the briefest moment, then says, “Gillian’s easy enough to persuade.”

But the way he shifts in his seat says otherwise.

“Why don’t you talk to her? Make sure she’s on board with the plan. And really play on the rivalry angle. Wind her up to the point where she is begging for a chance to let loose on Kathra.”

William grins mischievously. “Fine. But when the plan works out and we control Newmouse Enterprises...”

He tilts his head, pressing his paws together like a kit begging for a treat.

“Can I have Victor’s office? I kinda like the idea of having my own private Grandfather Clock entrance from the sky!”

JackRabbitt throws his head back with a laugh.

“When that day comes, William, you can have whatever office you want.

Hell, you can have the whole damn tree!”

Chapter Twelve

A New Note

In the center of Chenoa City's upscale shopping district, the Shabó Cosmetics Willow Tree draws in the city's most polished paws. Its long, ribbon-like branches sway gently around a curved glass entryway, where vines twist decoratively through lacquered beams. Nestled into the base of its trunk, sleek double doors with frosted inlays glide open as Mikki steps forward.

She pauses at the threshold.

Her journeys beyond The Ranch have been few, but therapeutic. Slowly, she's begun to trade quiet trails and familiar gardens for the world outside.

The Willow Tree pulses with motion behind the glass—noise, color, attention.

She exhales. Soft and steady. And steps inside.

The lobby gleams with natural light filtered through the willow's green curtain above, casting sun-dappled patterns across the marble floor. Boutique displays stretch across one half of the space, with rows of shimmering products, makeover stations, and mirrored counters buzzing with sales associates. The other half curves toward a darker hallway, where a brushed metal sign reads: Corporate Offices.

Mikki barely gets a few feet through the door before a chipper sales chickadee appears, feathers ruffling, sample bottle ready.

"Free spritz?"

"Oh… I'm actually just headed to—"

Pssst!

A cool mist shoots into the air just above her shoulder.

"Have a great day!" the chickadee chirps, already fluttering away.

Mikki's nose twitches, catching a hint of salty sweetness.

For a moment, she considers drifting into the boutique—just a peek—but instead, she chooses the hallway.

The boutique's buzz fades with each step, replaced by a quiet, modern corridor of cool lights and deep forest green wallpaper.

Mikki walks slowly, heels echoing on the floor as she reaches the executive lobby. A glass display case spans the far wall, showcasing a lineup of vintage perfume bottles—slender, colorful, and arranged by season. One for every era of Shabó Cosmetics.

The receptionist desk is empty. Beyond it, vertical blinds stretch across a large office window, closed tight.

Mikki draws in a quiet breath and turns toward the tall door just ahead.

She lifts a paw, holds it in place... then knocks.

Laughter filters through the door.

"Enter at your own risk!"

William's voice.

Mikki steps fully into the room, her long, slender tail slipping through the tailored slit at the back of her skirt, swaying with quiet rhythm.

JackRabbitt pushes off his hind legs and springs to his feet.

"Mikki! Just the mouse I was hoping to see!"

"Well, aren't you two hares looking happy today? Let me guess... something to do with summer sales? This old tree is really hopping today! I barely made it through the lobby without getting lured into the boutique. But I did get a drive-by spritzing."

She lifts her wrist and gives it a delicate sniff. "Ocean Breeze is simply divine."

"Mikki, that scent is my personal favorite," says William enthusiastically.

Without missing a beat, he slips into a his commercial announcer voice, like he's stepped straight into the fragrance ad.

"Refreshing top notes of sea spray and whispering waves."

He gives her a wink. "That's straight from my own ad copy. It's good to see you, Mikki. You're looking well."

"I'll say!" JackRabbitt's eyes brighten. "You're looking incredible! Has something changed with your fur?"

Mikki dips her head, wondering if the change is as noticeable as they make it seem. She smooths the elegant fabric of her silky magenta blouse, its long straps tied into a bow just below her chin. Paired with a smart pencil skirt, she's dressed for success, hoping to exude both professionalism and charm.

"Why, yes... something has changed," she admits, her eyes shimmering with a mixture of excitement and uncertainty. "You know, Kathra's idea has really sparked something in me."

"Mikki has been very busy lately."

JackRabbitt turns to William, bringing him up to speed.

"She's working on a fantastic charity event for the Forest ReLeaf Fund." He lightly touches her elbow. "Please, have a seat, and tell us more about it."

The topic lifts Mikki's spirits instantly. "Well, I don't want to give away too much..."

"Come on, Mikki!" William coaxes, jumping up to offer her his chair. He circles around, pulls it out with a little flourish, and sweeps his arm invitingly toward the seat. "You have to give us some details. How else are we going to arrange a donation?"

Mikki sinks into the chair, still unsure of how much she's ready to share.

William settles beside her, paws folded neatly in his lap.

Across from them, JackRabbitt sits behind the desk, watching with quiet encouragement.

"Well, since you asked..." Mikki begins softly. "Picture this... The Colonnade House. A silent auction. A lantern-lit path through The Meadow. And a dance floor beneath the stars."

She looks up, a touch of charm in her gaze. "And maybe... just maybe, a Shabó Cosmetics fall sampler among the auction items?"

"You can count on it!" JackRabbitt flashes a wide grin, his front teeth peeking out. "Mikki, it's so good to see you this way. Look at you! You are glowing again!"

"Thank you so much for saying that." Her cheeks warm beneath her honey-blonde fur. "This event has been just what I needed to take my mind off of... well, everything." She looks down, letting the thought settle. "I guess the only downside is that I'm not quite sure what I'll do with myself in a few weeks, after it's all said and done."

"Funny you should say that."

JackRabbitt casts a quick glance at William—somewhere between mischief and strategy.

"I have an idea that I think you'll find intriguing."

"Oh really?" Mikki narrows her eyes, sensing something has been cooked up. "What's that?"

JackRabbitt leans in, gives it a moment—then strikes.

"Mikki, I think Shabó Cosmetics could use your talent. And your style. What would you say to becoming a spokesmodel for some of our key products? *Furspray. Furshimmer. Claw Color.* I could see you in print ads from here to The Outer Forest."

She gives her hair a nervous toss. "Oh, JackRabbitt... I don't know about... modeling? Me?"

With perfect timing, JackRabbitt turns to his partner in crime.

"William, back me up here. Wouldn't Mikki be an incredible face for the fall line?"

William's eyes spark, already swept into his own vision. "I can see it now. A full campaign. Our own launch event with the showstopping reveal of Mikki—the star of the fall line! The crowd will eat you up."

Mikki's head swirls—too many compliments. She shakes it off.

"You two are dangerous when you put your heads together."

The words hang there.

She doesn't even know how true that is.

JackRabbitt doesn't flinch, but his stomach knots.

Beside him, William freezes, then flashes a warm smile to keep the fire burning. "Just imagine the press—everyone will be talking about the products, the venue, the food, the guest list."

JackRabbitt moves in for the win. "We could do a fashion tie-in with Forest Creations."

He lets the silence be there—just long enough, then—

"Say, Mikki, aren't you friends with Arik and Bridge Forester? Do you think you could contact them for us?"

Another look passes between JackRabbitt and William—barely perceptible, but sharp.

Mikki opens her mouth, then closes it again. Her furry brow wrinkles as she shifts slightly in her seat.

"Oh, well... yes. I suppose I could do that. Arik and Bridge have never turned down the opportunity for a fashion show. And I'm sure they have some fabulous new items in their fall collection they'd like to have featured."

And just like that, she takes the bait.

She pulls her planner from her bag—a leaf-leather-bound book adorned with a curling rose design. Then, with a flick of her paw, she turns to a fresh page.

"You know, a harvest theme could really accentuate the seasonal product change. Maybe we could even invite some local artists to help with the decor. Ooh! And a local chef could cater some delicious gourmet treats!"

Her voice grows more animated with every word, her eyes shining with ambition.

"You're onto something big here!" JackRabbitt leans back in his chair, satisfied with a job well done.

Together, they continue tossing around theme ideas like leaves in a playful breeze—festival colors, forest accents, local sponsorships. The energy is light, hopeful.

William springs to his feet and breaks into a goofy dance—all exaggerated hips and shameless jazz-paws.

Mikki throws her head back and laughs at him.

JackRabbitt watches her laugh—*really* laugh—for the first time in a long while.

The sadness that once weighed her down seems to lift, replaced by a comforting sense of purpose.

She rests her paws on her outfit, feeling that it does indeed emphasize her newfound hope.

But then—

A sudden flicker of trepidation crosses her face.

"But... I'm not sure I'm ready to be in the public eye so soon after, you know... Victor."

JackRabbitt hesitates, weighing his words like they might break something.

"But, Mikki. This could be just the thing to bring the community together after the death of such a... titan of industry."

He suddenly finds himself caught somewhere between compassion and disgust.

"Chenoa City needs someone to look to right now. Someone strong. If they see you thriving... they'll believe they can, too."

He leans over the desk and holds out his paws for her to take them.

She does.

"You could be that symbol. A role model for all mousekind."

She suppresses a surge of tears.

"I... I don't feel like a role model."

She draws her paws back quickly.

JackRabbitt sees her sinking and is desperate to throw her a life raft.

"But you *are* a role model, Mikki. You *are*! You have been to the bottom and you have risen to the top. The forest will want to see that. They will want to see *you*."

"I guess I've almost forgotten what it feels like to be seen."

She shrinks, ears wilting.

And as the room grows heavier with emotion—

It's William who breaks first.

"Well, I have a... meeting to get to. Right?"

He looks down to the nonexistent watch on his bare wrist.

"Right."

JackRabbitt and William lock eyes—a moment of unspoken understanding passing between them.

William steps beside Mikki.

He places a paw gently on her shoulder—a rare moment of stillness from him.

"Mikki, you would make an incredible spokesmouse."

He lingers, just for a moment, then sails out the door.

JackRabbitt senses Mikki drifting further away.

"Mikki Mouse? What are you thinking? Talk to me."

She turns her attention to him, voice steadier now.

"If we do this, it has to matter. It has to mean something. It has to benefit more than just the cosmetics line."

"Absolutely. For every product sold from our new collection, a portion could go toward The Forest ReLeaf Fund... or the Woodland Wellness Initiative... or The SORAS Foundation. You name it."

A quiet confidence settles into her posture. Her mind turns back to imagining the possibilities.

Then, something deeper rises—a chord that hasn't been struck in forever.

"I haven't performed in ages. But maybe I could play something? Just one piece. On the piano?"

She stops herself.

"But the modeling, the campaign... being the face of it all—that's a whole new version of me I'm not sure I've met yet."

She meets his eyes.

"I promise I'll think about it."

Her fingers trace the bow at her neckline like they're testing out forgotten keys.

JackRabbitt watches closely, relieved to still see the excitement in her eyes.

A quiet rhythm settles between them, full of promise, like a melody just beginning to play.

Chapter Thirteen

Revolving Door

Built beside The Great River, The Chenoa City Country Club rests at the water's edge, its marina lined with sleek boats swaying in the breeze. Past the docks, the grounds stretch wide with lush greens, a neatly trimmed widget course, and winding paths that lead toward The Clubhouse.

Inside the grand revolving door entrance, The Clubhouse has all the amenities its wealthy members could want—a bar and fine-dining restaurant, private lodging, a fitness center, and a gift shop where last-minute valentines and birthday baubles are often bought just hours before the event.

Deep in the cellar lounge, the sharp spice of rolled hickoryleaf smoke curls through the polished wood air. Leaf-leather-backed chairs sit deep and worn, inviting long nights of drinking and quiet scheming. Here, the pawshake is firm, the smile is convincing—and the fingers are always crossed.

When the sun goes down, the cards come out—and everything's on the table. No ledgers. No paper trails. Just the bet, the payoff, and the shifting of fortunes.

There are those who know how to play the game.

And then—there's William Abbitt.

Lounging at a secluded card table near the bar, his long ears tilt lazily, half-listening to the room, half-tuned to the quiet *shuffle* of a deal.

One arm drapes over the back of his chair, the other rests on his chips. His brownberry bourbon waits nearby, untouched but not forgotten. His sandy-colored fur glows by the firelight, hazel eyes gleaming with something unreadable as he watches the game unfold.

The pot is big. Too big to resist.

"Raise," he drawls, flicking a stack of chips toward the center of the table.

He grins. A well-worn bluff.

Across from him, a fox scowls. His whiskers twitch. Just slightly. Just enough to notice. He's losing confidence—William can see it.

This is where they usually fold. But this one doesn't.

"Call," the fox mutters, shoving his chips forward.

William runs his tongue across his top incisors thoughtfully. A tiny reaction. He's not worried. Not yet anyway.

Slowly, deliberately, they lay down their cards.

First, William.

A full house. A damn good spread.

The room stills. No one speaks. The flames *crackle* quietly in the hearth.

The fox grins and flashes his cards.

Four of a kind.

The table erupts.

The fox slams his paws on the felt as he rakes in the pot.

A couple of lady hares at William's side cackle with mocking laughter.

"Darling, you might be the worst gambler I've ever met."

William just grins, his nostrils flaring faintly with amusement.

"Oh, honey," he says, lifting his glass for a slow sip, "you should've been here last night."

The fox shakes his head, still grinning.

"You don't seem too upset."

"Of course not." William leans back, his long legs stretching beneath the table.

"Losing's part of the fun."

Around him, the club carries on, full of laughter, the clinking of glasses, and the shuffling of cards. The night is still young, and William is exactly where he wants to be.

And yet...

An itch that hasn't been scratched.

Above him, in the second-floor gym, Victoria throws another punch.

She drives her fist into the heavy bag, the impact sharp, controlled, relentless.

Victoria hates this club.

The polished wood. The perfectly arranged floral displays. The quiet, privileged murmur of old money and old expectations.

Her family's name has been on the membership list for as long as she can remember.

When she was young, she loved having the run of the grounds with the other club kits. But now...

Now, she's only here because the gym is the one place, other than The Crow House, where she can actually breathe.

Sweat clings to her fur as she drives her fists into the heavy bag, rhythm steady, controlled.

Thud. Thud. Thud.

Her tail curls with each strike, adjusting for balance as she shifts her stance and throws another hit.

She welcomes the burn, the sting, the distraction.

Her father is gone, yet he is everywhere.

His legacy. His name. Creating an expectation of who she's supposed to be.

She throws another punch, harder this time, her jaw tightening with the force of it.

It doesn't matter. None of it matters.

Move far away from here and go to college.

Or just stay in Chenoa City and work in the mailroom at Newmouse Enterprises.

What difference does it make?

The walls around her *creak* faintly—the restaurant below, alive with conversation and clinking silverware.

The world she was born into. The world that wants her. The world that she wants nothing to do with.

She swings hard, hitting the bag wrong. Her wrist bends too much on impact, sending a sharp sting up through her arm.

She curses under her breath, steadying the bag with both paws, claws pressing lightly into the canvas.

That's enough.

She peels off her gloves, wipes the sweat from her brow, grabs her bag, and heads down the stairs toward the exit.

She doesn't notice the chain hanging loose.

And she doesn't notice her small, brass wristwatch slipping free, tumbling silently onto the carpeted stairs just before she reaches the main floor.

Below, in the lounge, the night carries on.

William takes the last sip of his brownberry bourbon, then pushes himself up with a stretch. He murmurs something about fresh air, swiping his jacket from the chair as he heads up the stairs.

At the same time, Victoria reaches the main floor.

She steps down.

He steps up.

They pass in the foyer, just inside the revolving door.

She sweeps through the spinning door and out into the night. William doesn't notice her—he's too busy adjusting his jacket.

But as he steps forward, something catches his eye.

A watch, lying just beside the stair rail.

He pauses, bends down, and picks it up. It's small. Not a buck's watch. Brass. A little scuffed from wear. Could've been here for an hour, or a minute. No way to tell.

He flicks it once, spinning it around his fingers, then shrugs and locks it into his grasp. No point thinking too hard about it.

William makes it exactly three steps toward the exit before deciding that the night air is probably overrated.

It's damp. Unpredictable. Full of… responsibility.

The bar, on the other paw, is warm, well-stocked, and full of bad jokes just waiting to be made.

He pivots smoothly, as if this had been the plan all along, and beelines for the restaurant bar instead. The air is thick with quiet judgment, but at least the chairs have better cushions. William slides into one, absently setting the watch down on the bar top beside his emerald green cocktail napkin with The Chenoa City Country Club logo embossed in gold.

The restaurant is bathed in a low amber light.

The leaf-leather-backed menus are heavy in the paw, the kind that remind you that nothing here is cheap.

A waiter in a crisp vest glides past without acknowledging him, more concerned with the kind of guests who expect their melt mushrooms to be seared at exactly 120 degrees.

Not that William minds. He's not here to eat. He's here to drink.

As he leans against the bar, rolling an empty glass, his eyes drift to the watch.

He picks it up, twirls it again between his fingers, then turns it over in his paw.

The back is engraved.

He tilts it toward the light, squinting at the delicate design etched into it:

A pair of wings—intricate, feathered, stretched wide as if caught mid-flight. The carving is worn at the edges, softened from years of use, but the detail is still there—the fine grooves catching just enough light to give the illusion of movement.

An oddly detailed engraving. Wings. On a wristwatch. Not the kind of thing you pick up from a shop shelf.

A deep scratch runs along the back—maybe from being stepped on, maybe from being on the floor longer than it should have been.

"Sentimental value," he mutters, half to himself.

The bartender glances over. "Somebody lose that?"

William twirls it once more, debating. There's something about it—not quite curiosity, but the barest flicker of interest.

But not enough to keep it.

He shrugs, tossing it lightly onto the bar top.

"Guess it wasn't mine to begin with."

The bartender scoffs, shaking his head.

"You're lucky you don't care about money, Abbitt."

He smirks.

"Luck is just skill dressed in the right suit."

William pushes off the bar, straightens his jacket, and strides toward the exit without a second thought.

The revolving door rotates as he steps out.

A moment later, it rotates again as Victoria steps in.

Her eyes sweep the room, ponytail still damp, breath still cooling from the workout.

She knew she had it when she left the gym, but somewhere between the stairs and the door—it was gone.

She moves quickly, scanning the floor first, but then—something familiar catches her eye.

She looks up.

There. On the counter. Near the bartender's reach.

Her watch is sitting—set aside, like somebody meant to return it.

She exhales, pressing her lips together as she picks it up.

Warm, familiar, safe in her paws again.

She secures it back onto her wrist, the weight of it settling against her fur like an anchor.

She never notices the rabbit who found it.

And he never sees the mouse who came back for it.

Chapter Fourteen

Sunsetters

On the terrace of The Country Club, the sun sinks low over the marina, burning in streaks of orange and gold as it nears the horizon. Its final light spills across the rippling water, turning the waves to liquid fire. The air carries the clean scent of the river, fresh and sharp.

Jon Abbitt sits near the railing, right where Kathra expects him to be. The evening breeze ruffles his once-tan rabbit fur, now streaked with gray. He watches a cargo ship unload—calm, content. A tumbler of salted brandy rests in his paw, beads of condensation sliding down the glass.

Kathra moves with purpose. Unhurried. Untouchable. Conversations dip as she passes. The rings on her toes shift with a soft chime, her talons clicking sharp and steady against the stone floor. Her sharp blue eyes scan the space, calculating.

Jon notices her the moment she steps onto the terrace. His ears twitch slightly, the fur there a little longer than it used to be. A small smile tugs at the corner of his lips. He begins to rise, ever the traditionalist, but Kathra waves him off with a quiet motion, already settling in.

"Kathra." He smiles. "To what do I owe the pleasure?"

The server moves swiftly, pouring her a drink before retreating into the background. She lifts the glass but doesn't sip just yet. Instead, she studies Jon, her gaze sharp enough to cut the glass she's holding.

"Tell me something, Jon," she says, her voice light but purposeful. "Is this what retirement looks like? Sitting alone out here, staring at boats?"

Jon lets out a quiet chuckle. "It suits me just fine."

"Someone should really set you up with a social life."

Jon raises a brow, amused but not surprised. "If that's your way of asking whether I need a matchmaking service, the answer is no."

"Jon, if I thought you needed a matchmaking service, I'd have sent somebody far more qualified than myself."

A deep horn bellows from the cargo ship as it slides by, cutting through the evening air. Kathra stills, waiting for the sound to fade, then resumes as if nothing had interrupted her.

"I'm just here checking in to make sure you're not making any... foolish decisions with your spare time."

Jon chuckles, shaking his head. "So, you're here to give me your opinion on Gillian."

Another long horn blasts from the cargo ship, echoing across the terrace—louder this time. Kathra's expression tightens. She exhales slowly, swirling her drink with just a little too much force.

"Gillian isn't an opinion. She's a disaster."

Jon sighs. He knows what is coming, but he makes a conscious decision to let Kathra get it out of her system.

She watches him for a long moment, weighing her next words very carefully.

"You might not see it yet, but—"

A third, sharper horn cuts her off mid-breath. This time, she sets her glass down with a crisp, decisive *thunk*. She adjusts her chair, scooting it around, as if a new angle will erase the irritating horn from existence. But the sound of the chair scraping across the stone floor is somehow louder than the blast itself.

"You were saying?" Jon asks, with a quiet, playful smile.

Kathra, however, does not smile.

She lets a long, painful silence stretch between them as she eyes the cargo ship, willing it to leave. She watches it drift into the distance before recommitting to the conversation.

She gathers her composure—

leans in—

parts her beak to speak—

And then—

SCREECH!

Kathra's beak snaps shut.

Her head jerks skyward.

Her neck tilts up, down, and all around, scanning the sky for the shrieking hawk that is circling above them.

"Oh, for heaven's sake. Is that Gillian circling?"

Jon doesn't bother looking up.

"Gillian's still a squirrel last I checked."

Kathra raises a brow, undeterred.

"She's leveled up, Jon. Evolution comes for us all."

Kathra ruffles her wings once, letting the tension drop.

Jon looks amused, but responds with ease.

"Gillian and I have been divorced for years."

"Are you going to deny that you've been seeing her?"

"Kathra, we were married. We have a son."

"You also had an ugly divorce."

"And that's exactly why we're trying to stay on better terms. I've seen her, yes—but I don't think she's trying to rekindle an old flame, if that's what you're worried about."

"Gillian doesn't rekindle old flames. She reignites them... just long enough to burn through them." She gives him a moment to let the words settle. "I would hate to see you reduced to kindling."

Jon exhales and leans back, his gaze drifting toward the marina. On one of the boats, a crew member climbs the rigging, moving with the ease of experience. Jon watches for a moment before turning his attention back to Kathra.

"I know exactly who Gillian is, Kathra. I don't need a reminder."

"Good," Kathra says simply. "You'd be wise to not let history repeat itself."

Jon turns a small card over in his paw, running a claw along the edge.

"You didn't come here just to talk about Gillian. What's on your mind?"

"Really, Jon. What are you doing sitting here enjoying all of this... miserable peace and quiet when you could be back at Shabó Cosmetics in the thick of things?"

Jon flips the card again, unreadable.

"Kathra. You also didn't come here to convince me out of retirement. So, I'll save you the trouble of the soft sell and guess that you're really here to talk about JackRabbitt."

Kathra leans back, adjusts her feathers against the breeze, then folds her wings neatly in front of her.

"Darling, I just think that, since you've taken a step back, it's left him without a..." She searches for the words. "Guiding light."

Jon finally sets the card flat against the table.

"I took a step back from my company. I didn't take a step back from my family."

"Well, yes. Of course. Jon, listen, dear. You know I respect you. I've always respected you. You and I share the same values. The long-standing traditions. The tried and true methods. I need a CEO at Newmouse who thinks like we do."

Jon doesn't look up. His paw turns the card again.

Kathra continues, "I'm not against progress, you see. But JackRabbitt's got these wild ideas about trade deals with The Outer Forest, and it's not going over well with the rest of the board."

Jon tilts his head. "You think he's making enemies?"

"I think he's underestimating certain... special interests."

Jon watches her, reading between the lines. Then, he leans forward, resting his forearms on the table.

"And what about *your* interests, Kathra?"

Kathra brings one wing to her throat, the tip grazing her jewels before settling softly against her chest.

"What *about* my interests?"

Jon's smile is too knowing now. "Come on, Kathra. Your investments are at stake here. Your company needs those domestic building contracts with Newmouse. Your interests are in line with how Victor ran the company... not with how JackRabbitt wants to run it."

"Darling, I won't deny it. My interests and Victor's interests were often aligned. But Victor knew how to play the game. JackRabbitt wants to change the game altogether. And I can assure you, there's more at stake here than just my investments."

Jon exhales, rolling the card between his fingers.

For the first time, he flips it face-up, pressing it against the table.

It reads:

Jon Abbitt. Founder and Chief Executive Officer. Shabó Cosmetics.

Kathra's eyes flick down, just for a second.

She sees the card. Registers it. But says nothing.

Instead, she lifts her glass and waits.

"Kathra," he says, his voice steady, "I'm not getting involved in Newmouse Enterprises business. Jack is his own rabbit, and he's going to do what he's going to do, whether I step in or not. If you came here thinking I'd put a leash on him, you're wasting your time."

Kathra's gaze sharpens. "Jon, I came here because he listens to you."

"JackRabbitt listens to me when he wants to, and ignores me when he doesn't."

Kathra holds his gaze for a long moment. There's something behind her eyes—not pressure, not plea, but history. Memories. A mutual respect that doesn't need to be said aloud.

Then, slowly, she leans back, smoothing the tablecloth with a measured touch.

He exhales slowly. "Alright. I'll talk to him. But I won't interfere. That's as much as I'm willing to offer."

"That's all I could hope for, my dear."

Jon lifts the card again, holding it between two fingers. The setting sun catches the gold lettering, glinting off his name. The light is lower now, softer. The sky, once painted in fire, cools to a deep indigo.

"You know," he says, turning the card one last time, "I always thought I'd know when it was time to let go."

Kathra watches him carefully.

"Well, my dear," she says, lifting her glass, "the sun also rises."

Jon chuckles, shaking his head.

"Live until you die, Kathra."

She tilts her glass in a silent toast.

"Nothing less, Jon."

Jon watches the marina for a long moment after Kathra leaves, lightly grinding his teeth and watching the sunset. The card lingers between his fingers before he finally tucks it into his coat pocket.

The last sliver of sun disappears beyond the horizon.

But maybe the sun hasn't set on him just yet.

Chapter Fifteen

The Abbitt Warren

The Abbitt Warren is a welcome refuge after another long day at the family business. Nestled beneath a flowering bush, the home is burrowed deep into the earth, its entrance hidden among the blossoms. Guests are welcomed on the grand porch tucked beneath the blooms... but beyond that, the underground is reserved for the family alone.

With its curved tunnels and wide chambers, the burrow is stately and elegant, yet its enclosed nature gives it a sense of intimacy. Glazed stone and crystal walls catch the soft glow of lanterns, while fresh flowers brighten the entryway. Every room is rich with trinkets and ornaments—each one a token of a life well-lived in the forest.

The dining room is where the family spends most of their evenings together, and tonight is no different. The smooth wooden table gleams, freshly polished. Fine porcelain plates and shining silverware have been arranged with precision around it.

The aroma that fills the air is one of tradition: long-held recipes of hearty roasted vegetables, savory herbs, and warm, golden bread just from the oven. Maw, the housekeeper, has outdone herself again.

The family settles back in their chairs—Jon looking pleased, JackRabbitt and Ashlyn still dressed for the office, and Macy, younger by several seasons, sitting quietly at her usual spot.

Macy runs her fork through the food on her plate, slow and methodical. Her soft tummy presses gently against the edge of the table, the fabric of her oversized knitted cardigan bunched awkwardly around the middle. She doesn't like to eat in front of others—not even the family. Besides, Maw's honey-glazed carrots taste better cold, snuck from the fridge by the pawful.

"Did you know William is with his mother tonight?" Macy's voice is soft and sweet—and always a bit too cheerful.

Jon and JackRabbitt squirrel in their seats at the mention of Gillian's name.

Ashlyn, the chemist, steps in like she's stabilizing a volatile compound.

"Uh. Macy, why don't you tell everyone the good news about your writing? I think they'd love to hear about it."

Macy's cheeks flush slightly, but her gaze flickers with an inner glow. "Oh... well. Ok. So. My short story will be published in the college newspaper next week," she says, her voice growing more sure as she speaks, though the words are still soft. "It's kind of surreal. Between that and prepping for Tanny's gig, I haven't really slept at all."

JackRabbitt, swirling the last of his drink in his glass, says smoothly, "You've got a voice, Macy. On the page... and on the stage. That's power."

Jon turns to her with genuine warmth. "That's wonderful, Macy. We're all so proud of you. Communication is an important skill, you know."

Macy offers a small bob of her head, her pale blonde fur shifting with the motion.

But just as quickly as Jon praises his youngest daughter, his attention shifts to Ashlyn.

"And Ashlyn," he says with pride, "I suppose you've got a few new projects to show us too? The whole town's talking about your summer line."

He raises his glass for a toast.

"To Ashlyn—my beauty—and your incredible success. I can't wait to see what you're cooking up in the lab for fall."

JackRabbitt raises his glass, offering his approval as the eldest sibling... but he isn't celebrating summer colors. He's celebrating this brief, quiet moment. The calm before the storm.

"To Ashlyn," he echoes. "And to the future." He grins.

"Thank you!" Ashlyn's eyes sparkle as she lifts her own glass in return.

But as she notices all eyes on her, Ashlyn feels the slightest twinge of guilt. Without meaning to, she's shifted the spotlight away from her sister. She glances across the table—and just as she expects, Macy is already gathering her plate.

Ashlyn stands. "Come on, Macy," she says, light and encouraging. "Let's clear the table. I want to talk more about your future career as a prize-winning novelist slash singer."

Instead, Macy steers the conversation toward her crush on the Abbitt family gardener-turned-executive. "Or... you could just tell me what Brack was wearing at the office today." Her face lights up with a sly smile, her little tail giving an excited wiggle. "Oh, please tell me it was the tight black pants!"

Their conversation trails off as they make their way toward the kitchen, laughter echoing softly down the tunnel.

JackRabbitt leans back, pressing a paw to his stomach.

Indigestion.

Probably the carrots.

He's got bigger things to focus on.

He pushes back the chair, stands, and stretches his arms as he often does after a big meal.

"I'll join them. And I'll do my best to steer the conversation away from... Brack-a-licious."

He begins to leave. But Jon's voice stops him.

"JackRabbitt." His tone is serious. "I need to speak with you."

JackRabbitt freezes, his ears flicking forward before he forces them still. Suddenly, he feels like a young buck again, caught after sneaking the boat out for a midnight ride. Slowly, he lowers himself back down into his chair.

"What is it, Dad?"

"I've noticed something." Jon leans in closely. "You're tired, son. I think you're pushing too hard. You're not taking care of yourself."

JackRabbitt exhales, letting the tension in his muscles relax. His father doesn't suspect he's up to anything. He'll find out soon enough about the Newmouse takeover.

But not now. Not yet.

He would only try to stop me.

"Dad, I've got it all under control."

"I know you're in control, son. And I'm proud of you. So proud. I've always known you were capable of great things."

Jon settles back, crossing one leg over the other in a single, fluid motion—smooth as water, effortless as the tide.

"But I'm also worried. The extra responsibilities—CEO of

Newmouse Enterprises? You didn't take that position just for the title."

His arms fold across his chest and he tilts his head.

"I know you. You're trying to change the world. Trying to make it a better place. And that's an awfully tall order for one rabbit."

A deep *pressure* coils in JackRabbitt's gut.

"A little *pressure* never hurt anyone," he mutters.

A *sharp* twist tightens beneath his ribs.

"Besides... it keeps me *sharp*."

Jon wrinkles his forehead. "Running a publicly traded company with a board of directors is not the same as running our family business, is it?"

Instantly, JackRabbitt feels hot all over, searing from the inside out.

"Oh, I see. So, Kathra's been working overtime." He knew this was a possibility. "How resourceful of her."

"Yes," Jon says tentatively, "Kathra came to me with her concerns." He shifts forward, resting his arms on the table. "But my concern is you."

JackRabbitt takes a deep breath, preparing himself. "Well, go ahead and tell me. What did the wise old owl say?"

"Alright." Jon reaches for the pitcher of milk thistle at the center of the table and sets it down with a soft *thunk*.

"She said the Newmouse Board of Directors expects Newmouse Enterprises to be run the way Victor ran it."

JackRabbitt releases a quick, disgusted snort.

"Victor had a talent, I'll give him that. He built a hell of an empire out of stealing mining rights."

A quiet pause.

"Was it stealing?" Jon lifts the pitcher. "...if they signed it away?"

The liquid flows in a steady stream into his glass. The soft trickle breaks the silence.

"The Abbitts refused to sell. But there were families who were happy to take the scraps they were offered and start anew."

He sets the pitcher down again, resting his paw against the cool glass, the condensation wetting his fingertips. Thoughtfully, he remembers an old saying, then recites it aloud—

"Music comes from an icicle as it melts, to live again as spring water."

Jon slides the pitcher back across the polished wood. The *clink* of melting ice echoes faintly inside as its weight settles between them.

Suddenly, a searing pocket of pressure swells in JackRabbitt's gut. It burns like lava surging up his throat in an invisible eruption.

"How can you say that, Dad? The families who built this city deserve more than scraps."

A belch rises, thick with bitterness, but he forces it back down.

"Victor swindled them. He bought out their legacies for less than they were worth, and then gave nothing back to the community."

Jon picks up his milk thistle glass.

"You don't think a thriving economy is good for the community? Creatures have jobs. Creatures have homes."

He takes a slow, cool sip. His gaze never falters as he sets the glass back down with a quiet, deliberate *tap*.

JackRabbitt grunts, the heat still crawling up his throat.

His paw moves instinctively.

He grabs the pitcher, clenching the handle tight.

He loses control. The pitcher hits the rim of his glass with a *clang*.

A stream spills across the dark wood table.

He doesn't clean up the mess.

Instead, he lifts the glass and drinks—one, two, three quick gulps.

And then slams it down on the table harder than he meant to.

The liquid lingers in his stomach, the coldness battling the burn.

Jon waits patiently for him to finish. His eyes hold the quiet stillness of deep water, unaffected by the movement of the tides.

"Son, did you know the name 'Chenoa' means peace?"

Jon's voice is soft, steady.

"Peace is the foundation of our culture."

Jon closes the space between them, his presence unwavering.

He's the same Dad he's always been—the one who stayed when she didn't.

She never stays.

Not for Macy.

Not for Ashlyn.

Not for me.

"Long ago, we signed a treaty that allows us to live without fighting each other."

Jon rests a paw on his son's shoulder.

"Without hunting each other."

He gives a light pull and a small affectionate shake.

"Without devouring each other."

He lingers just long enough to let the gesture land, then pulls his paw away.

JackRabbitt releases the breath he didn't realize he was holding.

The burn in his body cools, just a little.

It wasn't the milk thistle he needed. It was his father's touch.

And the heat had nothing to do with the carrots.

He's been raised on his father's ideals since he was young— peace, equality, opportunity. He wants all of those things for Chenoa City... and for himself too.

But peace doesn't come without a push.

"Dad, I admire the hell out of you. I wish I could be half the rabbit you are."

His chin dips for a brief moment, trembling.

"You've given me a foundation, and I want to build onto it. I want to build something the next generation can stand on."

He lifts his chin, pushes back his shoulders, and straightens his spine.

"I want a family and a legacy of my own."

And I will be a hero...

Even if they never call me one.

Chapter Sixteen

Dedication

Snip!

Victor flinches.

"Got me on the ear again, doe!"

He presses a paw to his ear, feigning an injury.

Grace tilts her head toward him, smiling faintly as the ceremonial scissors are removed from her paws and replaced with her trusty cane.

All around them, the Pumpkin Acres Dedication Ceremony is alive with spirit and celebration. It's a triumph for Grace... and a milestone for Southbrook. The twelve homes sit nestled side by side, each one lovingly crafted for comfort, warmth, and everyday living. The walls still glow with the pumpkin's original hue—soft orange against the green rolling hills. Garden beds wait in every backyard, mailboxes stand ready for letters, and porch chairs rock gently in the breeze... like they've been waiting for this day all along.

Grace can't see it, but she knows—her vision has come to life. She hears the laughter of baby animals frolicking on the playground, feels the *thwack* of rackets reverberating from the new peaball court, and smells the pies and casseroles wafting from the community potluck.

Nearby, the low murmur of elders drifts from beneath a shady tree, their voices weaving together in soft memory. Grace tilts her head, ears twitching. She swears she just heard her father's name. Her heart swells with the quiet certainty that she's made her parents proud.

Gratitude radiates from the families surrounding her.

"Thank you, Miss Grace," says a mother rabbit, cradling her youngest kit while her older children cling to her skirt. "We never thought we'd have a place of our own."

"You've given us hope," says a squirrel with a shy smile, slipping a small corsage of bluebells onto her wrist.

Grace blushes under their praise. She shifts her weight on her cane and nods politely.

"I'm just glad we could make it happen."

Despite her modesty, the crowd's affection carries her from one group to the next, each eager to thank her personally. She lets their enthusiasm guide her from one kind word to another—until a scruffy-looking mouse steps forward and stops her.

He's thin. His coat is worn. One paw grips his hat with quiet desperation.

"Miss Grace," he begins, his voice trembling slightly, "I hate to bother you, but I was wonderin'... when might there be more homes like these?"

She angles one ear slightly forward, adjusting to the direction of his voice.
"More homes?" she asks gently.

"Yes, ma'am. Winter's comin', and it's lookin' to be a harsh one. My wife... well, she's expectin'. It'd mean the world to us to have a place like this to raise our litter."

Grace's heart aches at his plea.

I know how cold the dark can be.

She tightens her grip on the cane, considering her response.

While she must be cautious about making promises, the joy of the day emboldens her.

"We are doing our best," she assures him. "More homes will be built. I'll make sure of it. There's still time before Winter hits. We are not done here. Not by a long shot."

The mouse's face lights up with gratitude. But before Grace can respond further, the crowd begins chanting, "Speech! Speech!" She's caught off guard, her ears swiveling toward the makeshift stage adorned with balloons and banners. Paws guide her forward, and much to her surprise, she soon finds herself at the center, gripping the podium.

The noise quiets, leaving her with an expectant silence.

"I... I don't know what to—" she begins, a nervous laugh escaping as her fingers tap against the wood, searching for the right words. "But, um..."

She pauses, steadies herself, and then continues:

"Thank you. Thank you all for being here today. None of this would have been possible without the hard work and dedication of so many. They worked day and night to make these homes a reality."

The crowd cheers, and she feels the warmth of their approval. "And I think we all owe a special round of applause to our very own Construction Manager, Biff Milson! Come on up here, Biff! Take a bow!"

Her words ring out as Biff bounds onto the stage, shaking it as he stomps up to take his place proudly beside her. He gives an over-exaggerated bow, his big, burly tail swinging forward— flopping clean over his head. He pops back up with a toothy smile, then tops off his moment of glory with a little jig for the crowd. He's unusually animated today. Perhaps it's the barley juice.

As the attention shifts back to Grace, she freezes, unsure how to proceed. Then there's a sound—a subtle, quiet clearing of a throat. Unmistakable. Grace knows exactly who it is.

"And I would also like to personally thank the newest member of the construction team... Mr. Victor Miller!"

Victor doesn't wait for an invitation. He strides onto the stage with an air of confidence, nudging Biff aside and positioning himself next to Grace. Biff stumbles back, tail twitching. His smile remains out of habit, but his eyes betray the truth: Victor just chased him out of his own tree.

"Thank you, Grace," Victor says in his grandiose corporate tone. "I only hope the outhouses can live up to the occasion."

The crowd laughs—some louder than the joke probably deserved.

Biff fake-laughs along with them—loud, forced, and about three seconds too late. Then, with a final scoff under his breath, he steps back, tail in a twist, and fades into the background.

Grace chuckles softly, then turns to Victor.

"Your ideas and your input have been so valuable to the team... and to me."

Victor threads his fingers through hers, like they've done before in private—

But never in front of anyone.

The audience cheers and whistles.

At any other time in her life, Grace might have felt embarrassed by this surprise display of public affection.

But today, her smile runs deep and wide, steady as the river behind them.

She roots herself in its current, the rush around her only lifting her higher.

This moment, this feeling—it's what she's been striving for all along.

She is happier now than she's ever been.

But as the applause begins to ebb, a new wave crashes over her.

She thinks of the scruffy mouse—of his anxiousness and hope.

She thinks of how much this moment means to him, too.

She feels the pull of responsibility. The need to do even more.

Somewhere below, a young voice calls out,

"You're a hero, Miss Grace!"

Hero.

The word startles her.

She's never thought of herself that way.

But now it's been said—and there's no giving it back.

She has to live up to it.

Grace lifts her head and, with newfound confidence, she speaks.

"Southbrook is the Glowstone of The Great River. And we've only just begun to shine! I know many more of you need this housing... and that's why I am promising you that we are committed to building twelve more homes before Winter!!!"

The crowd erupts in thunderous cheer—louder than before.

Every nerve in her body is humming and tingling.

And it feels like flying again.

With no hesitation, Victor hoists their paws together toward the sky.

The crowd is roaring.

The ground is vibrating.

And all she can think is...

I cannot let them down.

Chapter Seventeen

Old Habits

The late morning sun beats down on the riverside meadow, and the Pumpkin Acres construction crew gathers under the leafy shade of the open-air pavilion. The workers chatter amongst themselves, snacking on nuts and berries, their water canteens sloshing up and down as they hydrate. Tongues hang out, panting in the summer heat. Fur sticks slightly to the skin. Comments about the sweltering day sprinkle through the conversation like sands through the hourglass.

Victor sits at a wooden table near the center of the pavilion. His ruggedly handsome features and easy demeanor make him the center of attention, even as he concentrates on the game before him.

Across the table sits Barney, a sleek orange barn cat whose whiskers twitch in concentration.

The two are locked in a fierce game of Chessnuts.

Victor's paw hovers over a nut-shaped gamepiece, representing his Queen. He glances at the board, then at Barney. A slow smile spreads across his face as he moves his Queen with deliberate precision.

"Checkmate," he declares.

A moment of silence falls over the pavilion before it erupts into cheers and exclamations.

"Victor just beat Barney! He really beat him!" shouts a squirrel, his tail swishing excitedly.

"A mouse beating a cat. How about that?" adds a gopher, his eyes wide with amazement.

Bets begin settling quickly among the crew. Scraps exchange paws as winners gloat and losers grumble.

"You lose! Pay up!" a badger purrs, pocketing his winnings. "That'll be twenty drift coins!"

Victor smooths his mouse 'stache as he leans back in his seat. The crowd surrounds him, clapping his back and praising his skill. Despite the heat, his composure remains intact, his fur barely ruffled. He extends a paw toward Barney, who looks both surprised and slightly annoyed by his defeat.

"Good game, old boy," Victor says. "You're a worthy opponent."

Barney's green eyes narrow briefly before he chuckles, shaking Victor's paw.

"You're a hell of a competitor, Victor."

"As are you," he replies. "We must do this again."

Before the camaraderie can continue further, Biff stomps into the pavilion, his broad shoulders and dusty fur giving him an imposing presence. The good mood of yesterday is gone, replaced by a marked urgency. He takes one look at the lively group and gruffly interrupts.

"Okay, okay. Let's get back to work," he says, his voice carrying over the commotion.

The crew protests, groaning in unison.

"Aw, Biff, we still got two minutes left on break!" a fellow squirrel argues.

Another voice chimes in,

"Biff, you shoulda seen it. Victor beat Barney at Chessnuts!"

Biff waves a paw dismissively.

"Guys, we ain't gonna finish building these new pumpkin houses by sittin' around playing games. Come on, I know it's hot, but winter's coming fast. And there's families that need these homes!"

A reminder of the importance of their work silences the complaints. Heads nod as the animals begin gathering their tools and cleaning up the remnants of their break. The crew disperses reluctantly, though admiration for Victor lingers in their glances and murmurs. The chatter dwindles into silence, punctuated only by the clinking of tools and the crunching of feet over dried grass.

As the pavilion empties, a gopher named Diggert approaches Victor. Diggert is built like a small bulldozer, his shoulders hunched slightly from years of grinding at the earth. He carries a small sack tied with twine, its contents clinking faintly with each step.

"Victor," he says. "Hey, 'preciate you comin' out yesterday. That damn pulley would've been the death of me. Buddy, you're a pretty good engineer. You could be a real success someday!"

Victor is more amused by the compliment than he lets on. A wide grin spreads across his face as he leans back on his heels and lets out a soft, "Hee hee hee."

He takes a breath, places a paw on Diggert's shoulder, and says, "Perhaps."

Diggert shakes his head, raising the sack.

"My wife and I thought maybe you could use this."

He thrusts it toward Victor, who hesitates.

"Oh no, Diggert. You don't have to pay me."

"Well, I know you said no scraps, but this isn't scraps."

He forces the sack into Victor's paws.

"It's just a little coal. Thought you could smoke yourself up a nice dinner."

He leans in and whispers,

"My wife insists."

Victor feels the weight of the bag and the rough texture of the nuggets inside. He unties the string and sniffs the contents, the familiar earthy scent of coal filling his nose.

The gophers always know where the coal beds are. Every town. Every time.

He nods appreciatively, then turns his head to both sides, instinctively checking to see who else is around.

He'd gone to help with the pulley, but he'd also seen the untouched vein—the fortune buried in Diggert's backyard.

The gopher was clueless of its worth.

Victor could've taken it.

Could've fast-talked his way into the deed.

Could've set up shop in Southbrook... or taken off for another town before Diggert even knew what he'd signed.

But he didn't.

He didn't do it.

Diggert shakes his head.

"Still got some cracked beams down there. Reckon I'll have to figure somethin' out."

Victor nods once and gives him a pat.

"Yes, I'm sure you will figure something out."

His attention drifts to the edge of the meadow.

He spots Grace—the glow of her ivory fur darting toward the big barrel barn. She glances over her shoulder, moving as though she doesn't want to be seen.

Using his lightest steps, he follows, peeking through the slightly ajar door with stealth. The cool dimness inside the rounded barn contrasts with the blazing heat outside.

In a corner, Grace hunches, something in her paw catching the faint light.

Victor's mind races.

Is something wrong? Is she hurt?

Without further hesitation, he steps forward and throws open the door.

"Grace, what are you doing in here?"

"Victor!" she exclaims, a thin wisp of smoke escaping her mouth.

"What are *you* doing in here?"

His eyes hone in on the cigarette in her paw—a rolled broad leaf with a faint ember of sage glowing at its tip.

"You're smoking?!" he says, incredulous.

Grace lifts her chin defiantly.

"Yes, Victor, I'm smoking. I'm smoking, okay?"

She takes another puff and blows it out.

He's suddenly shocked.

"Well, I didn't know this about you."

She's suddenly defensive.

"Well, maybe there's a lot of things you don't know about me!"

Whuff.

The words hit harder than she means them to—and land like an invisible punch to his gut.

There are a lot of things you don't know about... me.

They both go quiet for a long moment, the smoke curling between them.

"I'm sorry," she says finally, breaking the silence. "That came out wrong."

"Don't apologize. You're... not wrong."

"I guess old habits die hard?"

She flicks the ash off the end of her cigarette and offers it to him with a faint smirk.

"Want a puff?"

"Hell no," he replies instantly, wrinkling his nose.

Grace laughs, swaying her small hips.

"Scared?"

Still riding high on his Chessnuts victory, Victor's pride flares.

"Pfft. I'm not scared of anything."

He looks away, then slowly back.

"Alright, then. I'll try it."

She passes the cigarette to him, and he takes a deep inhale.

Immediately, he coughs violently, doubling over.

A chuckle slips through Grace's lips, though her amusement fades as his coughing continues.

She pats his back.

"Oh dear! Are you okay?"

"I know for sure I'll never do that again," he rasps. "What the hell good is a cigarette for anyway?"

Grace's expression turns serious.

"Calms my nerves."

"Your nerves? What are you nervous about?"

She sighs. "Come on, Victor. The clock is ticking for Pumpkin Acres. I promised twelve more homes before winter. I need to deliver on my word."

Victor steps closer to reassure her.

"And you will. Progress is progress. The weather's been dry, the workers are steady. Big Biff's barely letting anyone take a break."

Grace smiles slightly, then fumbles for a nearby water canister to extinguish the cigarette—part of her sneak-smoking routine.

Victor smirks. "Besides, I can ease your nerves better than any cigarette."

He pulls her into a smoky-flavored kiss, the taste of sage

lingering faintly between them.

She exhales softly as they part.

The kiss did what the cigarette couldn't.

"Now that's more like it." Her smile sharpens—clearer, brighter. "Come on. These pumpkins aren't gonna turn themselves into houses."

Victor places a paw at her waist, lightly guiding her toward the door.

They step out of the barn together and into the sun.

Off in the distance,

Biff watches—

and seethes.

Chapter Eighteen

Bridges Burn

JackRabbitt leans into the hum of a fan at the edge of the grand oak boardroom table. It should be a relief, but it barely cuts through the thick, stagnant heat of the day.

He sits with his collar loosened and sleeves rolled up. He drags a paw through his dampened fur bangs and angles closer, but its breeze only teases... never cools.

His focus drifts beyond the glass of The Sky Chamber, out to the glittering sea where he'd rather be. The water may as well be a mirage—distant and useless.

A small radio crackles from the credenza at his back, its metallic voice narrating the misery outside.

"...Chenoa City's heat wave stretches into its sixth day, with record highs and no relief in sight. Officials urge residents to stay cool, stay hydrated, and—"

The radio cuts off.

Silence.

He turns.

Kathra is standing at the credenza, one wing resting lightly on the dial.

"Do you ever knock?" He exhales slowly, pushing his paperwork aside.

"Why? Do you have something to hide?"

Kathra glides into the seat across from him, wearing a light orange summer kaftan. Her silver feathers are cool and soft, untouched by the summer's weight. She doesn't fan herself or search for the breeze. If anything, she seems to absorb the heat and render it irrelevant.

He rolls his sleeves back down, collecting himself—ready to make his move.

But Kathra beats him to it.

"JackRabbitt. Newmouse Enterprises is in need of your..." She searches for the words. "Considerable charm."

Intrigued, he leans back, paws folding behind his head.

"Go on..."

"The Agricultural Agency is predicting this will be a harsh winter. There are concerns—some of them valid—about the availability of housing. That's why we need you to hold a press conference."

His smile tightens.

"A speech? Me? And what, exactly, should I be telling them?"

Kathra spreads her wings gracefully, gesturing as if delivering the speech herself.

"Tell them we are breaking ground on The Everwood Condominiums. Tell them no one will be left out in the cold. Tell them it will be... finished before winter!"

Quietly, she folds her wings back in.

JackRabbitt shoots forward in his chair.

"Before *this* winter? Kathra! Be reasonable. It took six years to build Newmouse Tower, and you want to build another one in a couple of months? It's impossible."

He swipes his bangs from his face, only to have the fan's lazy current push them forward again.

"It's not impossible." She smooths the feathers around her face. "No, not impossible at all. Not if we scale back the exports and commit all of our available resources to completing it."

His eyes flick to his magnificent 3D model of the forest collecting dust in the corner of the room. He doesn't speak. He simply clenches his jaw, grinding his teeth—until finally, he forces out a tight, measured response.

"But that would kill our trade network."

He scrapes a claw along the wood table, like striking a match.

"Do you really want to burn bridges over this?"

The fan sputters. Its weak breeze barely stirs the silence between them—but still, it sweeps his bangs into his eyes. Again.

He brushes them away. Again.

Across the table, Kathra sits unmoved, not a single plume out of place.

She lifts one shoulder in a slow, graceful shrug.

"Bridges burn."

His ears lower pointedly at her.

"And not all of us have wings."

She tilts her head slightly, the corner of her beak lifting in quiet amusement.

She lets the silence hang—just long enough to be deliberate.

"A new name has surfaced on our shareholder reports.

Watership Inc. The company is acquiring Newmouse Enterprises stock at an aggressive pace. You wouldn't happen to know anything about that, would you?"

JackRabbitt doesn't flinch.

"No," he says lightly. "Are you looking to sell?"

For a fleeting second, something soft—almost reluctant—flickers in her expression. But then, like a stone skipping across a lake, the moment is gone.

She folds her wings in front of her.

"You have always been ambitious."

"Why, Kathra! Is that a compliment?"

"No, my dear. It's a warning."

She sits still, daring him to speak.

He shifts back, throws his arm up, and gestures broadly to the large empty room.

"Oh, sure! Why build a future when we can sell condos instead?"

Kathra clicks her beak twice in quick succession.

"Now there's the tantrum I remember. You know, you used to do the same thing when you were a little kit, and your father wouldn't let you steer the boat."

"A tantrum?" he says—of his tantrum. "Is that what you see? Kathra, you brought me in to do a job, and you won't let me do it."

A flash of arrogance crosses his face—entitled, expectant—like a prince who's never been told no.

But Kathra has seen many princes rise and fall.

She leans forward, folding her wings neatly over the table.

"Your father knows when to push and when to pause. You've got all of his intelligence... but none of his patience."

Her body softens.

"Darling, I admire your drive."

She looks at him—almost motherly.

"Actually, you remind me of a creature I once knew."

She inhales deeply, her gaze lifting upward.

"He was a brilliant strategist. Always planning, always positioning, always five moves ahead."

She sighs.

"He thought he could outmaneuver anything."

JackRabbitt rolls his eyes, shifting his head to one side.

"Oh yeah? And what happened to him?"

Kathra motions subtly to Victor's portrait on the wall.

"He's dead."

JackRabbitt runs his tongue over his front incisors, battling his instinct to bite back.

Kathra studies him. Then nods to herself, as if coming to a conclusion.

"Listen, dear. I know you want to make your mark."

He looks away.

But she draws closer, beckoning him.

"Look at me, JackRabbitt."

He bobbles his head, considering whether to comply—but finally meets her stare.

"The Everwood Condominium project will create plenty of jobs and beautiful new homes.

Darling, you'll be seen as a hero of industry.

And that's what Chenoa City needs right now."

With quiet finality, she stands and smooths the drape of her light orange kaftan.

She slips past the fan without so much as a ripple, then rests a warm wing on his shoulder.

"Get the project on track for the new deadline, and call a press conference for this week."

He watches the old owl move toward the door, the back of her kaftan trailing behind her, talons clicking steadily on the floor.

Until—

She stops.

For a moment, she doesn't turn.

For a moment, she doesn't move at all.

But then, she speaks—

"Oh, and JackRabbitt?"

Her head rotates slowly—her body remaining still.

"Do it…

Or you're out."

THE FAUNA AND THE FLORA WILL CONTINUE...

ANNOUNCER

"Fall in love with the colors of the season."

CUT TO: A delicate glass pot opening, revealing a rich, berry-hued lip stain.

ANNOUNCER

"Try our classic potted lip color in a variety of new fall shades. Made using this year's harvest of berry juices."

CUT TO: A rabbit leaving a kiss mark on a crisp autumn leaf.

A squirrel sips from a teacup, her lips leaving a perfect berry print on the rim.

A mouse smirks as she presses a playful kiss to a love note, sealing it with color.

ANNOUNCER

"For lips as lush as the season."

CUT TO: The product lineup, each pot shimmering in warm autumn tones.

ANNOUNCER

"*Berry Cherry Lip Stains* by Shabó Cosmetics. Dip your lips and make a kiss!"

FADE OUT.

Chapter Nineteen

Squirrel Puppet

JackRabbitt sits behind the immaculate desk at Shabó Cosmetics, every pen aligned, every paper clipped.

Across from him, William reads a marketing report, one paw tugging at his necktie like it's trying to strangle him.

"Grnnnh." He yanks at it again.

But it's not the tie that's really bothering him—it's what's coming.

"The press conference is tomorrow. Are you sure you know what you're doing?"

JackRabbitt doesn't look up from his file folder. He doesn't need to.

"I've been in this business since before you could tie a tie—a skill you have yet to master."

William looks down to the mess at his collar.

JackRabbitt gives his folder a quick tap against the desk.

"Trust me. I've got everything under—"

Suddenly—

A loud commotion erupts outside the office.

JackRabbitt and William.

Both.

Immediately.

Regret.

This.

The unmistakable voice of Gillian rings out through the executive lobby.

"—Excuse me, *excuse me*, do you know who I am?"

JackRabbitt glares at William.

"Tell me you didn't send her through the lobby. This is supposed to be a private meeting!"

"Have you ever known my mother to be *private* about anything?"

A squirrel silhouette flutters wildly behind the vertical blinds. Gillian is making a meal out of JackRabbitt's wimpy assistant, Zippy.

In a streak of dark brown fur with frosted blonde highlights, she pushes her way past poor Zippy and bursts through the door.

Zippy follows behind, apologetically.

"Listen to me very carefully," she continues, loud enough for everyone to hear. "I am not some... basic pedestrian walking in off the street. I was married to Jon Abbitt. And while I am certainly not a rabbit—thank gawd—I am an Abbitt by way of my darling William."

William's ears flatten. "Don't bring me into this."

Zippy throws a panicked look—one that begs for mercy—then closes the door and makes his escape.

Gillian has already moved on, fidgeting with her jewelry like it's planning its own escape.

William takes a good long look at her outfit and cringes.

It's—impossible. A leopard-print skirt suit, a leopard print pill box hat, an enormous chunky gold necklace, and sky-high heels that click across the polished floor with zero regard for how inappropriate they are in this setting.

And over all of it—over her own fur—she wears:

A fur coat.

In the middle of summer.

Gillian doesn't register her son's reaction.

Instead, she sweeps her teased tail behind her in a perfectly rehearsed flourish that bounces back with the resilience of a beauty pageant hairdo.

"Surprise!" she announces, as she holds up a bottle of champagne. "I know, I know, this is a very exclusive little gathering, but who couldn't use a little mid-day bubbly?"

She moves with complete confidence, her tail bouncing behind her in a firm hairspray hold, settling into the office as if it were her own.

With a flick of the wrist, she tosses her coat over one of the chairs—but it misses and lands on the floor. She either doesn't notice or doesn't care.

She places the bottle of champagne smack dab in the middle of JackRabbitt's neatly organized desk and flops into a chair.

He waits until she is still, then lifts the bottle and relocates it just out of reach.

"Gillian. Are you drunk?"

"Just barely!" she croons, while rummaging through her purse for a corkscrew—the wrong tool for the job, but dramatically correct. "And don't start with that tone. I can hear it. We're all family here! Well, sort of."

She snaps her fingers at William.

"Sweetheart, be a dear and open that for me?"

William opens his mouth instead... and lets it hang there.

"You brought champagne to a business meeting?"

"Oh. Are we... not celebrating?" she asks, genuinely surprised. "Because I certainly am! JackRabbitt, it's about time you finally recognized my brilliance."

Without a word, JackRabbitt reaches across the desk and gently removes the corkscrew from her paw, griping it with care, as if it were a grenade. He sets it down at the far edge of the desk, then folds his paws in front of him like nothing happened.

"Yes. Gillian. I do see your... potential. And that's why we need to talk."

She tosses her purse onto his desk, her big brown eyes narrowing slyly as she shifts in her seat.

"JackRabbitt, darling. Why don't you call me Mom? Is it because you're afraid I'll enjoy it?"

JackRabbitt freezes.

William dry heaves into his sleeve.

Gillian waits for a reaction.

"Nothing?" she sighs. "Oh, you really are dull without me."

"Gillian..." JackRabbitt erases the last seven seconds from his brain and begins again. "We need you to focus."

"Oh, fine." She waves a dismissive paw, sinking into her chair.

"You two are so serious. Honestly, I almost said no to this meeting. Do you know how much I despise CEO offices?"

She gestures grandly to the elegant but conservative décor.

"But then I thought, 'Gillian, darling, if you don't show up—who's going to bring the class?'"

William drags a paw down his face.

"So, let's talk about this position you're offering me over at Newmouse Enterprises. First of all, I love that you're thinking of me for it. Truly. But, before we get into all that…"

She leans forward, eyes glinting mischievously.

"Have you considered making me the face of Shabó Cosmetics? Because honestly, darling—if anyone can sell glamour, it's Gillian Abbitt."

JackRabbitt exhales slowly, then straightens, slipping into the role he plays best—the closer.

"Gillian, let's talk about opportunity."

She raises an eyebrow, tilting her head like a jewelry display in a shop window.

"Darling, I am always ready to talk about opportunity."

"Good," he says smoothly. "Because I have one for you."

He laces his paws neatly on the desk, meeting her gaze with a look of absolute confidence—despite the fact that he only vaguely knows what this position even is.

"Newmouse Enterprises. I want you on board."

Gillian laughs.

"JackRabbitt, please. I'm flattered, but you and I both know I am *not* an acorn counter. That's what accountants are for."

"It's not Accounting."

She sighs. "Operations?"

"Not that either."

Her nose wrinkles. "Oh, gawd, you're not asking me to run HR, are you? I am not interested in mediating the squabbles of the interns and their tragic little love lives."

JackRabbitt wiggles his long ears charmingly.

"Marketing."

William jerks upright like he misheard.

"Marketing?!"

Gillian blinks, glancing between them.

"Marketing?"

"Yes." JackRabbitt nods like this was always the plan. "You, Gillian, are the perfect representative for a company like Newmouse. Charismatic. Stylish. You know luxury. You define it! Who better to help craft a legacy brand than somebody who lives that image?"

"Lives that image?" Her faux lashes flutter. "JackRabbitt, darling, I invented it."

"Exactly. You see... a visionary like you belongs at a place where your influence can actually make an impact. Think about it—strategizing brand campaigns, building exclusivity, making sure our real estate projects reflect your impeccable taste."

Gillian sways her head in thought as she considers it.

"And?"

JackRabbitt leans forward slightly.

"And… I want you to use that influence where it really matters.

Not just in marketing. But at the table too."

"The table?"

"The boardroom table."

Gillian snickers. "Oh, JackRabbitt. You're adorable. What on earth would I be doing on the board of Newmouse Enterprises?"

He shrugs his shoulders.

"Well, Kathra is on the board."

Gillian blinks once.

Then twice.

"Kathra."

Oh yes.

"Kathra is on the board."

A short snort.

"Oh, I swear, she collects seats of power like they're cocktail rings."

She lifts her chin, imitating Kathra's stately posture, her lips pursed into a faux beak.

"And she always looks at me in that… judgmental, *owlish* way."

JackRabbitt nods in solidarity. "Like she's… above you?"

Gillian snaps her attention to him.

JackRabbitt doesn't flinch. "Like you don't belong at the table?"

She sucks a sharp sound through her long front teeth.

He presses on.

"If Kathra deserves a seat on the board, then so do you."

Gillian stares at him for a long moment.

"I know exactly what you're doing, JackRabbitt."

She pauses.

"But damn it... you are right.

Kathra has spent years treating me like some... frivolous little gold digger. Like I don't belong. Like she earned her position, and I just... landed in mine. But this?"

She leans forward, tracing an invisible circle on the desk.

"This would prove otherwise. Kathra would have to look me in the eye as an equal."

She taps a manicured nail against the surface, letting the silence stretch.

"A board seat?"

JackRabbitt nods. "A real seat at the table."

She narrows her eyes a bit before flashing a grin.

"I have to admit... it's a compelling offer."

She leans back, crosses her legs and stretches her arms wide over the back of the chair.

"But I can't help wondering... what exactly do you get out of all this?"

He dips his head and swivels one ear in that irresistible

JackRabbitt Abbitt way.

"Can't I simply want to see an incredible *squirrelle* get the recognition she deserves?"

Gillian sneers. "Oh, please. You are many things, but altruistic is not one of them. I know you, JackRabbitt. You want something from me."

"What I want... is for you to have a real voice at Newmouse."

Gillian hums, unconvinced. "A voice. Yeah, sure. But not *my* voice. *Your* voice. You want me to be your little... squirrel puppet."

JackRabbitt folds his paws neatly.

"You'd be a partner, Gillian."

She lifts a shoulder, the tension easing.

"Well. I am between jobs right now."

He lets out a small, satisfied breath—but before he can say anything, she lifts a finger.

"I'll sleep on it.

But I will not be your squirrel puppet, JackRabbitt."

He just smiles.

"Heaven forbid."

William eases himself between them.

"Why don't we talk about it over at dinner, Mom?"

Gillian's ears perk at that.

William picks her coat up off the floor and holds it open.

Gillian rifles through the desk hunting for her purse, knocking over a picture frame and sending a pen clattering to the floor.

"Oh, sweetheart. If you're bribing me with dinner, you should have started with that." She gives JackRabbitt a pointed look as she slips into her coat. "Take notes, JackRabbitt."

Then, she spins around.

"Oh, William—your tie!"

She gasps, clutching her chest like she's witnessing a crime against fashion.

She steps closer, adjusting the knot.

William tilts his head back, accepting his fate. "For the record, I hate tying these things."

She finishes up, giving it a pat.

"Alright, darling. Let's discuss this properly over a meal. But just so you know, I don't do casual dining."

William is unsurprised. "Perish the thought."

"You're lucky to have such a charming brother, JackRabbitt."

He pushes back his chair and stands. "Don't I know it."

"...And I'm taking this, of course."

She reaches across the desk—too close for JackRabbitt's comfort —and lifts the champagne bottle, tucking it under her arm like it's an award.

She gives him a wink and sashays toward the door.

She flings it open, crying out into the executive lobby:

"Skippy, hold my calls."

Zippy flinches as she struts past—heels clicking, tail swishing.

"My name is Zippy," he mutters under his breath.

But in his mind, she says it again—*Skippy*—just before leaning in and purring,

"Good boy."

Chapter Twenty

Rose-Colored Blazer

William waits until the door is sealed shut before glaring at his brother.

"You seriously owe me for that."

JackRabbitt takes his seat again, crossing one leg over the other.

"It'll be worth it to see Kathra's face when Gillian's *Furfume* cloud takes over the Newmouse boardroom."

William slowly gathers his briefcase, waiting just long enough to not have to bump into his mother again.

"If she's still in the lobby, I'm grabbing a branch and swinging out the window."

He moves to the door, eases it open an inch, peeks out, then nods.

The coast is clear.

"You can thank me later—with hazard pay."

JackRabbitt lets one corner of his mouth curl.

"I'd offer you a raise, but you'd spend it all on therapy."

William doesn't bother to dignify that with a response.

He slips out of the office, yanking his tie loose, his eyeballs twitching with post-Gillian trauma.

He rounds the corner past the executive lounge—only to nearly collide with Macy coming from the opposite direction.

They sidestep once, then again—like two rabbits dancing the

shuffle.

William adjusts his jacket with pretend patience.

"You'll get the hang of hallways someday."

Macy rolls her eyes.

"You know, William, technically I'm older than you."

He grins devilishly.

"Not in this book."

And with that—he sails down the hallway like he just dropped the punchline to a joke only a true fan would appreciate.

Macy adjusts the strap of her purse over her shoulder and heads toward the CEO office.

She is wearing a rose-colored blazer with standard-issue shoulder pads and the sleeves rolled up to her elbows. Her pleated gray skirt crinkles softly as she walks through the door.

JackRabbitt is busy restoring order to his desk when Macy glides up quietly behind him. She notices the overturned family picture frame and gently returns it to its usual position.

"Rough meeting?" she asks.

He glances at the frame, then at her.

"You have no idea.

Come on in. Sit down."

He gestures to the chair across from him, leaning back with an exhale as if he's just now catching his breath from the air Gillian sucked out of the room.

Macy hooks her purse around the back of her chair.

"Are you testing some kind of new *Furfume* today? That scent... it's very... *distinct*."

JackRabbitt dodges the question, while simultaneously realizing he will be stuck with the aroma of Gillian for the rest of the day.

Macy begins to settle in, tugging at the hem of her shirt like it's clinging too close.

"You wanted to see me? What's up?"

He watches her for a second, then folds his arms.

"I need you to attend my press conference tomorrow... as a reporter. To cover it."

"What?" Her posture stiffens. "JackRabbitt, I'm a fiction writer. I'm not a reporter. And it's not like I have some massive fan following like Lee Ann Lovely and her gossip column."

JackRabbitt's whiskers twitch at the mention of her name—a reflex he refuses to acknowledge.

"But that's exactly why I need you there. Look, if Lee Ann does show up, she'll be there to spray trouble all over the place."

Macy presses her lips together, sealing in a laugh.

"So what you really want... is for me to shield you from your ex?"

He doesn't deny it.

"She's unhinged."

Macy smiles gently. "She's not that bad. Just... misunderstood, maybe."

Sure. She's not that bad—until she is.

He shakes it off.

"You just had that story published in the college newspaper, right? You've got access. And you've got a voice readers trust."

She frowns. "That was a short story. One time. I'm not on the staff."

"Then ask the editor. See if they'll let you cover it. You've already proven you know how to write. You're thoughtful. You're fair." He lifts his glossy black pen with a gold nib and taps it on his leaf-leather planner. "That's exactly who I need sitting in the press row—someone who'll ask the right questions."

She squints. "The right questions, huh?"

"Macy, you've got a good head on your shoulder pads."

They both share a laugh, the force rocking her forward as a blonde curl tumbles in front of her face. She gently brushes it back, still smiling.

"Well, it could be interesting," she says—then pauses.

"But you're not going to try to... pressure me to spin things the way *you* want them to be spun?"

JackRabbitt shakes his head, holding up a paw in pseudo solemnity.

"I wouldn't dream of trying to influence you. I just thought it would be... beneficial all around."

Kindness is often mistaken for weakness—but Macy Abbitt is no fool. She knows her big brother too well. She watches him closely, reading past the charm, searching for signs of manipulation. But beneath all the bravado, she chooses to believe his heart is in the right place.

She lets out a soft sigh.

"Alright. I'll do it. I'll talk to the editor. For you."

He nests his gold-tipped pen across the leaf-leather planner's edge.

"Atta doe, Macy! You're the best."

Her ears do a cute little shimmy.

"You're lucky to have me."

He rises and buttons his jacket in one swift, silent motion.

"Don't I know it?"

She gives him a warm look—the kind you only get from someone who really loves you.

But then—

She pauses, studying him like she's just cracked the code.

"Hold on a minute," she says, hesitating.

"I see it now."

She leans in, almost conspiratorially.

JackRabbitt stiffens.

Macy's eyes widen.

"You've got that *I-skipped-lunch-again* face."

Her expression softens.

"I know—how about I bring you an eggplant panini from Zeena's? It's your favorite!"

He relaxes, waving it off with a shake of his head.

"Tempting. But I've got too much to do. Rain check?"

"Oh, I'm holding you to it, mister!"

She stands, pulling the bunched fabric of her shirt back down and gathering her purse.

"Well then, I'm off. I... think I'll go pay a visit to Brack on my way out."

JackRabbitt's head drops instantly.

"Maaaacy," he groans, drawing out her name in that long, disapproving tone she's all too familiar with.

"JackRabbitt, don't start," she says, heading for the door.

He follows.

"Brack Squirrelton is bad news. You're too good for him!"

She puts one paw on the doorknob, then turns around.

"Don't you have a speech to be thinking about?"

"I just don't want to see you get hurt. He's not right for you."

She lifts her chin, stubbornness flashing in her soft blue eyes.

"I think *I'll* decide what's right for me, thank you."

He bites his lower lip, clearly holding back more words.

She releases the doorknob, takes a step backward, and gives him a quick hug.

"See you tomorrow! Break a leg."

Before he can say anything else, she slides out the door.

Naturally, JackRabbitt has no intention of breaking a leg.

But he might break something else.

Chapter Twenty-One

Press Conference

The air outside Newmouse Tree Tower is thick with anticipation. The rustling of leaves blends with the quiet murmur of the gathered reporters. Cameras fashioned from hollowed-out logs sit atop sturdy wooden tripods, their vine-woven wires snaking toward a small power station. A crew of mice monitor the flow of electricity, adjusting the dials with their deft paws. The microphone—an acorn shell affixed to a spiraling birchwood stand—hums to life as the event begins.

In the front row of the press section—*she's* already written the ending.

Lee Ann Lovely.

Skunk first. Perfume second. Everything else, a distant third.

The monochrome menace with a gossip column, an advertising budget, and absolutely no boundaries.

Of course she would be here.

JackRabbitt doesn't need to see her to know she's there.

He can smell her.

The same Lee Ann who once faked an exclusive interview just to ambush him at a charity gala. The same Lee Ann who once swore she had "proof" that his boat club was rigging races—only to admit later, with a wink, that she'd made the whole thing up to get his attention. The same Lee Ann who, after a very brief and very regrettable involvement, had taken their fallout as an open invitation to use her gossip column to insert herself into every single scandal Chenoa City had to offer.

And now here she is.

Back at it.

Waiting for him to slip.

JackRabbitt steps onto the platform.

The late-morning light catches the rich hue of his fur, and it shines like caramel. His hair is coiffed, every wave of his fringe falling just-so across his brow. Today, he has chosen a tie that nearly matches his eyes—tidal blue—anchored beneath the deep navy of his tailored suit.

His tall ears twitch, just slightly. Not enough for the cameras to catch, but enough to release the tension he's hiding beneath the surface.

He *should* be here announcing the export plan, the trade agreements, his vision for Chenoa City.

Instead, he's here to pitch another monument to Victor Newmouse.

The pain in his stomach flares, a slow burn beneath his ribs. He inhales through his nose—steady and controlled.

Not now.

Beside the podium, an easel is draped in a satin cloth, teasing the attendees with a hidden surprise. He scans their curious faces. Then, with a flick of his wrist, he straightens his cuffs. He steps forward, nodding and waving to a few female fans in the bunch.

"Good morning, Chenoa City," he begins. "What an honor it is to be—!"

Before he can continue, a harsh *crackle* bursts from the

microphone, followed by a shrill *screech*.

The noise jolts through the front row.

A frazzled mouse technician scrambles at the power station as sparks briefly flicker along the vine wiring.

"Oh! My bad!"

Lee Ann sing-songs from her seat in the press section, daintily adjusting her chair.

With an innocent little scoot, she frees its leg from the wiring—*oops*.

She offers an unapologetic smile.

"I guess there must be a gremlin out here today."

JackRabbitt's smile tightens, but he doesn't flinch.

Oh, she's loving this.

The noise dies down as quickly as it came.

"Well, that certainly woke everyone up," he announces, effortlessly reclaiming control.

A few chuckles scatter through the audience, pulling the attention back to him—exactly where it belongs.

"Today, I'm here to talk to you about the future of Chenoa City. And how Newmouse Enterprises can be a partner to our community in building that future. Now, I know there's been a lot of talk about the weather lately. We've had a scorching summer, and now there's a forecast for a harsh winter."

He rests his paws on the podium, steady.

"Well, I'm here to tell you—Newmouse Enterprises is reading the wind before it shifts.

We're not just weathering the storm.

We're making sure every tail stays warm."

A wave ripples through the audience—some nodding in approval, others watching him with wary curiosity.

A raven with a press badge hanging around his neck scribbles a few notes, his beady eyes keenly observing every movement JackRabbitt makes.

He pauses, letting the last word settle into the crowd like a coal ember.

He steps back from the podium—slowly, deliberately—and turns toward the easel, still draped in its satin covering.

He clasps his paws behind his back as he approaches, the cloth fluttering slightly in the breeze.

He lifts a single paw.

"That," he says, "is why I'm proud to share something we've been working on for quite some time."

His voice rises.

"A project born from our belief that no one should be left out in the cold."

And with one swift motion—*fwip*—he whips the cloth away.

"We call it Everwood. You'll call it home."

JackRabbitt is smiling ear to ear.

That famous smile.

Two perfect front teeth shining like twin spotlights.

For a second, it's hard to tell if the cameras are flashing—or if it's just him.

The audience leans in to get a better view of the unveiling: a stunning painted portrait of the towering pine tree, transformed into a vibrant, multi-level living space: Wooden walkways and breathtaking terraces sprawling through the branches; winding paths and lush gardens spilling into the surrounding cityscape from the base.

But the reaction is mixed.

Some reporters scribble furiously, while others glance at one another in confusion.

He sees the hesitation, so he chooses his next words carefully.

"I know—it sounds ambitious. That's because it is!

But get ready for new homes, new jobs, and new opportunities—all before the first frost!"

An impatient squirrel in the front row raises his paw.

"Mr. Abbitt, this project is… enormous… and you're claiming it'll be finished before winter? Where are those resources coming from? What are you telling the traders?"

JackRabbitt scans the crowd, as if the answer is not just for one squirrel, but for the whole city.

"Tell them we need the supplies… and we're willing to pay.

Newmouse Enterprises is putting everything we've got into this project to bring new homes to our community before winter."

"Follow-up! What about the export market? Are we really sacrificing trade to build condos?"

A murmur runs through the row of reporters as Kathra's words echo in his mind.

Do it... or you're out.

He takes a deep breath.

"You're worried about exports, Stuart? I'm worried about families with no homes this winter. Surely, you've seen The Agricultural Report. I think the real question is: Why aren't more companies like Newmouse working to get ahead of the weather? Chenoa City should be everyone's priority."

The crowd still isn't sold. He can see it.

But they don't need facts.

They need a symbol.

So he gives them one.

"Victor Newmouse built this Tree from the ground up."

He's almost disgusted with himself.

Almost.

"And today, we're continuing that legacy. He may not be here to finish it, but Everwood was *his* design—*his* final blueprint. Every detail, every promise—it comes from him." He throws his paws up. "I'm just here to make sure his vision lives on."

Then—

With perfect timing, a skunky-sweet voice, drenched in mischief, sprays through the air.

"JackRabbitt."

Lee Ann's crazy blue eyes are fixed on him, like he's already guilty.

"This all sounds incredible..."

She taps her notebook once, the glossy blonde streaks down her back catching the light—just enough to remind him who he's dealing with.

"But tell me—how does it *feel* to be pitching somebody else's dream instead of your own?"

A few reporters shift in their seats, pens poised, waiting.

The question hangs like a shining wire.

JackRabbitt doesn't react. Not at first.

He exhales slow and steady, holding her gaze.

Then, he flicks his head and whisks his bangs from his eyes.

"I've always believed that progress means knowing when to let go...

Especially when it was never yours to begin with."

Lee Ann reaches for her tail, flinging it up over her shoulder like a boa.

Still grinning.

Because she knows—

He felt that one.

The cameras flash.

Another voice rises above the murmurs of the press.

"Mr. Abbitt! What kind of jobs will this project create?"

His ears perk at the familiar voice.

Macy stands among the journalists, her soft blue eyes steady, her notepad in paw—a lifeline thrown right when he needed it.

JackRabbitt doesn't miss a beat. He turns to her with a confident nod, effortlessly shifting the energy of the crowd.

"Excellent question."

He gestures to the easel.

"We're creating real, solid jobs here—construction, landscaping, hospitality, security. It's the kind of work that puts food on the table and keeps a city running.

We'll have builders shaping homes right into the pine tree. Gardeners bringing the place to life with color and texture. A full hospitality team running the restaurant and event space. And, of course, top-tier security, so everyone can rest easy—day or night."

Another reporter, a red-breasted robin with an eager glint in her eye, chimes in.

"So... are we talking spa tubs or just basic bird baths?"

JackRabbitt's grin widens.

"Ah, now we're getting to the good part."

He spins slightly, motioning toward the easel painting.

"Not just spa tubs. Full spa-inspired bathrooms.

Plus, each home has a lavish bedroom suite.

A custom kitchen.

Plenty of storage nooks.

And for those who love a starlit evening?

Private terraces for nights under the sky."

He winks at the red-breasted robin reporter.

"Romance optional."

Oh yeah.

The crowd is leaning in now, drawn into the world he's conjuring.

A ripple of excitement moves through the air.

A few reporters nod approvingly.

He hears the whispers—

Everyone is going to be talking about this.

He straightens, placing both paws firmly on the podium.

"We're rewriting the story of Chenoa City here.

Not to erase the past—

But to grow something new from it.

And this version?

Trust me—

It's one you won't forget."

Chapter Twenty-Two

The Golden Grotto

A lone swan perches in her nest, a delicate mirror cradled in her wing. She tilts it, studying herself. The silvered glass does not lie. Her feathers, once radiant, seem dull. The skin at her throat pulls just slightly, softened by time.

A whisper of air escapes her beak.

She snaps the mirror shut.

Then, with a powerful push, she lifts into the sky, wings slicing clean through the late morning hush.

The world beneath her begins to blur as she glides toward the spa hidden behind the falls.

She lands on a flat stone ledge.

The waterfall crashes down in front of her, a roaring curtain shielding the entrance.

She slips behind the veil.

The Golden Grotto.

The quartz-encrusted entrance surrounds her in a gentle radiance, as if stepping into a fractured geode. Her webbed feet press against the smooth stone path as the cavern widens into a luxurious spa and salon.

In the center of the cave, steaming water flows gently beneath a skylight, the scent of lavender and mint swirling through the mist. Forest creatures of every kind drape themselves along the edges of the hot spring, half-submerged in the golden water—soaking, unwinding, and surrendering to the warmth.

The tension in her shoulders melts away.

She has arrived.

Mikki and Kathra settle into their moss-covered resting spots, sinking into the velvet-soft mounds with a shared look of peace, each waiting for her turn to slip behind the curtain of hanging ivy where private treatments await. Beside them, shopping bags from Venmore's Department Store spill into a colorful mound, brimming with silk, satin, and sparkle.

"I think we outdid ourselves," Mikki sighs, taking a sip of her hot rainwater tea. "I have to say, that was the most fun I've had in months." She reaches out to tickle a delicate red ribbon from one of the bags. "And the best part? The Gala is actually coming together. The caterer's booked, the invitations are out. I really feel on top of things."

Without warning, Kathra extends her long legs in a relaxing stretch, nearly upending Mikki's entire moss pile.

Mikki scrambles to rescue her teacup as she steadies herself.

"I almost wore that," she mutters, brushing a droplet off her nose.

Kathra remains unaware that she nearly toppled her tiny friend.

"That's wonderful, dear. It's about time you felt like yourself again. You took a spill... but you landed on your paws." She pauses, then adds, as if suddenly remembering something vital, "Oh, and Mikki... about the cake."

"The cake?"

Kathra lifts a feather, precise. "A tiered centerpiece. Elaborate but elegant.

And it must be green.

If the theme is Green Gala, the cake should be exactly that."

Mikki nods, already making a mental note. "Got it. A giant green showstopper."

But Kathra doesn't look convinced. "Actually... I'll go to speak to Zeena myself. You know how particular I am."

"You don't trust me to relay the message?"

Kathra's eyes flicker with amusement. "I simply want to make sure the cake is perfect—down to the last detail."

She reaches for her tea, but there's something unspoken in the way she exhales, as if she knows perfection only happens when she does things herself.

With a dramatic sigh, she adds, "At least I can trust the caterer to follow instructions. If only I could say the same for JackRabbitt..."

Mikki tips her head back against a plush fern pillow as the steady rush of the waterfall fills the space around them. "Why are you so unhappy with him? His press conference was great. The whole town is excited about the new condos. Isn't that what you wanted?"

Kathra makes a small, polite noise, somewhere between acknowledgment and deep disapproval.

"You have to admit," Mikki props herself onto her side, facing Kathra, "He's a great leader. He's smart and charming!"

Kathra keeps her gaze straight ahead.

"Smart and charming are a dangerous combination."

"Oh, Kathra." She waves the comment away. "You're so conservative. Victor was the same way. JackRabbitt simply has a more... liberal view." She gives her honey blonde hair a toss and lays back down. "I think his ideas are fresh. I trust him."

Kathra raises a feathered brow.

"Are you sure you can trust him?"

Mikki props herself back up on both elbows, puzzled by the question.

Kathra shrugs her shoulders.

"Darling, he's the one holding all of *your* power."

"Kathra! Of course I trust him." Mikki reaches for her teacup and saucer. "Look," she says, taking a sip, "I hold the majority stake of Newmouse Enterprises until Victoria and Mickolas are old enough to take over. If I didn't have complete faith in JackRabbitt, I wouldn't have recommended him for the CEO position."

Kathra adjusts the silver feathers along her wing with slow, meticulous care.

"And how fortunate for him that you did."

Mikki's whiskers twitch—just once—a quick, involuntary reaction.

She firmly clinks her teacup back into its saucer.

The teacup rattles.

Outside, against the porcelain—

and inside, somewhere deeper.

Kathra nods her head and pulses a wing.

She's made her point.

Mikki releases the teacup as if letting go of the thought itself. Then, shifting her focus, she nudges one of her Venmore's shopping bags with her toe.

"Enough of this," she deflects. "Let's talk about something truly important—our gala attire!"

Mikki practically bounces with excitement as she pulls a soft garment bag onto her lap. "I cannot wait to wear my dress." Her eyes dance as she turns to Kathra. "But I'm really just over the moon about your magnificent headpiece. Oh, Kathra! It goes perfectly with your feathers! You are going to look stunning! Now, be careful that you don't steal the show. I want everyone looking at the auction items... not just at you."

Kathra, ever the picture of elegance, beams with quiet pride. "Well," she muses, "I do have a way of commanding attention."

Mikki clasps her paws together. "Ooh, can I see it again? Just one more time?"

Kathra lets the moment stretch, savoring the build-up. "Well... if you insist."

With grace, she lifts a lush jewelry box from one of her bags, her every movement deliberate. She takes great pleasure in the anticipation, drawing it out just long enough for Mikki to squirm with impatience.

Then, with a soft *click*, the box pops open.

But before either of them can comment on the shimmering masterpiece inside, they are startled—not by what's in the box, but by who is standing behind them.

The scent arrives before she does—floral, aggressive, and absolutely everywhere.

Mikki's ears flicker.

Kathra's eyelids lower.

It's Gillian.

The Golden Grotto is no longer peaceful.

"Nice crown," Gillian drawls, her teased, two-toned tail twitching impatiently. "Have you appointed yourself the Queen of Chenoa City?"

Kathra's face remains perfectly still. "I don't need a crown to be a Queen."

With one fluid motion, she snaps the jewelry box shut, the satisfying *click* echoing in the cavern's soft acoustics.

Gillian grins devilishly.

She rolls her eyes and flops onto the moss beside them, sinking in with an exaggerated sigh.

"Mmm, cozy," she groans, grinding her teeth and letting her legs stretch out as if she belonged there all along. "So... what are we chatting about?" she continues, tone falsely casual. "I thought I heard something about a party? Did I miss the invitation?"

Mikki sits up straight, already sensing the tension coiling in the air. She lifts her paws in a placating motion, trying to steer the conversation back toward neutral territory.

"Oh, Gillian. It's just a little gala...," she says lightly, choosing her words with the delicacy of someone defusing a bomb. "It's for the Forest ReLeaf Fund. You wouldn't be interested."

Gillian slaps a paw to her chest, gasping theatrically. "I care about the environment!"

Kathra and Mikki exchange a glance.

Mikki presses forward in her polite but desperate attempt to move this along, "Yes. Well. It's next week. I'm sure you wouldn't be able to fit it into your busy schedule."

"Try me."

Mikki hesitates, wishing she could rewind this entire conversation. Still, she forces a tight, diplomatic smile and says, "It's Thursday night."

The explosion is immediate.

"You can't have a party on Thursday night!" Gillian's eyes go wide with horror, her voice pitching upward into a near shriek. "*I'm* having a party Thursday night!"

Kathra, still perfectly poised, folds her wings in her lap and exhales, settling in for the long haul.

Gillian continues her tirade without waiting for a response. "We can't both have a party on the same night. You'll have to cancel."

Mikki's politeness fractures. "Gillian, we are not canceling The Gala."

Kathra leans forward, her tone smooth, yet precisely cutting. "Yes, Gillian, we are not canceling The Gala because you've hired a couple of... cocktail dancers to prance around half-dressed in your living room."

Gillian gasps—offended, scandalized, personally attacked.

"Cocktail dancers?!" she sputters. "I'll have you know that my party is every bit as sophisticated as yours. Besides, you're just jealous that I still have gorgeous young bucks begging for my attention, when you're just a dried out old prune!"

Kathra turns her head in disgust. "Oh, please! Mikki, don't even bother wasting your breath on this one. Gillian is just a...," She searches for the words, "Tramp."

Gillian's claws twitch, then—*CRACK*—she slaps a paw down hard against the stone beside her. The sound echoes against the walls of the cave like a shot that has just been fired in public.

"You know what, Kathra? You like to pretend that you're soooo much better than everyone else. But the fact is, you and I really aren't all that much different."

Kathra's eyes flash red. "Gillian, you and I are nothing alike. I don't have to steal nuts in order to get them."

Gillian gasps—loudly—one paw flying to her chest. "How dare you! The nuts came to me!"

Kathra sits up taller, feathers ruffling. "Flip just... came to you? Is that how it happened?"

Gillian gasps with outrage. "Oh, don't start."

In one sharp motion, she pushes herself up from the moss, standing now, tail bristling.

Kathra rises just as smoothly, keeping her regal composure, but there's an unmistakable edge of steel in the way she squares her wings.

Mikki scrambles upright, quickly wedging herself between them, paws raised. "Alright, let's all take a breath, shall we?"

Neither moves.

The hot spring suddenly feels too hot.

Kathra leans in close. "You slithered into my nest, and you flaunted yourself in front of him."

Gillian cuts her off with a wave of her paw. "Stop. I didn't steal Flip. We were in love." She smirks, tail flicking. "And if you hadn't been such a bitter old bore, he might not have needed me."

Kathra's brows lift, dangerously calm.

Gillian shrugs, her voice too smooth to be sincere. "Not that it mattered, in the end." She leans in, the accusation gleaming behind her teeth. "Because you went and drove him right off a cliff, didn't you?"

Mikki inhales sharply.

Kathra's beak tightens, but she doesn't flinch.

"You were a distraction, Gillian. Nothing more. Honestly, it's a wonder any male survives you. You sink your claws in, drain them dry, and then scamper off to the next poor victim."

Gillian huffs, crossing her arms. "Oh, excuse me for being irresistible."

Kathra curls her beak upward. "Right. I'm sure that's exactly how Jon Abbitt would describe it too."

Gillian's eyes narrow. "Jon Abbitt and I had a very passionate marriage."

Kathra waves a wing. "Oh, I'm sure it was passionate—right up until it crashed and burned." Her voice is light. "The smartest thing Jon ever did was divorce you," she says smoothly. "And you're not going to sink your cheap press-on claws into him ever again."

Gillian's fur bristles, her tail twitching.

Kathra leans forward, her voice carrying across the spa with unmistakable authority.

"Not over my dead body!"

Kathra and Gillian both stand firm, staring each other down. Mikki remains in the middle, tense, trying to keep the peace.

Suddenly, Gillian lifts her snout and sniffs the air. "Wait. Stop! I smell something."

Kathra doesn't miss a beat. "Amazing you can smell anything over yourself."

Gillian cuts her off with a sharp *shhh*, her nose twitching.

Just then, a wave of scent hits them all—roses, cedarwood, and something distinctly... skunk.

"Ooh, did somebody say dead body?"

All three heads snap toward the entrance.

It's Lee Ann Lovely—blonde streak blazing through her inky fur, tail curled like punctuation, and eyes scanning the room for a scandal that hasn't happened... yet.

This just got so much worse.

The one thing Kathra, Mikki, and Gillian can all silently agree on is that there is nothing more dangerous than Lee Ann Lovely with a headline.

Mikki is the first to break the ice, plastering a too-wide smile on her face, her voice suddenly sugar-sweet. "Lee Ann, darling, we were having a friendly little moment of... feminine bonding."

Kathra waves a wing dismissively. "Just catching up on old times."

Gillian forces a charming smile. "You know how we girls get."

Three pairs of eyes blink in perfect unison.

Lee Ann squints at them, suspicious.

They're lying.

She knows fake when she sees it. She built a career on it. The second she walked in, everything shifted. The air changed.

They think I don't belong here.

She adjusts her tail. Smooths it. Fluffs it. Too fast. Fluffs it again. Slower.

They were at each other's throats a second ago, and now they're... civil? Please.

She might deal in drama, but she can spot a cover-up like it's a mud mask.

Kathra didn't even look at her. Mikki gave her that sugary voice she saves for guests who stay too long. Gillian... well, Gillian is just mean. But even she didn't throw a compliment or a jab. Nothing.

Dead silence? That's worse than insults.

You're not imagining it.

They were fighting.

You walked in, and now they're unified... in ignoring you!

Her smile twitches. She reins it in. Tilts her head. Eyelashes up.

Show them you're unbothered.

You're unbothered.

You are so unbothered.

She spritzes a puff of perfume into the air around her—not because she needs it, just... ambiance. Identity. Comfort. Her scent is her signature.

Fifteen years in this business, and they think they can keep secrets from me?

She licks her teeth. Eyes dart. Still no one's reacting. Still pretending like she's background noise.

You are not background noise. You are Lee Ann. Lovely.

Then, quietly—almost under her breath—her tail curling tighter across her shoulder:

They can't take the funk? They don't get the skunk.

Again.

They can't take the funk? They don't get the skunk.

She breathes in the floral fog she made for herself.

It doesn't calm her.

But it reminds her:

Better to be feared than adored.

She snaps back to reality.

Kathra, Mikki, and Gillian are all frozen—three perfect smiles. No one has breathed in at least seven seconds.

"Oh," Lee Ann chirps. "Did I just zone out? I do that sometimes."

She flutters her lashes, gives her tail one last unnecessary fluff, then pivots on her heel.

"Well, if no one's going to die in a fit of rage," she calls over her shoulder, trotting toward the reception desk, "I'm here for my seaweed wrap."

She flashes the receptionist an expectant look.

"Lee Ann Lovely. I'm sure you've heard of me."

The moment her stripe disappears behind the ivy curtain, Kathra, Mikki, and Gillian all exhale in unison.

"Well. She certainly left her mark." Kathra waves a wing through the air, as if trying to clear the aftermath. "And her scent."

Gillian huffs, picking up right where she left off... in her own mind. "You wanna know what really bugs me?"

"No, but I'm sure you're going to tell us anyway."

"You two act like I planned my fabulous party just to compete with your boring tree-hugger gala."

Kathra doesn't bother looking at her. "I don't believe in coincidences."

Before Gillian can respond, a soft chime rings through the cavern. A spa attendant, a petite rabbit with a serene smile, steps forward.

"Mrs. Chansoar, it's time for your talon sharpening."

Kathra turns smoothly. "Good. I like to keep them razor-sharp." She glances at Gillian—just long enough for the message to land —then reaches for her shopping bags.

"And Mrs. Newmouse, we're ready for your blowout."

Mikki claps her paws, scooping up her bags. "Finally! Some fresh air."

Kathra adjusts the handles of her shopping bags before turning her full attention to her new jewelry box.

She lifts the box lid open—just a sliver.

The glowstone headpiece gleams inside, catching the light from the waterfall. She studies it for a long moment, as if committing its brilliance to memory. Satisfied, she snaps the lid shut.

Mikki grabs her bags, ready to follow, but Kathra is already gliding toward the treatment room.

Before Kathra disappears, she pauses beside the spa attendant, lowering her voice just enough to seem polite—but loud enough to echo. "Derek really ought to be more selective about who he lets into this cave."

And with that, she disappears behind the ivy curtain.

Mikki follows, tossing one last exhausted glance at Gillian. She opens her mouth like she might say something... then closes it.

Some conversations aren't worth salvaging.

Gillian waits until they're gone. Then, with an exaggerated sigh, she drops back into the moss, sprawling out like a queen claiming her throne.

She stares up at the skylight, the shimmer of filtered sunlight playing across the cave's ceiling.

Slowly, a knowing smile spreads across her lips.

Oh, this isn't over.

Not even close.

Chapter Twenty-Three

Aromalottis

"Don't get your tail in a tease, Gillian."

"Zeena, my tail has been in a tease since before it was fashionable."

"But I already told you. I'm sorry, I just can't do it."

Zeena's voice is warm but firm—the kind of refusal that leaves no room for negotiation.

Gillian leans against the hostess stand, tapping her claws on the wood. "Now, let's not be hasty. You *could* cater my event. You're just... choosing not to."

Zeena exhales. "I'm already booked. The Green Gala has been on my calendar for a month."

Gillian scoffs. "A month? That's hardly a commitment."

She reaches into her purse and pulls out a small velvet pouch, sliding it across the hostess stand with the air of somebody offering a perfectly reasonable solution.

Zeena doesn't even glance at it. "Gillian."

Gillian snatches the pouch back, stuffing it into her bag. "Fine. Be difficult." She straightens, smoothing her fur. "But don't blame me when my event steals the spotlight."

Zeena smiles, her dark eyes unreadable against that bright white mask. "Enjoy your evening, Gillian."

Gillian huffs and heads toward the bar.

Zeena Aromalotti is no stranger to a bribe. She's an Outer Forest opossum with a felony rap sheet. Bribery was practically a family tradition.

But that's not who she is anymore.

Now she owns the hottest restaurant and nightclub in town, serving up live entertainment and authentic old-world recipes to Chenoa City's finest fur and feathers.

She started out as a singer at Joe's Supper Club years ago. When Old Joe decided to sell the business, she saw it as an opportunity to make a new life for herself—to start a clean slate. She bought it and renamed it:

Zeena's Place—

Where the tables are intimate, and any private conversations are most definitely, never ever, secretly overheard.

It took some work to turn the old hollowed-out hill into an upscale eatery, but the place had sturdy beams and loads of charm. The domed ceiling follows the natural curves of the hillside, and the arched entryway blooms with seasonal wildflowers, tangled reeds, and bits of salvaged thread—humble materials arranged like art. Pure Zeena.

Through the front door, a central hearth welcomes guests with warmth and ambiance. The scent of roasted nuts and cooking wine wafts from the kitchen, where Zeena manages the daily menu and the catering orders. Most of her staff came from the same kind of past she crawled out of... and she wouldn't have it any other way.

In the back, near the bar, a light rhythm flows from the musicians' alcove, where a small group of forest creatures are playing backup for Tanny Aromalotti's light vocal stylings.

Tanny, Zeena's brother, is a rising star, born to be on the stage.

His cockatiel wings flutter gently in time with the music, the tension rising as his voice fills the room with a haunting crescendo.

Just behind him, Macy Abbitt stands near the microphone, harmonizing softly. Her voice blends into Tanny's, light and effortless, never drawing too much attention to itself. She keeps her eyes closed, focused on the rhythm, her paws clasped on the microphone in front of her as if she'd rather disappear into the music than be seen.

Back at the hostess stand, Zeena greets a pair of newcomers, directing them toward the dance floor. Couples sway in slow, effortless circles, the melody just upbeat enough to keep the energy light but relaxed.

As Tanny's ballad fades to a close, the crowd applauds, and a few voices chime in with a heartfelt "Bravo!"

Tanny scans the room. His eyes land on a beautiful, beaming white dove. He flutters his eyes irresistibly, blows a kiss, and says, "That one was for you, Priss."

Then, to the audience, he offers a warm, humble smile. "Thank you, everyone! And how about a round of applause for the band?"

Beside him, Macy gives a small, nervous laugh, tucking a strand of fur behind her ear.

Gillian maneuvers her way to the bar with purpose. She gives a half-hearted clap for the song, then slides onto a barstool, crossing one leg over the other. She signals to a young otter waiter moving through the crowd with a tray of drinks.

She catches his sleeve lightly as he passes. "Oh, you look like you could use a break."

The otter balances his tray, blinking at her. "Uh. Yeah. Busy night."

Gillian tilts her head, studying him. "What's your name, darlin'?"

The otter hesitates. "Um. Leo?"

Gillian hums in approval. "Leo. Handsome name." She taps a nail on the bar top, low and conspiratorial. "Listen, Leo, I'm coordinating The Green Gala, and I have a few... thoughts on the menu."

Leo frowns. "You're... with The Green Gala?"

Gillian rests a manicured paw on her chest, feigning humility. "Head planner, actually. And naturally, I have some notes."

Leo glances toward the bustling restaurant, clearly pressed for time. "What kind of notes?"

"Oh, nothing drastic," she says, waving a paw. "But the cake? It needs to make more of a statement. I'd like to discuss some... adjustments."

Leo shifts uneasily. "I—I'd have to check with Zeena."

"Oh, don't trouble her," Gillian says, curving her mouth, leaning in closer. "You seem perfectly capable of handling it. After all, a strong, capable male with your... talent... should be used to handling all the details."

She holds his gaze for one calculated beat.

Leo hesitates. Then nods, just slightly. "I... guess I could check."

Gillian smiles. "That's all I ask."

Before she can push further, a familiar voice cuts through the moment.

"Am I too early?"

Gillian turns as William strides toward her, tall ears relaxed, jacket crisp, smirk already in place.

"You're always too early," she says smoothly. "Clearly, you take after your father. Not a trace of squirrel in you."

William grins.

"Nature's coin toss."

She waves a dismissive paw at the waiter. "Leo, darling. I'll follow up later. We'll finalize the details, ok?"

Leo nods quickly and disappears.

William exhales, shaking his head. "You are impossible."

Gillian twirls the stem of her glass between two fingers. "And yet, you suggested having dinner."

"Maybe I just enjoy the entertainment."

"Flattery will get you everywhere."

William signals for a drink. The bartender sets down a glass, the ice clinking softly.

Gillian shifts toward him, scooting her seat closer. "Now, tell me. How am I supposed to enjoy my evening when Kathra is actively trying to upstage me? You see, I'm throwing a fabulous party on Thursday night... only to find out that Kathra scheduled The Green Gala on the exact same evening."

William pauses mid-sip, lowering his glass. "You're throwing a party?"

"Of course I'm throwing a party."

He tilts his head. "Since when?"

Gillian rolls her eyes with a dramatic sigh. "Since before I even knew about The Green Gala. I've been wanting to host something for ages."

William raises an eyebrow, clearly skeptical. "And you two just happened to plan your event the same night?"

She taps her claws against her thigh—impatient, irritated, or just itching for drama. "Yes! It's called timing, William. Kathra's trying to push me out of the spotlight, as if she has the monopoly on attention."

William smirks, sipping his drink.

Gillian narrows her eyes. "What?"

He shrugs. "This is the first I've heard about your party. Can't help but wonder if you invented it after you found out about Kathra's Gala."

"How dare you?" She tosses her tail. "I have had this party planned for months."

William sets his glass down, his expression growing serious. "Let's talk about the job, Gills."

She sighs, reclining back in her chair. "Must we?"

"Yes."

Gillian waves a paw lazily. "Fine. Go on, sell me on my brilliant future at Newmouse Enterprises."

William's nose twitches as he shifts toward her, angling his seat. "Mom, it's more than just a title. You want to be the center of attention? You want to be taken seriously? This is how you do it."

She lifts a brow. "Oh, do tell."

"You'll get your name in the right places. You'll sit at the table with the creatures who actually run this city. And you'll prove that you're not just—"

Gillian's eyes sharpen. "Not just what?"

William pauses. His long ears dip back, just for a second. "Not just a socialite."

She tips her head, thoughtful. "Hmm... And what do you get out of this deal?"

William shifts in his seat. "Freedom."

"Freedom from what exactly?"

He takes a slow sip before answering the question.

"Freedom from the Abbitt name. From all of it. JackRabbitt and I —we're building something that isn't tied solely to our father's legacy."

His grip tightens around his glass.

"Newmouse is practically ours. I want to make sure I can do what I want without having to run every decision through somebody else."

Gillian watches her son for a long moment. "Sweetheart, if you think JackRabbitt is ever going to let you run things your own way, you really don't know your brother."

William throws his head back. "JackRabbitt and I are partners."

"Are you? Or are you just another piece on his Chessnuts board?"

Gillian's lips twitch.

William runs a paw down the back of his neck, like he's trying to keep the steam from rising. "You're deflecting."

"Oh, darling, I excel at deflecting."

He curses under his breath. "So, that's a no, then? You won't take the job?"

Gillian taps a single claw nail against the bar top, slowly. "I didn't say that. It's just… it's a commitment."

"Yeah, and we all know you can't handle a commitment." He downs the rest of his drink and signals for another.

"Is that a dig about your father and me? Because I'm doing everything I can to correct that mistake. Jon and I have been… seeing a little more of each other lately."

William groans. "Please, no."

Gillian's attention drifts, something deeper behind her eyes now.

"When we first met, Jon Abbitt was so powerful. So in control…" She sighs. "These days, he just putters around The Country Club, letting his brats run the business, claiming he's"—she makes air quotes with both paws—"'*semi-retired.*'"

"And?" William asks.

"And… he seems depressed."

Gillian tilts her head thoughtfully.

"Do you think it's because he misses me?"

William stares at her blankly.

"Sure, because nothing says *love* like years of resentment."

Gillian ignores him completely and smiles to herself. "He and I have been connecting. *Really* connecting. Maybe things could be different now. Maybe we could make it work this time."

William studies her, as if trying to locate the part of her that actually believes this. "You're not seriously considering trying to get back together with Dad, are you?"

Gillian lifts a shoulder. "We have a history."

"And a divorce."

She shrugs. "Details, darlin'."

William shakes his head. "You are unbelievable."

"You say that like it's a bad thing."

William lowers his glass with the kind of care that means he's trying not to throw it. "So? The job?"

Gillian exhales, pretending to think it over. Then, with a slight grin, she says, "I'll consider it."

"That's the best I'm going to get, isn't it?"

She clinks her glass lightly against his, even though he's not holding it.

"For now."

Behind them, a server weaves through the crowd, carrying an ornate ceramic tray with a single cup of tea.

Gillian doesn't notice.

Neither does William.

Their conversation moves forward, words slipping between them like cards at a dealer's table.

The server disappears into the crowd, just after the tea is set down...

In front of Kathra.

As she lifts her cup, the curved surface catches a faint, distorted reflection.

Gillian gesturing, William shifting beside her.

Kathra sips her tea.

She does not turn.

She does not glance.

Gillian keeps talking. William keeps pushing back.

And Kathra remains exactly where she is.

Chapter Twenty-Four

The Colonel

The vast wooden beams of The Crow House stretch high above Kathra's head, the dim lantern light casting elongated shadows across the floor. She pauses just inside, considering her next move.

So... JackRabbitt and Gillian are in bed together.

Not literally—though it wouldn't be a stretch.

And William, the forest flunky, is begging for leftovers. Predictably.

JackRabbitt actually thinks he's going to stack the board at Newmouse Enterprises and get away with it.

But if Mikki could be convinced to take back her board seat... or to transfer it—

Well, that would put a stop to their plan, wouldn't it?

The delicate thing, of course, is that Mikki is still grieving. Recovery takes time. And there's no need to push her into something she isn't ready for.

But...

This isn't a push.

It's just a gentle tap.

Kathra steps forward, calling softly, "Mikki? Darling? Are you in here?"

She looks up and around, her jewels clicking softly against the wooden planks.

Silence envelops the place, save for the distant rustling of leaves outside.

It is empty—eerily so.

Just then, a voice cuts through the stillness.

"Well, now! What a pleasant surprise!"

The sudden exclamation echoes against the walls, and from the far end, a figure emerges—a crow, impeccably dressed, his oily black feathers neatly tucked beneath his trademark ascot.

Colonel Austin Douglas—

The Colonel.

He moves with great effort, his gait assisted by the steady rhythm of a cane. Still, each hobbled step exudes an old-world charm.

"Kathra!" His voice rings with warmth as he approaches. "Lovely as ever!"

His sharp, beady eyes twinkle with admiration for her.

He pulls her in, placing a polite, pecky kiss on both sides of her face, the smoothness of his feathers brushing against hers. His scent—a mix of cold wind and a faint trace of pipe smoke— lingers around him.

"Colonel Douglas," she says, smoothing her facial feathers back into place.

The Colonel steps back, smoothing his ascot back into place too. "I'm surprised to see you here."

"Yes, well, I am looking for Mikki," Kathra replies, sweeping a keen gaze across the space. "She's not at the main house, she's not in the rose garden, so I thought she might be here with

Victoria."

"She's not here, I'm afraid."

The Colonel's tone shifts, a note of wistfulness creeping in. His wing gestures absently, the air now quiet and subdued.

"The Crow House has been unusually quiet today, since there are no marching orders. It hasn't been the same since we lost the old boy. It seems like just yesterday, Victor was standing right there in the center of the amphitheater. I can almost hear him now."

His voice softens. "I do miss him, you know?"

Kathra studies him for a moment, her sharp blue eyes reading his pain through the dimness of the lantern light. "You poor thing. You've been carrying this weight all alone, haven't you?"

With a slow motion, he brushes a wingtip beneath one eye, as if wiping away dust... or something more.

"Darling," she says, "You can't keep holding it in. You have got to get it out. Talk to me. Tell me what happened that day—the day of the Outer Forest crash."

The Colonel exhales, ruffling his feathers before smoothing them down again.

"Well, I can tell you I'd never seen him so angry... and I've seen him plenty angry."

He pauses, clicking his beak lightly.

"He was bonkers! Ab-solutely bonkers! He summoned me to the rooftop of Newmouse Enterprises and ordered me to take him out of Chenoa City at once!"

Kathra remains still, waiting.

"I didn't think twice about it," The Colonel continues, his voice steady but edged with something heavier. "I figured I'd have a chance to talk to him eventually, after he burned off the energy."

"Did he say where he was going?"

"Well, that's the puzzling thing about it." The Colonel's eyes narrow slightly, his wings twitching at his sides. "He wanted to go... *beyond* The Outer Forest. Only gawd knows what's out there."

Kathra blinks, her eyes reflecting the dim lantern light. "And he didn't say why?"

The Colonel shakes his head. "He wasn't in the mood for a chat, my dear. He filed the flight plan, and I followed it."

He shrugs it off, but the moment lingers. "The trip had become long, and we were both knackered, so... we stopped for a rest."

"Go on..." Kathra urges, her voice eager but measured.

The Colonel leans into his cane, shifting his weight from one clawed foot to the other.

"He was having a rest on a log, you see, and I went searching for a bite to eat."

His head lowers as if the memory itself carries weight.

"Suddenly, I heard a commotion! He was running toward me shouting, 'Go! Go!'"

He pauses, his beak tightening.

"So, I..."

"Went?" Kathra presses.

"Mmm."

The Colonel lowers his gaze again, absently kicking a stray twig.

"Something wasn't right.

I could feel it then, and I can feel it now.

But I can't put a feather on it."

He hesitates, his expression darkening.

"It was as if... he wasn't himself. It was as if... he was a *different* mouse."

Kathra leans in slightly, her feathers rustling. "A different mouse?"

The Colonel nods, his movements unsteady now.

"During the takeoff, he had no grip. No control. His tail was flopping around behind him. It was as though he had suddenly forgotten how to fly!"

His voice wavers, and he dips his head down, plucking at the dirt with his beak.

"He fell."

Silence hangs between them.

He looks up to find Kathra making a slow, circling motion with her wingtip, urging him to continue.

"When I dove back down to get him, I—"

The Colonel swallows.

"I was gobsmacked."

His voice drops to a whisper.

"There he was. Victor Newmouse. My boss...

My... friend.”

He straightens, smoothing his ascot with a trembling wingtip.

“He was dead.”

His voice cracks mid-word.

For a moment, he tries to swallow it down, then fails.

Tears spring from his eyes.

Then, with a sudden lurch, he drops his cane and throws his wings around Kathra.

She stiffens immediately, wings pinned awkwardly to her sides.

He sobs into her feathers, shaking with unrestrained grief—each cry louder than the last, echoing through the cavernous rafters.

He drags his beak sideways along her silver shoulder—*Snnrfff!*—wiping his nose on her perfect plumage with all the grace of a toddler.

He releases her, still sniffling, bending to retrieve his cane.

Kathra glances down.

Slow. Mechanical.

Subtly inspecting her snot-streaked feathers.

The Colonel continues, planting his cane firmly on the ground.

“I’d broken my talon during the commotion, and I couldn’t very well haul him all the way back to Chenoa City with one foot. So, I left the scene and came back to The Crow House for help.”

He stands a bit straighter, adjusting his composure and what remains of his pride.

"We organized a procession of our finest crows to bring the old boy home for a proper burial."

He meets her gaze again and does what any self-respecting crow would do after an emotional meltdown:

Pretend it never happened.

"Kathra, you know the rest. You were there when I brought him in."

Still staring at her shoulder, she replies, "I signed the death certificate myself." She says it as if confirming it to herself as much as to him.

But then—

The Colonel hesitates, glancing around, his demeanor suddenly cautious.

He leans in, his voice lowering conspiratorially.

"But I'll tell you something, Kathra."

She tilts her head, waiting.

He looks around once more, ensuring they are alone.

"I've been hearing the strangest rumors flying around the forest."

His tone is hushed, but there's an unmistakable weight behind it.

"I dismissed it at first, of course, but the more I think about it—"

Kathra narrows her eyes. "Well, what is it?"

The Colonel hesitates just a moment longer.

"The strangest rumors indeed."

PROMOTIONAL CONSIDERATION PROVIDED BY...

ANNOUNCER
"True elegance never announces itself."

CUT TO: A refined female squirrel in a well-kept tree hollow, brushing her tail in front of a mirror.

A delicate glass bottle of *Furfume* sits on the vanity.

She lifts it, dabs a touch behind her ear, and smiles.

ANNOUNCER
"A fragrance so light, so subtle... they'll never know it's there."

CUT TO: A woodland gathering at dusk. The squirrel gracefully moves through a small, candlelit table setting.

Gentle conversation, soft laughter.

A fox pauses, tilting his head slightly—as if catching something in the air.

She smirks.

ANNOUNCER
"Just a whisper of sophistication. Nothing more."

CUT TO: The squirrel stepping onto a moonlit hill.

The breeze moves through the trees.

She closes her eyes, content.

ANNOUNCER
"*Furfume*, by Shabó Cosmetics. Effortless. Timeless. Unmistakable."

FADE OUT as the bottle of *Furfume* glows softly in the moonlight.

Chapter Twenty-Five

Time Pieces

Another late summer night fades away, and a hot orange sunrise burns into the Southbrook sky. The rooster crows wildly in the farmyard as Grace stands over the kitchen cooktop, stirring a hot pot with a wooden spoon. Steam rises from two coffee cups positioned on side-by-side table settings.

Victor cruises into the kitchen, wasting no time before drawing the hot chicory brew to his lips. The morning breakfast routine that was once polite and cordial has now become a comfortable courtship over cereal.

"That rooster is in rare form. Does he have to be so... chipper in the morning?" Victor asks, rubbing his eyes and taking a seat at the table.

"You stop pestering A.J.," Grace teases, carefully dishing two bowls of hot cereal. "He's doing his job! This old farm is full of clocks, and he's the best one!"

Victor smirks. "He's a cock of a clock, alright."

He clangs his cup onto the saucer and reaches into his pocket.

Click.

He flips open the cover of his watch.

"Victor, this watch. You check it habitually!" She shuffles to the table, delivering their breakfast bowls. "Where did you get it? May I hold it, please?" She takes a seat and reaches her paw out expectantly.

He closes the cover—*Snap!*—and places it in Grace's paw.

"It was a gift from my mother..."

"Oh, how lovely!"

"...on the day she left me at the orphanage."

Clunk.

"Oh." She slides her fingers over the engraving on the cover, trying to decipher the design.

Victor takes a sip of his chicory coffee, the steam moistening his mouse 'stache. "What was that bit of wisdom you had? 'I can't miss what I never really had?'"

Wings. The watch cover design is a pair of wings.

"My father, the coward, abandoned his own family when I was just a pup. Mother didn't have the means to care for a child alone. She tried for a while. I suppose she did what she thought was best."

Grace holds the pocket watch a moment longer, feeling its weight—not just the brass, but the burden. Then she holds out her paw to return it.

Victor retrieves it and continues, "This was my father's. It was the only thing she had of his belongings. She gave it to me and told me to hold onto it."

He shifts in his chair.

"She said she was coming back... but she never did."

He looks at the old brass watch with loving contempt.

"Perhaps it's time I got rid of it."

"Victor, no. It's a part of you. You can't just throw the past away."

The irony of this statement is not lost on either of them.

"Yes, well... Perhaps running is all I know how to do.

I ran away from the orphanage after a year of hopelessly waiting for her. Eventually, I just wised up. I wandered in and out of the forest—occasionally at campsites, but mostly just alone. I could never quite commune with the other mice. I found brotherhood instead with the birds: first with the seed-eaters, then eventually with the predators."

We have more in common.

He catches himself slipping into an old identity and clears his throat to adjust.

"I'm a mouse who was born to fly too, Grace. I always wanted to be more, to do more, to go higher. I think that's why we get along."

He leans in close to her and nuzzles her nose with his own. "You and I are birds of a feather..."

"Not me, Victor!" she says, surprised by the comparison. "I've never left this town. I've barely ever left this farm."

"Well, that takes a certain kind of bravery too, now doesn't it?

After a while, I had drifted for so long, I became afraid to stay anywhere. I traveled from town to town on business for many years. I never much felt at home anywhere... until I met Mikki."

Grace swallows hard. "You have never really talked much about her."

Suddenly, Victor has lost his appetite. He pushes the cereal bowl forward, then pushes his chair out from the table. He sits for a moment, as if he's considering whether to run.

"Mikki was the love of my life. I gave her everything—probably too much. Still wasn't enough to keep the marriage from crumbling. And just when I thought we were finding our way back from the divorce... she decided to hop along with a rabbit.

And not just any rabbit, mind you. A smug trust-fund phony. I despise that hare as much as he despises me."

Victor stands from the table and moves toward the window.

"She'd rather spend her days with him? Fine. She made a fool of me twice—I wasn't going to leave room for it to happen again."

"...but do you still love her?" Grace asks, now having lost her appetite too.

Leaning on both paws over the sink, Victor gazes out the window, looking for the answer to her question. Instead, what he sees is Biff barreling toward the tree stump farmhouse in a huff.

"I wish I could answer that, my dear, but right now we have a visitor. Here comes Big Burly Biff. And he looks angry. Maybe somebody stole his nuts."

"Victor, you rascal."

"He has a crush on you, you know."

"He most certainly does not!" she insists, standing up and clearing the table. "He's a good friend and a capable construction chief. Besides, Biff and I have known each other forever."

"And he's probably wanted you for that long. Trust me. He loves *you* as much as he hates *me*."

"You're just being silly." She shuffles to the sink where Victor is still gazing outward. They share a smile, a chicory-flavored kiss, and an embrace before Biff's knock shakes the stump door.

Grace opens up for a greeting on the back steps. Biff is relieved to see her, but his relief quickly turns to grief when Victor appears in the doorway behind, smoothing his kissed lip fur back into place.

Biff has seen Victor as a threat from the beginning, and now that threat is confirmed.

But there will be time to deal with that later.

Biff has news from Chenoa City.

"Grace, we got a real problem. I'm hearin' news about a press conference that just came out of Chenoa City sayin' that Stickum exports are being cut. Permanently!

They've stopped all the shipments that were scheduled to come down the river.

That dag-blamed Newmouse Enterprises is hoggin' it all up for their own housing projects."

Biff smacks his tail on the ground in a rage that rattles the kitchen dishware.

"They're cutting us off cold!"

Victor's blood cuts off cold, too.

Biff takes off his hard-shell hat and runs his fingers through his too-tan fur, trying to regain his composure.

"Grace, we've got a field of pumpkins that are gonna rot, if we don't do somethin' fast."

"We can't find a honeypot of Stickum anywhere else in the forest?" she asks desperately.

"You know those Newmouse scoundrels own the rights to the pine sap... and they hold the patent on the manufacturing process. We got nowhere else to go! I've been hoarding supplies all summer, but not enough to finish the whole project."

Grace stiffens. She tilts her ears toward Victor—just for a second—and then she's in motion.

"Biff, call the committee. I'll meet you at the pavilion in ten minutes."

She turns, taking her tail in paw and swooshing it back like the train of a gown. She stomps back up the stone steps, brushing past Victor's shoulder, then disappearing inside.

Victor stumbles out the door and down the steps, head spinning harder than on the day he died.

Biff stands firmly in his path—like a heavy bag on legs—daring him to swing.

"Where you headed off to, pip-squeak?"

"Not now, squirrel."

Victor tries to blaze past him, but Biff is persistent.

"You're gonna break her heart, you know!"

Victor freezes.

Biff continues, "You listen here! You may think Grace is tough as nails, but that doe in there has her limits. She's already had a lifetime of heartache. She don't need you pumpin' her full of false hope."

Biff kicks the dirt and stubs his toe, but doesn't let on how much it pains him.

"Southbrook cares a lot about her. *I* care a lot about her. And if *you* care about her at all, you'll get the hell out of this town. Go back to that dank forest you crawled out of."

Victor weaves around Biff, like a fighter trained to dodge the blow.

He doesn't look back.

He marches toward the forest, each step harder than the last, as if he could outrun the truth once again.

"She's better off without you!" Biff cries out.

And Victor stops. Just for a moment.

The words hit.

Because they're true.

Then—

Because he has to, he keeps moving.

And he doesn't stop.

Chapter Twenty-Six

Revelations

Furiously, he storms toward The Outer Forest.

It's not just my company…

He stomps down the cobblestone path.

It's me!

All the way past the mills.

It's my tried and true business plan!

All the way through the bean field.

Buy cheap, dig deep.

Smashing and tearing as much as he can.

It's the same damn plan I used in Morel Ground.

Into the grass.

And Acorn Alley,

Right to the edge of the forest.

And Chenoa City too!

He charges the burr bush that knots the entryway like a gate.

I never pulled a punch.

He smashes through it, but leaps back.

I can't do it.

He drops to his knees and hammers his fists into the ground.

"I killed Victor Newmouse, and still he lives!"

Just then—

A familiar voice seeps into the air above him.

"Come on now, Victor. You didn't really think you'd pull this off forever, did you?"

His head snaps up, eyes scanning for the source.

And there she is—

Perched on the branch of a teaberry tree, silver feathers glinting in the prairie sun.

"Kathra Chansoar?" He blinks wildly. "How the hell did you know I was here?"

She tilts her head to the side slowly.

"Please, Victor. You should know by now that I know everything." She says it as if it were a complete matter of fact. "Also... crows love to gossip."

Victor sinks his knees deeper into the dry ground, fists tangled in a snarl of burrs.

Of course.

Calling the crows.

That's when I gave myself away.

He grits his teeth and growls.

With a fluid motion, Kathra descends to the ground, but she doesn't approach him right away. She keeps her distance, studying him closely. But even through the burrs and broken pride, she knows—

This is still Victor.

She glides closer.

"My old friend. I've known you for a long time."

She touches a wingtip to his shoulder, inspecting the scar on his ear.

"I always saw something special in you."

She grins.

"Even back when you were wearing cheap shirts and running common cons from town to town."

Their eyes meet in a knowing glance.

"Now. You tell me the truth.

Why would you do this?"

"Kathra." He rises from the ground. "I didn't plan to lose my life. I just... found a hell of a deal on a new one."

He begins to pluck the little green burrs from his fur.

"All I wanted was to forget about Chenoa City. To forget about Mikki."

The scent of the damp pine from the forest fills his nose—and his memory.

"And to forget about her gallivanting around behind my back with that... Jackass Rabbitt!"

Kathra's feathers ruffle slightly.

"Mikki and JackRabbitt? For heaven's sake, Victor, what are you talking about?"

"I saw the photos of their... heartwarming affair." He rolls his eyes, curling his tail with disdain.

Her wings slide to her waist. "Really? Where did you get these photos? Where are they now?"

"They were delivered to The Sky Chamber by Anony-mouse Courier. And that is where I left them."

Kathra lifts her head high, slowly—then snaps it back down, pinning him with her stare.

"Now let me get this straight. You let everyone think you were dead over some photos of Mikki and JackRabbitt?"

Her talons tap impatiently on the dry ground.

"Did you talk to Mikki? Do you know who took the photos?!"

He doesn't respond, his eyes fixed on a fallen twig. He picks up the twig, rolling it back and forth in his paw.

"Look at me, Victor."

He lifts an eyebrow, then an eye, then his head.

"Darling, I don't know what you think you saw, but I find it very hard to believe that Mikki would be cheating on you with JackRabbitt. If she wanted him, she'd be with him right now. But she's not! She's devastated over your death!"

"You've seen her?"

"Of course I've seen her." Kathra shrugs. "Mikki is one of my dearest friends. And I know what's in her heart. She wanted to reunite your family more than anything. She's been inconsolable! She's barely left the house since your funeral."

My funeral.

"...and JackRabbitt has barely left Newmouse Tower since he was appointed as CEO."

Victor's ears peel back slowly.

"Now, hold on a minute. You're telling me JackRabbitt Abbitt is running Newmouse Enterprises?"

The twig bends under the pressure of his paw.

"That's right, my dear."

"Kathra! How could you let that happen?" He begins to pace. "No. That can't be. The board wouldn't just give my company over to the enemy!"

"Wouldn't they?" She turns her head, trying to keep the sun off her face, though it insists on following her. "It was chaos after your... departure. JackRabbitt stepped up, and the board approved him in the midst of crisis."

Crisis?

Crisis creates opportunity...

Kathra watches as the realization rolls over him, letting the silence be.

"And now JackRabbitt is buying up Newmouse shares under a shell corporation. He's trying to force the mice off the board. He wants to replace them with William and... Gillian."

The twig snaps between Victor's fingers.

"I'll be dammed."

JackRabbitt didn't just step up to run the company.

He maneuvered it all.

Victor's pulse beats faster.

His breathing grows louder.

His mouse 'stache twitches.

And then—

Kathra gives him the final push.

"He's… also got Mikki's voting proxy on behalf of the children."

Victor snaps.

"That pompous perfume peddler! He set me up!"

"Mmm, and that's why I'm here."

Kathra smooths the fine feathers around her face, longing for a rejuvenation treatment at The Golden Grotto.

This prairie heat is very drying.

"Listen, my dear, no one else suspects you're not dead, but I need Victor Newmouse to be alive."

She rolls a shoulder, weary.

"If I have to deal with Gillian for one more second, I think I'll strangle myself."

Her tone shifts, sharpening.

"And JackRabbitt is becoming dangerous. I've had my suspicions about him for a while now. I tried to warn him. Perhaps I could try talking to Jon again at The Green Gala, but—"

"A party?"

"Why, yes. Victor. Life did continue on with you."

He blows out a breath in an exaggerated huff. "Yes, that's a realization that's quickly dawning."

Kathra clears her throat. "The point is, JackRabbitt is far more devious than I gave him credit for. I think it's time for you to..." She searches for the words. "Resurrect."

"Resurrect? Now why would I want to do that?"

He turns away from her, gazing thoughtfully into the darkness of the forest.

"Damn it. I have a new life here. A simple one. Peaceful."

She gives him a moment, then, with just enough weight to make it land:

"Victor. Now that you know the truth, do you really think you can go on out here playing 'Little Stump on the Prairie'?"

His tail lashes at the ground. "Hell yes, I—"

"Do you have any idea how much guilt The Colonel is carrying? He thought you died on his watch. Turns out, you died on yours."

"I never intended to hurt anyone!" He bristles.

"You have two children in Chenoa City who think their father is dead."

"They're better off without me!"

He spins around, turning his back to the forest, gazing into the prairie.

"Darling, you're gonna hear this eventually, so I might as well be the first—

How could you let everyone believe Victor Newmouse is dead?

Victor Newmouse isn't dead.

He's on summer vacation!

Well, the summer is over, my dear.

Fall sweeps are coming.

JackRabbitt Abbitt is running your company!

And he's using Mikki to do it!"

Victor smacks his tail to the ground, stirring up a cloud of dust, but still refusing to turn around.

"Listen to me.

I understand you, Victor.

If no one else understands you…

I understand you.

But you have got to face this.

You have a family!

You have an empire!

You have a… *responsibility* to the life you built."

And with those words, he is just a mere pup again.

Sitting on the stoop of the orphanage.

Swinging his feet from the steps.

Twirling the tie on his knapsack between his fingers.

Not yet Victor Newmouse. Still Kristan Miller.

Waiting.

Day by day. Hour by hour.

Waiting for them to come back.

But they never did.

Abandoned.

By a mother and a father who buckled under the weight of *their responsibility*.

He takes a deep inhale.

"You're right. I can't keep running."

I am not going to abandon my family the way my parents abandoned me.

I am not going to let JackRabbitt get away with this.

And I am not going to let Victor Newmouse destroy Grace's dream!

He watches the prairie grass sway, like it's asking him to stay.

Southbrook has shown me what I could be.

But the forest is what I am.

Slowly, he turns around.

"I shall return to Chenoa City on Friday."

"Friday?!" she gasps. Even her shadow seems annoyed, stretched out behind her like it wants to retreat back into the forest immediately. "You expect me to keep up this facade until Friday?"

Victor crosses his arms and begins to rock back and forth on his feet.

"It's non-negotiable. I have some... business to attend to here before I go."

She considers him quietly, noting that he seems different

somehow.

"Alright, Victor. Attend to your... business. I will keep your secret for a few more days—but only because I don't want to be the one to tell Mikki."

Victor slips his paw into his pocket and takes a step toward her.

"Kathra, it's imperative that you make sure Mikki arrives at Newmouse Tower just before noon on Friday."

He pulls his paw out of his pocket, retrieving his father's watch.

Click.

Snap!

"I'll handle the rest myself."

Chapter Twenty-Seven

The End

Silver wings flicker in the moonlight that casts through the farmhouse kitchen window. It's past midnight. Grace sits at the dining table wearing her sleeveless mint-green nightgown and an aqua robe that doesn't match. It flows down her ivory fur like a waterfall to the floor.

She's lost in the flow of thoughts, tapping her fingers on the table, waiting for Victor to come home.

Home.

As he slowly twists the wooden doorknob, Grace thoughtfully twists the dial on a small sunflower oil lamp to light his way. The brightness of the flickering light illuminates the finality of their summer fantasy.

This is the night he says goodbye.

"Victor, come sit down," she softly commands.

"Grace..."

He moves wearily toward the table but does not take his seat.

"I have something to tell you."

But he struggles to find the words.

"You're not going to like it."

He closes his eyes, squeezing them tight.

"So, I suppose I'll just come out with it."

He takes a deep breath and braces himself.

"My name isn't Victor Miller. It's Victor—"

"Newmouse."

She knows.

"You know?!"

"Yes, Victor. I know."

"How?!

How do you know?"

"Victor, I have eyes and ears all over. I'm a businessmouse too, you know. You think I don't know who my suppliers are?"

His eyes widen in disbelief. After the conversation he had with Kathra tonight, nothing should surprise him—*and yet here we are.*

He plants his feet on the floor and folds his arms in front of him.

"Well, does the whole damn town know?"

She smiles lightly. "I doubt the whole damn town keeps up with industry news."

A burst of air vibrates over his lips, and his eyes scan the empty room, as if he's searching for the hidden camera.

"How long have you known?"

"Well," she replies, "the news of your death came downriver with the otters—right about the time you passed out on my kitchen floor.

The rest wasn't hard to piece together after I pieced together that expensive shirt of yours.

A satin weave, is it?"

Victor drags a paw down his mouse 'stache. He would be impressed if he weren't so in shock.

"Why didn't you tell me?" he asks.

"...and send you back out into the wild prairie with a head wound?"

"Two head wounds," he reminds her.

She nods, reluctantly amused.

"I knew your name, but I didn't know *you*. After talking with you that first time, it was clear you didn't want to be found.

So, I let you keep your secret—and, in the meantime, I rather enjoyed knowing The Great and Powerful Victor Newmouse was digging my outhouses."

Checkmate.

"As our friendship grew, I had hoped you would want to confide in me someday. I was never going to push—but now we have a problem on our paws."

He straightens. "Grace, I intend to fix this for you."

"Oh, I know you're going to fix it," she kindly demands, "and you're going to fix it now before I lose an entire year's investment."

Nodding to himself, he takes his usual chair beside hers at the dining table. "I'll put a stop to the forest real estate expansion, and I'll reinstate the exports to Southbrook."

The lamp light dances over her sleek, slender face, though she doesn't know it. He indulges himself with one last stolen look at her native beauty, then hangs his head and stands up from the chair.

"I just need to gather a few things for my journey back to Chenoa City. I can sleep under the pavilion tonight if you'll allow it. I'll be gone by morning."

"Oh, you're not going to Chenoa City alone," she explains. "Now *I* have a deal to propose to *you*."

She flattens her nervous paws down onto the table to keep them from moving.

"Victor, I want to go with you to Chenoa City."

He plummets back down into the chair. "No! Absolutely not. You are not going to Chenoa City, Grace. You don't even know what you're asking."

"Don't you dare presume what I know!"

Victor thrusts his paws to his face and groans. "My goodness, Grace, why on Earth would you want to go to Chenoa City?"

She shifts upright and stiffens her shoulders, preparing for the pitch of her life.

"For starters, I intend to oversee the correction of your mistake. I'll stand dockside to ensure those shipments go down the river if I have to."

She loosens her hard approach and continues in a gentler tone.

"More importantly, Victor, you've given me wings! Now, I want to meet more new creatures and experience more new things. I want to wear makeup and beautiful dresses. I want to go to restaurants, and eat melt mushrooms in the forest!"

"I'm afraid I may have oversold you on these mushrooms."

She sighs. "Victor, please be serious. The time we've spent here together has changed my life. I couldn't unwind this clock if I wanted to."

"Grace, you can't leave Southbrook. It's your home. It's your family. It's your dream to make Pumpkin Acres a success."

"And I will. I'll just have to... commute."

She grins—just a little—with self-satisfaction.

"Of course, I love Southbrook. It will always be my home, but I want to know other places too. Perhaps you could return my hospitality and be my guide through Chenoa City! I can find my own place to stay, or..."

We could be together.

She resumes the involuntary tapping of her claws on the wooden table.

"Think of it, Victor. We can do more for Southbrook *and* Chenoa City... together. We can combine resources, expand trade, and help both communities flourish. We could flood Chenoa City with farm-fresh produce while expanding the housing and commercial districts in Southbrook at the same time."

Victor looks wearily at the pure ambition that is electrifying her body.

He's seen it before.

Chenoa City has proven itself to be a cruel trap for many creatures. The allure of its mysteries, thrills, and opportunities have paved the way to countless crushing defeats. He can't protect her from that harsh reality.

Hell, he can't even protect her from himself.

Inside Victor's silence, Grace listens for signals of his response. She receives none but carries on.

"Victor, I've made up my mind. I don't want to go back to the way things were. I don't want to live the rest of my life in a... comfortable prison!"

She takes a deep breath and releases a cleansing truth.

"I don't want to leave *you!*"

This truth takes his breath away right along with hers.

He doesn't want to leave her either—but he knows that returning to Chenoa City will mean traveling down a tunnel of trouble with JackRabbitt.

And then, there's Mikki.

If the affair was a lie, where does that leave the love between them?

Where does it leave Grace?

Biff was right about one thing: Grace doesn't need false hope.

"My darling, I can't promise you the fairy tale forest life you're dreaming of.

Chenoa City is... complicated.

My life there is complicated.

Mikki, and the kits—"

He can't quite find the words to continue on.

So she does.

"I'm not asking for a promise.

I'm just asking for a chance.

For myself.

For us."

Dammit, she's beautiful and brilliant.

"Victor, I'm serious. If you won't help me, I'll find another way.

If I can fly a bird, I can ride beaver upstream all the way to Chenoa City on my own!"

It's true.

Once Grace sets her mind to something, she'll do it.

"What do you say, Victor? Do we have a deal?"

She's everything I am—plus everything I'll never be.

"Alright, Grace."

Victor places one paw on top of hers, and the other one follows.

"On one condition."

"Oh, really? I'm afraid you don't have much room to negotiate."

She arches a brow, curious now.

"Pray tell, what is it that you want?"

He smiles. "I want a proper date."

"A date?" Her ears twitch.

"One last night here in Southbrook. Together."

She hesitates. "Victor. The timing. Don't you think we should..."

"I've already made the arrangements."

He releases her paws, leans back in his chair, and crosses his arms.

"When?

When exactly did you have time to make arrangements for a date?

Sometime within the last 30 seconds?"

His mouse 'stache twitches as a slow smile rises at the corners of his lips.

"Well now, my dear, the truth is, before I knew we would be traveling to the city...

I planned to bring the city to you.

A gourmet dinner, candlelight dancing, a new dress, some cosmetics."

"Cosmetics?" She echoes.

"Yes, well...

Bubbly Bath, *Furfume*, *Berry Cherry Lip Stain*, things of the like."

He waves his paw around in a circle as if it is all just second nature.

"But, if you don't think you'd enjoy it..."

"No!" she interrupts quickly.

"I... think I *would* enjoy it very much."

"Then it's settled. Meet me at the pavilion at 6 o'clock."

He snaps forward in his seat and leans into her closely.

"Tomorrow night, we dine, we dance, and then... we begin our journey to Chenoa City."

Suddenly she begins to buckle under the weight of her own victory.

“I suppose it’s time.”

Gently, he caresses the fur on her cheek.

“Yes.

It’s time.”

Chapter Twenty-Eight

Big Burly Goodbye

Fragments of the Pumpkin Acres Dedication Ceremony slowly settle into the landscape. Flattened grass marks where the crowds once stood. Tattered banners hang from wooden posts. Paper lanterns sway lazily in the breeze.

The air is filled with the sounds of a peaball game being played on the community court—the *squeak* of shuffling feet, the *thip-thip* of the ricochet, and the *smack* of the paddle sending a painted yellow pea spinning toward the backline.

Grace rests her paws on the worn wooden picnic table, her cane leaning beside her. Biff sits across from her with hunched shoulders, letting the weight of her words sink in.

"You're leavin'?" His voice contains a mixture of disbelief and heartbreak.

Grace nods. "I have no choice. I've already spoken to the committee. I have to get the supply chain moving again."

Biff's big bushy tail swishes back and forth, tickling the grass behind him. "I know that, but..." He pauses, then thrusts his fists onto the picnic table, rattling it and startling Grace. "No! Forget it, Grace. Chenoa City is way too dangerous a place for you."

Grace's ears flatten, a rare sign of irritation. She fights hard to maintain her composure, but a lifetime of being told about the things she can and can't do boils over.

"I am so... damn tired of hearing that!"

"I... I'm sorry," he mutters, his gaze dropping to the ground.

Biff knows better than anyone what Grace has been through. He's known her as long as he can remember. He can recall their earliest days toddling around together playfully. She would cling to his arm with tiny paws, trusting him to guide her over roots and uneven ground.

As they grew, he'd walk her to the schoolhouse each morning, always a step ahead, calling out curbs and corners before she could stumble.

By their teenage years, they had fallen into an easy rhythm— Grace, sharp-witted and determined, and Biff, her self-appointed protector, always keeping an eye out, always ready to catch her if she needed him.

But she never did.

Grace always had a way of moving forward, of finding her own footing no matter the obstacles in her path.

And now, she is stepping into the unknown.

Without him—

and with HIM.

"I know you just care about me."

Grace shares all those same memories too.

"But I can do this! I won't be alone."

Suddenly, a sharp *crack* echoes from the peaball court, and a commotion interrupts them.

"You're out!" a voice yells, slicing through the air.

Biff's wide eyes become angry slits.

"Oh. Yeah. Right. Ok. I reckon *Victor's* goin' with you to Chenoa

City?"

Grace both recognizes and resents his disapproving tone.

She straightens her back and assumes a professional posture.

"Yes. Victor will be accompanying me. He will be my guide. Victor knows Chenoa City very well."

Biff shakes his head, trying hard to think of some way out of this.

"Hey, I got an idea. Why don't you just let me go in your place? You stay here, and I'll go."

Grace is not amused.

"What?! Biff. A blind mouse can't manage the construction crew. My skills are best suited to negotiating the restoration of the Stickum supply."

She inhales deeply, growing impatient.

"Please, Biff. You have to stay here. You have to see the project through. Southbrook needs Pumpkin Acres.

And Southbrook needs *you*."

Biff opens his mouth, then closes it.

"But I need..."

You.

He stops himself before accidentally saying it.

The truth is, he didn't take on the Pumpkin Acres project simply because he loves Grace, or because he wants to help build her dream. He didn't take on the project hoping that someday they would build a life together, although that's true too. Biff took on the project because he sees the faces of the families who need this housing every day on the street. He knows that his hard work can make a difference in their lives.

He sighs a heavy sigh. "Yeah, Grace. Yeah, okay. I'll stay in Southbrook," he says at last, his voice hulking with resignation. "I can keep the project movin' for a couple more weeks before the supply runs dry."

"That's all the time I need," Grace says, with relief.

A paddle twirls on the peaball court. The referee's whistle *shrills*.

"When will you be back?"

"I... I don't know."

"But you will be back... Won't you?"

Grace hesitates. She's learned her lesson in not making promises she can't keep. But this is not a matter of promise. It's a matter of fact.

"I *will* get those exports flowing again. There's not a doubt in my mind. And I *will* return to see those houses built."

"Okay. Okay." Biff puts his big burly paw on top of hers. And for the first time, she becomes aware that Victor was right about Biff's feelings for her.

But they are feelings she does not return.

"Goodbye, Biff," she says softly.

She removes her paw from under his, then stands slowly and retrieves her cane. As she begins to walk away, she reaches up to place a paw on his shoulder. His big burly body melts under the weight of her tiny touch.

"Goodbye, Grace," he replies, as she disappears behind him.

Her cane taps softly through the grass, brushing past clover and the crushed heads of a few forgotten bluebells.

He is tempted to watch her walk away, but he refuses to turn around.

He can't break.

He has to remain strong.

For Southbrook.

And so—

The love she *should* have chosen lets her go.

But inside, Biff's big burly heart... is breaking.

Chapter Twenty-Nine

Around The Clock Work

Yet another late night has crept up on JackRabbitt.

And yet another battle is being waged at the grand oak boardroom table in the Sky Chamber of Newmouse Tower.

But this time, the battle is internal.

He is alone in the dimness, the city's twinkling lights flickering through the tall windows.

His stomach sears—an ulcer, his apparent reward for perseverance.

He reaches for the bottle Dr. Hisstings prescribed: a wicked-tasting cocktail of cabbage juice, garlic, and honey. But it keeps the pain at bay.

The ulcer has been creeping up for weeks now, a slow-burning testament to the stress gnawing at him from the inside.

It's as if his body is staging a rebellion against his own ambition.

Dr. Hisstings warned him to take it easy.

As if he could.

As if anything worth building has ever been achieved by taking it easy.

His gaze lingers on the blueprints spread before him.

The Everwood Condominiums.

A gleaming high-rise, full of promise.

The city is rallying behind it. Investors are pouring in. The press conference was a resounding success.

And it is all going exactly as planned.

JackRabbitt knew, even as the cameras flashed, that he was going to sink the project.

The sails are raised. All he has to do now is let the wind take it.

It's not that it's a bad project.

In fact, it's good.

Too good.

So good that it blinds the city to the world just outside its borders.

The so-called visionaries believe that pulling up the drawbridge will make the kingdom untouchable.

But JackRabbitt has spent too much time past the riverbanks, seen too much to pretend that's true.

Without trade, without fresh minds, without a path to the greater world, the forest will fall.

And Everwood will burn the only bridge leading out.

His fingers trail over the blueprint title.

Phase One: Foundation.

If this project succeeds, the city will mine itself dry.

It's just what Victor Newmouse would have wanted.

He presses his paws against the table, staring down at the blueprints.

For a moment, he hesitates.

He could let this happen. He could let the city have its shining monument, its temporary success. He could let them live in the illusion a little longer.

But then what?

He swallows hard, his stomach twisting against itself.

No.

A few well-placed disruptions—delays, disputes, uncertainty. Just enough to shake the board's confidence. Just enough to stall the project before it locks the city into a future it can't escape.

The citizens will grumble. The headlines will shift. It's nice to have a writer in the family.

Delays plague the Everwood Project—Public trust wanes.

The stock will dip. The board will panic. The mice will scurry around looking for an exit.

And when they do?

He'll give them a solution.

A contingency clause—something Victor "left behind."

Not real, of course. But real enough.

Victor's signature—a swipe of the pen.

Authorizing a limited stock release.

No board vote required. No questions asked.

And when that new stock quietly gets bought up through shell companies and old family friends...

Mikki loses her majority.

I gain control.

And—

She'll never know a thing.

Because it won't look like a takeover—it'll look like leadership.

A necessary move during a critical moment.

It's business.

I'm looking after the company.

For the children.

For the future.

JackRabbitt leans back in his chair, stretching his long legs beneath the desk, letting the weight of certainty settle over him.

"Let's see how they handle a little controlled chaos."

With a renewed sense of self-satisfaction, JackRabbitt's eyes begin to grow heavier.

A slow yawn slips out, soft and heavy, the tide gently tugging him under.

He is standing tall at a podium, ears high, voice ringing clear and smooth over the sea of eager faces. The sun glints off the glass of Newmouse Tower.

But wait—

It's not Newmouse Tower.

It's JackRabbitt Tower now.

The iconic "NE" that once crowned the tower is gone, replaced with his own initials.

JR—

Gleaming in gold against the skyline.

His voice rings with triumph—smooth and commanding, the words flowing like a victory march.

"...And so, the mining rights have been returned to their rightful owners!"

A wave of applause ripples through the crowd, washing over him.

"To the families who built this city, who toiled for generations—your legacy is restored!"

His arms spread wide, basking in their adoration.

"And with our new trade deals in place, there will be resource sharing, profits, and prosperity for Chenoa City, the Outer Forest, and beyond!"

The cheer that follows is deafening—an uproar of approval so strong, he feels it even through the figment.

He sees business leaders nodding in gratitude, workers lifting their caps, young entrepreneurs calculating their futures.

Victor Newmouse who?

Chenoa City is *his* town, and it thrives because of him.

JackRabbitt's eyes scan the cheering crowd, then land softly on one face—his father's.

Jon Abbitt stands in the front row, tall and proud, his chin lifted, his blue eyes shining with something JackRabbitt has craved his entire life.

Approval.

Not just acknowledgment.

Not just measured patience.

But pride.

And respect.

His father nods once, slow and deliberate—the way he does when he sees a job well done.

And then—he smiles. A true, beaming smile, warm as the sunlight breaking through the clouds.

It's the smile of a father who believes in his son, who knows—without a doubt—that he has not only lived up to the family name... but elevated it.

The applause swells, but he barely hears it now.

His ears twitch. His breath catches.

And for a moment, he is just a kit again, sitting in the rowboat with his father's paw on his shoulder, pointing toward the endless horizon.

"One day, you'll see the bigger picture, son."

And he has.

And now, Dad sees it too.

He reaches for his father—

But the vision shifts.

The podium, the crowd, the tower—they all dissolve like mist.

And the roar of applause fades into birdsong.

The sunlight is softer now, dappled through high oak branches.

Beneath him is a blanket spread in the grass.

Beside him, a picnic basket.

He's on the Abbitt Warren's south lawn with a panoramic view of the natural countryside.

The tulips are in bloom, and the vast fields of sweetgrass are gaining their limey spring color.

He glances up.

The clouds are gliding by slowly, like sailboats on the sea.

He swings his head to the side—and there she is.

Mikki. As lovely as the day.

She's an angel.

No. Not an angel.

He knows she lacks perfection.

He loves those imperfections too.

And looking into her eyes right now, he feels that same loving acceptance reflected back at him.

He reaches for her paw, fumbling over the glowstone ring on her finger.

She's more than the love of his life.

She's his wife.

Their romantic picnic is suddenly spattered with the distant sound of a pup's laughter.

JackRabbitt swivels his ears in the direction of the sound, and his eyes follow toward the pond.

A spry young kit is running toward them, a toy fish on a pole bouncing behind.

As the youngster bursts into view, he wonders—

Is it a son or a daughter?

A rabbit like me?

Or a mouse like its mother?

Then, with an abrupt jolt, the dream vanishes.

His body jerks.

He leaps up.

He stands, wide-eyed in military alertness.

There's a sound of subtle stirring in the room.

He is not alone.

"Who's there?" he demands, lunging toward the electrical panel.

His heart pounds. His blood rushes wildly through his body.

And with the flick of a switch, the room floods with light.

It's empty.

It's all empty.

Only the sound of The Grandfather Clock.

Bong.

Bong.

Bong.

Bong.

He spins around, scanning for any trace of movement.

But there is nothing.

Nothing.

Except the haunting face of Victor Newmouse staring back at him—

From the portrait on the wall.

Chapter Thirty

The Lab

The Shabó Laboratory glows like a box of light—white cabinetry with glass-front panels gleaming under the fluorescence. The shelves illuminate rows of tools and tinctures lined up with obsessive symmetry. Even the air in the room is disciplined: imported prairie grass extract and pumpkin seed oil soothing the sterile bite of alcohol and steam.

It's not just The Lab—it's a reflection of the Abbitt at its center.

Ashlyn rises onto the pads of her hindpaws to reach for a bottle near the top shelf. She twists the cap open, nose twitching once as she sniffs it.

Satisfied, she carries the chosen bottle back to her workstation, setting it down between a set of glass pipettes and a burner plate still faintly warm. A teacup lingers near the corner, forgotten mid-sip. Above, a wall calendar hangs with tonight's Gala circled in ink.

Her dress has been ready for weeks. The Venmore's Department Store garment bag hangs in the corner beside a row of lab coats.

Ashlyn wears her lab coats like armor: stark white and barely blemished.

With concentration and composure, she measures a deep blue serum into a narrow test tube.

The liquid moves like silk, curling at the edges, dissolving into the pale gold mixture beneath it.

A reaction.

Subtle, but promising.

She tilts her head, watching the formula as it operates on instinct alone.

Even if she doesn't allow herself to.

Suddenly, the door swings open behind her.

"Ash?" JackRabbitt calls out.

His voice ignites like the flick of a match, crackling into her concentration.

She sighs, setting down the test tube with care and precision. "If you ruin this batch, I will ruin your life."

He ignores her threat, gliding into the room with that trademark JackRabbitt optimism.

He's feeling great this morning. Renewed, even. Light-footed and looser than usual. The hard work is paying off. The dream is tangible. Close. Everything is going to work out just fine.

His eyes scan the room. "Do you have it?"

Ashlyn doesn't bother looking up. "Have what?"

"The gift basket," he says, as if she should already know. "For the auction. The exclusive fall sampler?"

Ashlyn blinks, one ear tipping to the side. Then, for the first time since he entered, she smiles.

"Oh, that." Her tone shifts from cool to unmistakably pleased. "Yes, of course."

She moves across the lab with purpose, razor-sharp heels clicking against the tile.

A glossy, bronze basket sits on a side table, nestled in a bed of red tissue paper. The collection inside is pure perfection—limited edition lip stains, claw colors, pigments, and perfumes that she has personally refined over months of research. The scent alone is intoxicating—an autumn blend of spiced fig, warm sandalwood, and just a touch of smoked vanilla.

She picks up the basket and carries it over, holding it in one paw—just out of reach.

"You're lucky I love my work more than I dislike interruptions."

JackRabbitt takes one look at the basket—and his face lights up like a kit on Wishmas morning.

"Ash," he smiles wide, "You keep doing work like this, and... I'll keep taking all the credit."

He reaches for the basket—

But she pulls it back teasingly, just enough to make him work for it.

He shifts his stance, playing along. "Brilliant as always."

She presents it to him, her tail giving the slightest twitch of smug satisfaction.

"Careful, Jacky. You almost sound happy."

"I do love my life."

He lifts the basket with both paws, holding it up to admire it. "I'll give it to Mikki personally."

Ashlyn folds her arms, one brow lifting in quiet judgment. "Mikki, personally, hmm?"

He looks up from the basket, bracing for what comes next. "Ok. Go ahead. Spit it out."

She leans casually against the counter, the edge of her lab coat parting just enough to reveal the shimmer of her metallic dress.

Then, unable to stay still, she shifts, pulling in a tray of vials to work on.

"Just wondering what exactly this is. A charitable donation? Or a play for Mikki's affection?"

JackRabbitt smiles, shaking his head. "And here I thought you'd be flattered that I'm showing off your work."

"I am," she says easily. "But let's not pretend I don't know you."

Her paw hovers briefly, then she selects a vial filled with a soft amber gel.

"I hear Mikki's been a mess since Victor died."

JackRabbitt's jaw tightens at the mention of the name, but he keeps his expression neutral.

"She's grieving," he says firmly. "She needs a win."

Ashlyn peels an old label off the vial in one slow, even motion—*skrrch*—then rolls the paper between her fingers into a coil.

"And you're the one who's going to give it to her?"

He doesn't answer right away. Instead, he watches her work in silence, then nods toward the tray. "Is this your idea of stress relief?"

"Better than whatever you've been doing." She eyes him clinically. "You look like hell, by the way."

He gives her a sideways smile. "Thanks."

"I'm serious."

She presses a fresh label into place, smoothing it down with the back of her paw.

"You've been absent-minded lately. Burning the candle at both ends—Newmouse Enterprises and Shabó Cosmetics. Even for you, it's too much."

"Save it. I've already had this conversation with Dad."

He turns, half-ready to leave. "Besides, I feel great."

She uncaps her fine-point marker with a quiet *click*. "Right."

She glides the marker tip across the label in crisp, narrow letters.

"I mean it," he says, giving his lip a quick bite. "Let's just say... I had sweet dreams last night."

She finishes writing, pauses, then reaches for the next vial. "Whatever that means."

Then, without warning, a gust of hot air hits the lab as the door swings open again.

"Did somebody order a specimen?"

Brack Squirrelton steps into the room like it's scene one of something soft-lit and scandalous, his fitted shirt clinging to his chest with an eager embrace. His blackish brown fur catches the fluorescent light—slick and greasy.

His golden eyes lock directly onto Ashlyn.

He pauses, then strides in with a walk that says... he's not here to talk about chemistry. He's here to ignite it.

JackRabbitt mumbles under his breath. "Great. Golden Boing is here."

Ashlyn's ears arrange themselves into perfect professional

posture. "Brack," she says plainly.

Brack gives her an easy grin. "Miss Abbitt."

He flicks his golden gaze toward the basket in JackRabbitt's paws, feigning interest. "Well, now, what's all of this?"

JackRabbitt sets the basket back down on the counter for safekeeping. "It's a gift. Not that you'd know anything about giving."

Brack places a paw over his chest with exaggerated offense. "Jacky Cakes! Please. You wound me. I'm a giver."

JackRabbitt forces a laugh. "Oh? And what exactly have you been giving lately?"

Brack pumps a paw once. "Memorable experiences."

JackRabbitt pauses, like he's waiting for Brack to say something dumber. "Maybe you should try giving something someone *actually* wants."

Brack settles in beside the gift basket, idly winding the bronze ribbon around his fingers. "Say, Jacko. Don't you ever get tired of letting your sister upstage you?"

JackRabbitt swats his paw away from the basket. "Say, Squirrelton. Don't you ever get tired of being so... squirrelly?"

Brack rubs his paw as he draws it back. "Comes with the tail," he says, giving it a slow, impressive shake.

Ashlyn lets out a breath—loudly—then slides back to her workstation, collecting a fresh vial of serum. She's not about to waste her time watching these two circle each other in some kind of... male domination dance straight off the forest floor. She has work to do.

JackRabbitt waits for her to be fully occupied before shifting gears. His voice dips lower, quieter. Serious.

"Let's cut the act," he says, adjusting his stance. "I know what you're doing."

Brack blinks, wide-eyed with innocence. "Doing?"

A faint buzz hums overhead as one of the fluorescent lights begins to stutter.

JackRabbitt glances up at the flickering light, then back at Brack. "It's not all that hard to see, Brackpack. You're trying to claw your way up the corporate tree."

Brack chuckles, shaking his head. "Jacky, Jacky, Jacky. Always so suspicious."

"I've been suspicious of you since you were trimming hedgerows on my family's front lawn." His glare deepens. "But I still haven't figured out how you managed to sweet-talk your way into a sales job at Shabó."

"Oh, wow. Is that another dig about how I used to be a gardener? That's very original, Jackpot. You know, some of us peasants have to work for a living. Not all of us were given the whole nut pile at birth."

The fluorescents give another nervous twitch.

A beam of light flickers across JackRabbitt's face as he moves in closer.

"Let me illuminate the situation for you, Squirrelton. You're not climbing one branch higher in this company. Not now. Not ever. This isn't your tree—and you're sure as hell not going to use Macy to scurry your way up it."

Brack doesn't move.

For once, even his tail has nothing to say.

JackRabbitt watches him for a second, then gives a faint nod—like the matter has been resolved.

"Glad we had this little talk, Brackski. Now why don't you go *sell* something."

With a soft *snap*, the light overhead gives up entirely.

Ashlyn notices the subtle shift in her lighting. She crosses to a small control panel near the door, flips a switch, and the fixture buzzes back on.

JackRabbitt nods to her. "I'll have maintenance take a look at that."

He turns to the counter and lifts a jar from the gift basket— *Bonfire Balm*. Its burnished copper label gleams under the restored light. He turns it over in his paws.

"Gotta say, Ash, this one's impressive."

"Glad you approve." She snaps the panel shut. "It only took a decade of chemistry, research, and fending off executives who've never measured anything but margins."

He picks up the basket and heads for the door. "See you at The Gala tonight."

Ashlyn has already returned to her workstation. "Try not to embarrass the family name," she calls out, without looking back.

JackRabbitt chuckles, casting a glance over his shoulder. "Later, Brackstrap."

Brack's grin tightens as the lab door swings shut behind him. His claws trace the fur along his jaw in a calculated touch-up. Then, smoothly, he moves toward Ashlyn, slipping back into that easy confidence as if the previous conversation never happened.

"So," he says, sliding up beside her. "Let's talk sales. Any updates on the spring prototypes? I like to be ahead of the pitch, you know."

Ashlyn doesn't look up right away, carefully swirling the contents of her vial.

"Your department sells what's ready, Brack. Not what's still in development."

Brack leans against the counter beside her, watching with mild interest as she lifts the vial to the light.

"Can't blame me for wanting to get closer to the source."

Ashlyn laughs despite herself, shaking her head.

"You are unbelievable."

"I believe the word you're looking for is... undeniable," he corrects her, tail fluttering excitedly behind him.

She finally turns toward him, pulling the glasses from her face and tossing them onto the desk, resolved that no real work is getting done here.

"What is it that you want, Brack?"

"Just wondering if your schedule might allow for one little dance tonight. That's all."

She thinks about it for a second, then—

"Sure!

...But only if the forest catches on fire and you're the one blocking the nearest exit."

He flashes a grin.

"Then I'll make sure to stand strategically."

"Of course you will."

She peels her gloves off one finger at a time.

"You're so cold to me, Ashlyn."

She shrugs.

"Maybe I just have a better understanding of who you are than most."

He leans in deeply, voice rich, eyes sizzling.

"And who am I?"

She doesn't pull away.

If anything, she lets the moment stretch.

Then, with a quick smile, she pivots entirely.

"Macy has a crush on you, you know."

For the briefest moment, his expression goes still—

but then he's back to being Brack again.

"Ah, well, I *am* quite crushable."

Ashlyn brings her paws to her hips.

"I'm serious, Brack. She's inexperienced. You might need to find a way to let her down easy."

He puffs out his lips, looking almost thoughtful.

"You Abbitt rabbits, always trying to make a better squirrel out of me."

"No, Brack. We just know you won't do it on your own."

Ashlyn rolls up the sleeves of her lab coat.

Not because it's hot.

But because she needs to feel the air on her fur.

The fact that he's attractive is infuriating.

Damn, I hate myself for sleeping with him.

And even more—for wanting to do it again.

Chapter Thirty-One

The Green Gala (Part 1)

A Welcome Banner flutters at the entrance of The Colonnade House, stretched between two white log pillars:

WELCOME TO THE GREEN GALA
A Benefit for the Forest ReLeaf Fund
Root for a Better Tomorrow

Groups of well-dressed guests ascend the wide front steps, passing beneath the rippling banner before stepping into a bustling lobby.

An easel displays a carved wooden sign that reads:

INSIDE:
Silent Auction
in The Colonnade House

OUTSIDE:
Dinner & Dancing
in The Meadow

At the welcome booth, eager paws trade event tickets for lush gift bags filled with promotional treasures. Buried in the tissue paper are a golden leaf supporter pin, a pressed petal bookmark, and a seed pouch for the Midnight Moonflower Ceremony.

Deeper inside, the space unfolds into a wide, vaulted gallery, where towering sponsorship panels line the walls in spotlight. Beneath each crest or company name, auction items rest on mossy velvet cushions—exclusive products, concert tickets, vacation getaways—each one vying for attention, each one whispering its worth to the highest bidder.

Socialites circle slowly, sizing up their competition before pausing for portraits under the ivy-draped arbor. A slender garden snake strikes an elegant pose for the roaming photographer, a twinkle in her eye.

Servers in green satin-backed vests circulate with trays of forest-inspired cocktails—fizzing with golden liquid and rimmed in crushed mint.

A finely groomed fox lifts his glass and wanders through the garden doors, drawn toward the music and moonlight—

In The Meadow.

Down the back steps, flickering lanterns line a winding path, the gentle slope guiding guests forward, step by step. A pair of heels click softly on the stone walkway, the hem of a gown trailing behind.

Just beyond the curve, guests pass through The Grand Archway into The Meadow—a sweeping pasture of glowing green and glittering gold.

Beneath a canopy of starry lights, the refreshments display gleams, each tier glistening with elegant treats and fluted glass.

At the center of the display, a section of floor is roped off with green velvet cords, its emptiness humming with expectation. A cake cutter and stack of dessert plates rest neatly on a counter nearby—waiting.

Near the far end of The Meadow, on a rising stage, the woodland orchestra fills the air with enchanting music. A grand stag conductor stands tall, baton poised, eyes sharp as the band kicks in. Squirrels strum their harps, woodpeckers hammer out a crisp beat, and a chorus of songbirds burst in, harmonizing so flawlessly it's soul-stirring. At the keys, a mole plays with dramatic flair, the tails of his tuxedo jacket resting gently on the stage floor behind him.

And right beneath the stage, just past the glow of conversation and laughter, the dance floor awaits.

A polished stretch of wood.

An open starry sky.

A perfect night ahead.

◆

Macy passes through The Arch and into The Meadow, softly glowing of her own accord.

She has chosen a sage-green gown with a flowing chiffon skirt—the perfect match for her favorite necklace, a thin gold chain with a tiny leaf pendant that nestles quietly against her fur.

Her paw moves instinctively to her waist, fingers brushing over the gold vine embroidery stitched along the bodice. She feels the shape of herself beneath it, the subtle cling of the fabric reminding her just how far she's come.

Tonight, she feels beautiful.

Her eyes drift over the refreshment display—but it's the velvet-roped space in the center that really catches her eye. Plates perfectly stacked. A golden cake cutter gleaming under the starry lights.

Whatever is coming must be special—and definitely worth the wait.

But in the meantime…

The hors d'oeuvre table is stacked with delicate pastries, glazed fruits, and tiny golden tarts.

Everything looks so good.

She scans the spread, tail fluttering excitedly. A thousand choices, each more tempting than the last.

Finally, she reaches for a honey-drizzled fig, lifting it carefully between her fingers.

She hesitates. Just a second. Just to admire it.

The rich scent, the sticky sweetness catching in the candlelight. She can already taste it, already feel the burst of flavor, the warmth of something indulgent—something earned.

She parts her lips—

And then, a voice slices through the moment.

"Better not eat that, or you might bust out of your dress."

Laura Venmore.

That snotty little squirrel.

Laura laughs—one of those snide, stuck-up laughs—and glides away like she owns the place, her fluffy red tail bouncing with every self-satisfied step.

Macy grips the fig, stomach twisting.

It's bad enough she has to deal with Laura on campus—whispering behind her back, snickering during class. Always watching. Always waiting for an opportunity to take a pot shot.

And now she has to deal with her tonight too.

Macy looks down at the fig. The glow is gone.

She worked so hard to fit into this dress. She can't ruin it now.

Her paw tightens.

Then, with a sharp breath, she tosses the fig back onto the platter and walks away.

Not even hungry anymore.

◆

Victoria crosses through The Arch and strides into The Meadow like she knows exactly who she is.

She pauses at the threshold, scanning the crowd for her mother. Her fingers lift to the square neckline of her green velour gown. The heavy sleeve slips just past her elbow, and her wristwatch catches the light.

The engraving on the back remains hidden, but she knows it's there. It's always there.

As she moves deeper into The Meadow, her braided ponytail and braided gold belt sway in quiet rhythm with her tail.

She sees her mother now, buzzing around the glen—a honey-blonde hurricane in heels.

Mikki is in her element.

She adjusts the edge of a tablecloth with one paw while gesturing a caterer closer with the other—still managing to laugh at a donor's joke, all without missing a beat.

It's like she was born to do this.

Mikki floats between guests, a vision of hospitality in her gold-sequined gown with cap sleeves and a V neckline. The sequins are scratchy under her arms with every reach and twist, but she doesn't flinch. She just keeps smiling.

A glowstone pendant rests at her heart, warm against her fur. It gives off a quiet light as she turns, spotting Victoria. Her smile is instant, radiant.

Victoria moves toward her. "Nice party you've got here."

Mikki is startled, ears twitching. "Victoria, darling! You made it."

"Yeah. Would've been weird if I hadn't."

Mikki brushes past the awkwardness, ever the hostess. "Well, how do I look?"

Victoria glances her over. Her hair perfect. Her dress is flawless. Her smile seems genuine.

"You look good, Mom."

Mikki touches her bouncy blonde curls. "Well, I do try."

Victoria nods, quieter now. "I can see that."

For just a second, there's something unspoken between them.

A moment of peace.

But then—a panicky porcupine materializes at Mikki's side, holding what looks like a melted centerpiece.

Mikki doesn't even flinch. She squeezes Victoria's arm, light and brief.

"I'm glad you're here."

Then, as quickly as she came, she vanishes.

Victoria stays quietly put.

If she can do this, so can I.

The thought dissipates quickly as a hush ripples through the crowd.

✦

Kathra Chansoar has arrived.

The crowd parts with a whisper as she glides through The Grand Archway, making every step a statement.

She moves like a queen surveying her kingdom with smooth and effortless command. Her dark forest-green velvet gown features a high neckline and long, flowing sleeves that only enhance her regal presence.

But it isn't her gown that has the crowd hypnotized.

It's her headpiece.

From head to shoulders, individual strands of shimmering glowstones dangle like a beaded curtain that frames her feathery face.

Three teardrop-shaped emeralds rest against her forehead—one long in the center of her brow, and two slightly shorter on either side.

As she moves, the crystalline curtain sways gently, side to side, giving the illusion that this luminous veil simply hovers around her.

She stares into a nonexistent distance, not committing to eye contact with anyone or anything. She simply lets the surroundings absorb her. But the slight upward turn at the sides of her beak indicates that she instinctively knows she's the center of attention.

And she loves it.

Amid the quiet spectacle of her entrance, one glance slips toward Mikki. So brief it could be mistaken for nothing at all. But in this moment, Kathra is keenly aware of the secret she is keeping.

Victor is alive. And Mikki has no idea.

With a breath of quiet resolution, she floats toward her friend, expression smooth as ever.

Mikki immediately begins to chatter away, unaffected by Kathra's aura of authority. This, perhaps, is what Kathra likes most about Mikki's companionship. No pretense.

"You will not believe what just happened," Mikki huffs.

"I rarely do." Kathra vaguely scans the room for important faces.

"One of the mole waiters set a tray of hors d'oeuvres right next to one of the musicians. Turns out, she was a chameleon!"

"A chameleon?"

Mikki nods. "Perfectly camouflaged. Some poor fox nearly took a bite out of her!"

Kathra takes a sip from a glass she didn't seem to have a second ago. "And?"

"Took care of it. Apologized. She was very offended, but no one got eaten, so... I'm calling it a win!"

Kathra quickly presses a wingtip against her beak, suppressing a laugh so as not to break her air of superiority. Her shimmering headpiece catches the light as she dips.

Mikki points at her. "Oh, sure, go ahead and laugh. But if you were a mouse having to smooth-talk an angry reptile, you'd be sweating too."

Kathra waves her wing in a grand flourish. "Darling, you're handling it."

"Of course I am. And you know what else? The deer actually showed up."

Kathra raises a brow. "All of them?"

Mikki nods, smug.

Kathra leans in, lowering her voice. "We might actually pull this off."

Mikki nudges her. "Was there ever any doubt?"

Kathra tilts her head. "That depends. Where's the cake?"

Mikki waves her paw like she's summoning magic. "Your giant green showstopper is on its way."

Kathra takes a sip of her drink. "Good. Now—an important order of business. There's a... meeting at Newmouse Tower tomorrow. Just before noon. You *must* be there."

Mikki groans. "Tomorrow? All I want to do is sleep in tomorrow!"

Kathra leans in close, her tone like ice wrapped in silk.

"Darling, it's a matter of life and death."

Mikki sighs, resigned. "Fine. But only because you said it like that."

Kathra turns away, satisfied that she's been heard.

And for the first time, she looks around, truly taking in the elegant party. Guests laughing. Glasses clinking.

Proof of Mikki's hard work. Proof of her progress.

Mikki didn't just plan this night—she's handled every small crisis that's come her way. And that, more than anything, gives Kathra hope that she'll be able to do it again.

"You've come a long way, my dear."

She touches a wingtip lightly to Mikki's shoulder.

"And I will be here for you. Whatever comes next."

✦

At The Meadow entrance, Brack arrives through The Grand Arch, wearing a jade green blazer and a black silk shirt left unbuttoned.

Macy spots him immediately.

He looks like he's just been peeled off the page of Animal Magazine's 50 Most Beautiful Creatures list.

Subscription delivered.

She smooths her dress and fluffs the loose waves in her blonde hair—heart pounding, hoping that maybe tonight, he'll ask her to dance.

She takes a step toward him, mentally rehearsing something charming, something casual to say. But before she can say anything, he turns, catches her eye, and smiles.

This is happening.

He moves toward her in slow motion, her heartbeat syncing to his steps.

The scent of his cologne fills her nose, pulling her into his gravity.

The background fades. The noise disappears.

There is only Brack.

"Wow, Macy. You look amazing."

She was hoping he'd notice.

She can feel her body heating up. She absently touches the leaf pendant hanging around her neck.

A dreamy lull fills the space between them as she gazes into his golden-brown eyes.

Then, realizing the conversation has gone quiet, she quickly straightens her ears, snapping back to the present. "So, how's the job going?"

"It's incredible. It's the best thing that's ever happened to me, Macy."

He leans in slightly, voice just low enough to make it feel like a secret conversation...

Because it is.

"I've got a real career now. And I've got you to thank for that. It's almost hard to believe I'm the same squirrel who was digging up dandelions in the spring."

Macy beams, heart swelling. "You brought me a beautiful bouquet."

Brack leans in a little more, voice warm and familiar. "You believed in me, Macy. No one else has ever done that."

She flushes, touching her cheek without thinking. "Of course I believe in you, Brack. I always will."

He shifts, eyes scanning the room.

"Listen, Macy. We had a lot of fun this summer..."

Her ears bounce lightly as she nods in agreement.

"I owe you a lot, and so... that's why I need to be honest with you."

He taps his foot a few times.

"I just... I don't see a romantic future for us."

Wait. What?!

"You're incredible. Really. It's just that... you're more like... a really important friend to me. Family, almost."

This is not happening.

"I just think we're in different places, emotionally."

This doesn't make any sense.

"It wouldn't be fair to you, you know?"

It wasn't that long ago, he kissed me in the garden.

"I didn't mean to lead you on or anything..."

It wasn't that long ago, we were curled up in the grass.

"I was really into it at first. But..."

I convinced my dad to give him a chance!

"I think I just... respect you too much."

He made me feel like he wanted me. But all he really wanted... was the job?!

Brack hesitates, running a paw over the back of his neck. "I just don't think I'm what you need right now, Macy."

Before she can process what has just happened, he moves in close. Pats her on the shoulder. Starts to leave. Spins around like he's forgotten where he's going—then bolts without another word.

She doesn't move.

She feels ridiculous.

Like she should have seen this coming.

Like she should have known better.

Brack wanted something from her—but he didn't want *her*.

She stares at the empty grass where he was just standing.

The dress that felt so perfect an hour ago now feels too tight and clingy.

She sucks her stomach in and presses both paws over the fabric.

She feels a panic attack coming on.

She glances around. No one is looking.

Of course no one is looking. No one ever is.

I'm not Ashlyn—the brilliant chemist.

I'm not JackRabbitt—the charming CEO.

I'm just Macy.

The one who doesn't take up space.

The one who doesn't get picked.

The one who thought that for one summer—

Maybe she could be someone's number one.

But she was wrong.

Desperately, her eyes scan for the exit.

But the exit is also an entrance.

JackRabbitt and William step through The Arch together, dressed in duality—one wearing a showman's smile, the other clad in silent annoyance.

A camera flashes—

JackRabbitt strikes a perfect pose for the photographer, presenting his Shabó gift basket like a prized trophy.

"I'll be at the bar," William mutters, already loosening his tie. "Try not to be too insufferable."

"No promises," JackRabbitt says through clenched teeth, still smiling for the camera.

His eyes scan the party, spotting Mikki instantly.

He strides toward her, the deep emerald of his tuxedo sharp against the glow of the starry lights. His brocade vest gleams beneath the lapels, just a touch of that Abbitt flair.

"Mikki," he says, offering the basket with both paws as if it were the crown jewels. "For the auction."

Mikki sweeps her cascading curls over one shoulder, then stretches her arms wide to receive it.

"Oh, JackRabbitt. It's lovely. Thank you!" Her face lights up, and she leans in, whispering, "This may just send the socialites into a bidding war!"

JackRabbitt grins proudly. "Oh, I'm counting on it."

"Well, I had better take this up to the auction right away."

She raises the basket with a wink, already turning to go.

JackRabbitt doesn't miss a beat.

He gently eases the basket from her paws, tossing it into the arms of the nearest staff member.

"Find the auction table," he says, eyes still on Mikki.

"Hey, Mikki. Why don't you take a break with me? It's a beautiful night. Do me the honor of just one dance—with the most dazzling hostess in The Meadow."

Mikki's tail thrashes quickly behind her. "JackRabbitt, I can't slow down right now."

She begins to walk away, but he catches her arm—her fur brushing against his.

"Who said anything about slowing down? Just one dance. Think of it as a victory lap."

"It's still early. It's hardly a victory yet."

"But it will be."

He reaches for her waist and guides her in with one smooth motion.

"And then, there will be another victory.

Then another. And another. And who knows—maybe even an official 'yes' to becoming the radiant new face of Shabó?"

Mikki gives him an exhausted look, but before she can respond, a familiar scent creeps between them.

The camera flashes—

"Oh, JackRabbitt!"

Their two heads snap toward The Arch in unison.

"It just got Lovely in here."

Lee Ann Lovely stands posed at the entrance, eyes fixed on her ex, one paw lifted in a slow, annoying wave.

She turns to the photographer. "Stay close. I have a feeling it's going to be a very photogenic evening."

She sways toward them, midnight-black fur slashed with a streak of blinding blonde, her tail wrapped around her shoulders like she's wearing *herself*.

JackRabbitt closes his eyes for a second, collecting himself.

When he opens his eyes, Lee Ann has inserted herself directly between them... and into a conversation with Mikki.

"...And then he says 'It's not you, it's me'. Can you even believe that?"

JackRabbitt's nostrils flare with the stench of regret.

It was a couple of nights. A year ago! And she's still stinking up his life.

It was supposed to be casual. It couldn't have been more clear.

But apparently, Lee Ann Lovely doesn't do casual. She clings. She claws. She turns every crumb of affection into a headline.

One nasty byline in her column tomorrow, and this whole Gala becomes a joke. The sponsors, the donors, all of Mikki's hard work—destroyed.

And she'd do it for no other reason than to spite me.

So, he swallows the disdain, and smiles through gritted teeth.

"Lee Ann. Always a pleasure seeing *you*."

Her grin widens. "That's what you always say."

She leans in closer to Mikki and whispers, "But he never calls."

JackRabbitt runs his tongue along his teeth. "What can I say? My calendar is full."

Lee Ann lets out a dramatic laugh. "Oh, I know. Wheeling, dealing, disappearing—always scheming something, aren't you?"

Mikki's ears twitch, and she clears her throat, stepping between them. "Lee Ann, I didn't realize you were on the guest list."

Lee Ann gasps, giving her tail a stroke. "Mikki, darling! Of course I am. Big event, big names, big donations. It'll be tomorrow's headline."

Mikki's smile strains. "You're covering the Gala?"

"Oh, don't worry. I'll only print the juicy parts."

Lee Ann lifts a paw to JackRabbitt's lapel, straightening it unnecessarily.

"And I have a feeling tonight will be full of them."

◆

Suddenly—

Clatter.

Shatter.

Hissssssss.

A champagne bottle hits the floor near the refreshment display, spitting out foam and glittering glass. The fizz crawls across the ground as the trio stares blankly into the commotion.

The crowd goes quiet.

Someone claps awkwardly.

JackRabbitt turns back to Mikki—

But she's already gone—

And Kathra is standing in her place.

She trails a feather lightly along the rim of her glass.

"Some things shatter so easily, don't they?"

JackRabbitt freezes.

Lee Ann leans in.

"Ooh! Was that symbolic?"

Kathra turns her neck slowly, her glare locking in on the scandal-sniffing skunk.

Lee Ann shifts, suddenly self-conscious. "Who, me? I was just settling in here."

"Then by all means, do so... somewhere else."

Lee Ann scoffs. "You really don't like me, do you?"

Kathra takes a slow sip of her drink. "I like you... exactly as much as you deserve."

Lee Ann, unsure if that was a compliment or a cut, turns to JackRabbitt.

"Well, I'm not one to overstay my welcome."

"Could've fooled me," he mutters.

"Listen, darling. I'll be right over there. Just out of earshot. Surely."

She drags a claw lightly over his sleeve.

"Not that I need to hear anything. I always find out eventually."

Lee Ann smiles, tosses her tail over her shoulder, and sways away.

Kathra remains completely still.

"Funny, JackRabbitt, I would think someone with your problems might look a little more... concerned."

He grins. "And here I thought confidence was an asset."

Kathra lifts a wing and sets her empty glass onto a tray as it drifts past.

"It seems The Everwood Condominiums are having trouble getting out of Phase One."

He adjusts the knot of his bow tie, taking his time before speaking.

"Construction's a tricky business."

Kathra nods, slowly.

"Mmm. So many moving parts. So much that can go wrong."

She pauses.

"That wouldn't happen to be part of your strategy... would it?"

He moves one paw into his pocket, the other lingering on the button of his jacket.

"You give me far too much credit."

She studies him. Silent. Waiting.

He holds her stare.

One second. Two.

By seven, he's hoping someone drops another champagne bottle.

But Kathra doesn't blink.

The glowstone strands of her headpiece hang perfectly still.

Finally, JackRabbitt sighs and gives up.

"Now why would I make life harder for myself?"

Kathra lifts a wingtip to her face.

"No, of course not. That would be foolish."

She taps her feathers lightly, creating a slow, thoughtful rhythm.

JackRabbitt's eyes drift past her, noticing that Jon and Ashlyn have just passed through The Arch.

Perfect timing.

"Gee. As much as I love a good interrogation, Kathra, I think I'll take my chances with family. Enjoy your evening."

He gives her a wink and slides away.

Kathra watches him go.

Slowly, her beak begins to curl.

Almost a smile.

But not quite.

Not yet.

◆

Jon and Ashlyn arrive arm in arm.

Ashlyn's gold lamé gown flows like a foundry over her statuesque frame, draping off one shoulder and slicing high to the thigh.

When she throws off the lab coat, she really throws it off.

Her eyes sweep the refreshments display, landing briefly on the velvet-roped space at the center. "Is that where the cake is supposed to go?"

Jon follows her gaze. "You know Kathra. Even the dessert will be dramatic."

As they move deeper into The Meadow, they are greeted by a gentle symphony of soft music, light conversation, and the shuffle of heels scooting across the dance floor.

Jon moves with quiet authority, lifting two drinks from a passing tray. His deep green three-piece suit is impeccable, the gold vest gleaming beneath it as a quiet reminder of who he is—and who he has always been.

"Ashlyn, my beauty, the Shabó Cosmetics display looked wonderful in the lobby," he says, offering her a glass. "It certainly stood out among everything else."

"Of course it did." Ashlyn accepts the drink with a nod, her platinum-blonde fur catching the starry light.

JackRabbitt slides up beside them, smooth as ever.

"There you are." Jon welcomes him with a smile. "You know, you two never fail to impress me. An exclusive sampler of the fall line. Could be our biggest auction item yet."

"Even bigger than JackRabbitt's mood lipstick idea from last year?" Ashlyn pops an olive into her mouth. "I'm not sure blue was my color."

JackRabbitt nods begrudgingly. "Let's just say... it was ahead of its time."

Jon chuckles, shaking his head lightly. "Well. It's clear the company is thriving."

He taps his claw against the side of his glass. "And that's why I've made a decision."

JackRabbitt and Ashlyn exchange curious looks.

"I'm coming out of retirement," Jon says, voice confident and firm. "It's time I return to Shabó Cosmetics."

Ashlyn drops her glass onto a side table, eyes locked on her father.

"Daddy, that's amazing. We need you there."

JackRabbitt doesn't move right away. His smile stays in place, but his ears flicker—a quiet shift in power, instinctively recognized... but not unwelcome.

"Big news," he says, resting a paw on his father's shoulder.

Jon returns the gesture.

"I trust the both of you. But I've had a lot of time to think. And what I've realized is—I didn't leave because I wanted to. I left because I thought I was supposed to."

He sets his glass down without looking.

"I thought reaching a certain age meant I was supposed to be done. But I was wrong. I'm not done yet. I've still got a lot more to give."

JackRabbitt's ears perk up; Ashlyn's tail twitches.

"Glad to have you back, Dad."

"It was never the same without you, Daddy."

Jon runs his paw along the graying fur at his temple. "Well, I tried the quiet life." He chuckles. "Turns out, I prefer a little noise."

Before anything else can be said, Macy quietly joins them, stepping in close, her presence soft.

In this moment, she folds herself into the comfort of family, masking the ache she doesn't want to name.

Jon welcomes her in, gazing warmly upon each member of his family.

"You know, I don't think I say this enough. But I'm proud of you. All of you. It's true, we have an incredible family business... but more importantly, we have an incredible family."

"Hey, did you hear that?" JackRabbitt chimes in. "We're incredible."

Ashlyn rolls her eyes but smiles. "I mean, obviously."

Jon laughs, pulling them all in for a quick hug.

Macy lets herself sink into the solace, holding on a little tighter than usual.

And even in a moment like this, Ashlyn can tell that Macy seems... off.

As they pull apart, Ashlyn guides her sister aside, giving her a concerned look.

"You okay?"

Macy plasters on a smile. "Yeah. Just a long night."

She knows she could tell her family what happened with Brack. She knows they'd rally around her in an instant. But what would she even say? That she thought someone actually wanted her, only to find out that she was just a means to an end?

No thanks.

Ashlyn lifts Macy's chin, trying to get a closer look into her eyes.

"You sure you're alright? You're usually the first one crying at a sentimental moment like this."

Macy laughs weakly.

And suddenly, Ashlyn remembers—

Macy's crush on Brack.

She had warned him to let her down easy.

She had tried to soften the fall.

But heartbreak was inevitable.

She scrambles for something—anything—to say.

"Hey, maybe we should go back up to the lobby and bid on those tickets to the Firestorm Festival."

She gives her sister a playful nudge.

"Just imagine it—the two of us, in the middle of a wild music fest, surrounded by blacklight and body odor."

Macy snorts, shaking her head. "We'd last an hour."

"Please. Thirty minutes, tops."

It's a small moment, but it helps.

Macy will hold onto it: the way Ashlyn teases, the way JackRabbitt overprotects, the way Dad's hug still lingers.

It doesn't fix everything, but it reminds her—she isn't alone.

She will always have her family.

And for a second, it's enough.

But then—

She looks to the dance floor and sees them.

Brack—

With Laura Venmore.

That snotty little squirrel.

◆

Macy whirls around.

Her powerful legs launch into motion, and she bolts through The Grand Archway.

She tears up the winding path toward The Colonnade House—ears pinned back, vision blurred by tears.

She just needs air.

She just needs to be anywhere but here.

She just needs—

Smack!

In a split second, a colorful blur of cockatiel feathers flashes in front of her, and they crash together—like a hug at full speed.

Tanny Aromalotti?

He stumbles back, flutters, trying to catch his balance.

"Whoa! Hey, hey—Macy, where's the race?"

One paw flies to her mouth, then drops again as she reaches out instinctively.

"Tanny, I'm so sorry!"

"Sorry?"

His bright yellow crest springs upright.

"Don't be sorry! You're exactly who I was looking for. You're never gonna believe this—"

He breathes out a half-laugh, feathers still settling.

"Amy Chaméleon was supposed to do a duet with me tonight, but—"

"Tanny, I—"

"But she almost got eaten!"

"What?"

"Yeah! Something about a tray of hors d'oeuvres and a hungry fox. She's really shaken up over the whole thing."

Macy presses a paw to her chest.

"Tanny, I don't mean to be rude, but... what does that have to do with me?"

"Well, she won't go on stage! And the set list is locked. Can you fill in for just one song?"

"Tonight?" Her ears lift. "Right now?"

"Yeah. We go on in twenty minutes. You know *Restless Heart*, right?"

"Well, yeah, but—"

"Macy, you'd be doing me a huge favor. That song's one of my biggest hits."

The orange patches on his cheeks seem to glow brighter under the lantern light.

"Tanny, I... I just can't."

She flattens her tail tight against her back.

Tanny's head tilts sharply to the side as he studies her with one curious eye. For the first time since they crashed together, he notices—she's been crying.

Heartbreak is unmistakable to anyone who's known it.

He bobs his head in a gentle rhythm, like he's listening to a melody only he can hear.

"Okay. I get it."

He shifts, ruffling the feathers at the back of his neck.

"But, you know, Macy... sometimes the worst nights make the best songs."

She lets out a sharp breath. "Tanny, please. I don't need a pep talk right now."

He nods. "Alright. No pep talks. Maybe Laura Venmore's around —she's done this one with me before."

With a smooth hop and a flick of his wings, he glides away.

"No—wait. Tanny!" she calls out, thumping her foot against the ground.

He twists mid-air, swooping in a low circle before landing beside her.

His smile is so bright, it lights the way back to The Meadow.

He gestures down the path with an easy, open wing.

"After you."

Chapter Thirty-Two

The Green Gala (Part 2)

Ashlyn's eyes track Macy as she disappears through The Arch, her pale green gown vanishing into the darkness.

She springs forward, ready to follow—

but Jon's paw closes gently around her wrist.

"No, no. Give her some space. She'll be back."

After raising two daughters on his own, Jon has learned not to chase every storm.

His eyes linger on The Arch for a moment longer.

"I'll go make sure our dinner table's ready for when Macy joins us again."

He gives JackRabbitt and Ashlyn a nod, then slips into the crowd.

JackRabbitt tosses his arms up.

"Well, what the hell was that all about?"

Ashlyn's eyes scan The Meadow, searching for Brack.

And there he is.

Alone.

On the dance floor.

JackRabbitt follows her line of sight.

But Brack *isn't* alone.

Laura Venmore is circling him.

Paws on hips. Coming, then going, then coming again—thrashing her puffed red tail.

Full-blown squirrel quarrel in progress.

Ashlyn edges closer, and JackRabbitt falls in step behind.

Laura's voice slices through the music like a snapped string.

"You're dumping me?!"

The rhythm stumbles.

Heads turn.

Lee Ann Lovely quietly swirls her drink.

Brack's second breakup of the night is unfolding beautifully.

"Laura, it's over," he says. "I'm done pretending."

"Oh, sure," she scoffs. "Now you find your conscience. After you've already cashed in."

Brack fires back. "It wasn't about that."

"Puh-leaze. You used *me* to upgrade your wardrobe.

You used *the fat one* to get you the job.

And now you're sleeping your way up the family tree."

She pauses for a hair flip.

"Funny, I thought Ashlyn was smarter than that."

Lee Ann's ears perk.

JackRabbitt's paws curl into fists.

And Ashlyn feels something snap loose.

Laura storms off, leaving Brack shouting into the empty space she left behind.

"This isn't the same!

She isn't the same!"

He swipes a paw through the air, desperate and aimless.

"I don't *want* anyone else!"

Ashlyn's pulse skips a beat.

JackRabbitt's head snaps toward her, the truth written all over her face.

Brack lifts his head through the swirl of dancers—

and finds her.

Their eyes lock.

Ashlyn flinches like she's been struck.

And JackRabbitt doesn't wait.

He launches.

First, Brack feels the force of nature barreling toward him.

Next, Brack feels the paw that is clenching his shoulder.

Finally, Brack opens his eyes to find JackRabbitt standing nose to nose in front of him, growling.

"What the hell did you do to my sisters?"

Brack backs away, looking around at the crowded dance floor. "Jack-O-Lantern. Buddy. What's got you so lit up?"

JackRabbitt takes a step forward, closing the gap between them. "Answer me, Squirrelton."

Brack hesitates, sighs, then blurts it out.

"I did what you asked me to do, ok? I told the truth. You ever tried that before? It doesn't always go over well."

"Don't pat yourself on the back, Brack." JackRabbitt's paw flexes once at his side, then curls into a fist again. "Telling the truth doesn't make you any less of a coward."

"Hey, I wanted this to be easy, but it wasn't. It never is."

Brack starts talking faster.

"You think I like breaking someone's heart? Do you? You think I wanted to hurt her?"

His volume rises with his frustration.

"Oh sure! Brack's a stud. Brack's a gigolo. Brack only cares about himself."

Brack...

is too loud.

Hovering on the edge of the dance floor, Lee Ann whispers to herself, "Keep going, handsome. You're almost entertaining."

"I did what had to be done, alright? It was hard, but I did it."

His gaze drops to the ground.

He sighs, more of a broken whimper than a breath.

His whole frame seems to shrink.

For a second, Brack looks smaller than JackRabbitt's ever seen him, weakening under the weight of his own excuses.

And somewhere in the middle of Brack's tirade, it clicks for JackRabbitt.

He looks at the pitiful squirrel, still trying so hard to play the victim.

Always trying to make himself seem bigger than he is.

And suddenly, it's so obvious.

Brack…

is an ass.

"Stay away from my sisters!"

Brack smacks his tail down on the dance floor.

"Of course. I'm not good enough for your sisters. I'm not good enough to work at your company. I'm not even good enough to work in your garden. Please, tell me—Oh, Royal Prince—is there anything else I'm not good enough for?"

Lee Ann smirks behind her glass. "Oh, this is getting good."

JackRabbitt steps in close, his voice dropping to a low, dangerous rumble.

"Listen carefully, Brackski. I'll say this very slowly so that you can understand. Stay away from my sisters. And I do mean *both* of them. Or you won't just be digging dandelions. You'll be digging your own grave."

JackRabbitt drops his paw onto Brack's shoulder, way harder than necessary.

"Enjoy your dance."

Brack looks around for his date, but then realizes… he doesn't have one.

JackRabbitt staggers away, shoving through the crowd—and through Ashlyn—like she doesn't even exist.

Across the Gala, William pushes away from the bar, muttering to himself, drink untouched.

The two brothers cross paths mid-stride.

Neither stops. Neither slows.

Just a quick grunt of mutual irritation—moving in opposite directions.

✦

Inside The Colonnade House, Victoria steps into the lobby where it's quiet, a world apart from the lively party that is pulsating outside in The Meadow.

Instinctively and inevitably, her eyes land on the Newmouse Enterprises sponsorship display—an elegant, freestanding exhibit that stretches the length of a white wooden wall, framed by green and gold panels.

And at the center of it all, her father: Victor Newmouse.

A three-paneled timeline tells the story of his empire—on the left, grainy black-and-white photos of his first projects and blueprints sketched in a steady paw; on the right, newspaper clippings detailing the aggressive land acquisitions, record-breaking pine sap production, and the mining operations that fueled it all.

And in the center, photographs of Victor himself spanning decades: his younger years on dusty construction sites, accepting industry awards with a firm pawshake, and finally, standing atop Newmouse Tower, surveying the empire he built.

At the top of one panel, a quote in bold lettering catches Victoria's eye:

From the ground up.

Her father's famous words.

She stares at them, as if they are speaking to her directly.

Then, a gentle paw rests lightly on her shoulder.

Victoria turns, already knowing who it is.

Mikki.

She doesn't speak right away. She just follows Victoria's gaze to the display—the one she organized, curating every plaque and every image to honor both the company and the mouse behind it. Each detail has been arranged with care, as if tending to her rose garden—perfect, ordered, a tribute worthy of him.

"He was larger than life."

Mikki's fingers drift to the glowstone pendant resting against her heart.

"Everyone out there sees the legend, the powerhouse."

She exhales, adjusting a frame that doesn't need adjusting.

"But we knew the mouse behind the myth."

Victoria swallows. But the ache in her chest won't settle.

She blinks, but the tears come anyway.

Mikki doesn't say anything. She just stands close. Solid and warm. Letting her daughter have this moment that she needs.

After a while, Victoria gathers herself and straightens.

"I've made a decision."

Mikki's brows lift. "Oh?"

"You were right," Victoria says, nodding toward the display.

"About Newmouse Enterprises. I've been thinking a lot about Dad. About what he built."

She runs her fingers lightly over the delicate brass watch at her wrist, the weight of it grounding her.

"I'm going to continue the Newmouse legacy.

And I'm going to do it... from the ground up.

Starting in the mail room."

Mikki smiles. A real smile. Not the one she's had plastered on her face all evening, asking for donations.

She reaches out to her daughter, squeezing the same paws that were once so tiny, now fully grown.

"I'm so proud of you," she says simply.

Victoria looks at her mother, absorbing the words, wishing her father were here to say them too.

Mikki turns her attention to her favorite photo of Victor, then back to her daughter, eyes flashing back and forth between the two.

She nods to herself.

And then—an urgent voice calls out from across the lobby.

"Mikki!"

They both turn to see Zeena Aromalotti weaving through the entrance, her sleek white fur nearly glowing, her long fleshy tail following behind. She's slightly out of breath but grinning.

"Sorry to interrupt you, but... The cake is here."

Mikki's face lights up, her ears giving an involuntary flutter. "Oh, thank the stars," she whispers, half to herself.

Then, just as quickly, a flutter of guilt crosses her face.

She doesn't want to leave her daughter.

Not in the middle of the best moment they've had in years.

"I—I should—"

"Go, Mom. It's okay."

Mikki searches her daughter's face for any hint of resentment but instead finds understanding.

"Hey, it wouldn't be The Green Gala without the green cake, right?"

Mikki leans in, pressing a light kiss to her forehead.

Victoria tenses at first, then softens into it.

A small smile passes between them before Mikki hurries off after Zeena.

✦

Victoria watches her mother disappear into the crowd.

The room suddenly feels too small for the weight she's carrying.

A quiet instinct leads her toward the open air of the balcony, a pull she doesn't bother to question.

Her feet are moving, and she simply follows.

A soft breeze catches a loose strand of the long ponytail braid that rests on her shoulder. She tucks it behind her ear and rests her paws on the railing, gazing outward.

Below her, The Meadow party stretches out in warm, golden light—lanterns glowing, satin gowns sweeping across the dance floor, glasses clinking in a symphony of celebration.

Everything looks so effortless, so perfectly in motion. Her mother's doing. Yet, from up here, she feels like a spectator in her own world. As if everyone else has already found their rhythm.

But there's also something else. A whisper of déjà vu. Like she's remembering something that hasn't happened yet.

Then—a voice.

Low. Frustrated. Familiar in a way that doesn't make sense—curling up through the night like a mist.

"Always a game. Always."

Above her, Tanny Aromalotti's voice drifts up from the stage, lifting high into the open air with notes of hopefulness and joy.

But below her, the words cutting through the darkness are resentful and angry.

"She couldn't do this one thing. Just for me."

Who is that?

The courtyard beneath the balcony is wrapped in shadows.

Nothing but shapes and restless pacing below.

Victoria leans in—a little too far.

She loses her balance.

The voice rises—

dragging itself up the walls.

"It's my turn to build something from the ground up!"

She grips the railing, heart skipping once before steadying herself.

What am I doing?

But before she can answer that question, the wind shifts—carrying his voice away, scattering it like leaves.

She should go now. She knows that.

And yet, her feet won't move right away.

Something about the moment is holding her in place.

The cool summer night air sends a shiver through her body.

She reaches for a shawl that isn't there.

And below, William disappears back into the party.

✦

At The Grand Archway, a commotion ripples through The Meadow.

"She wasn't invited, was she?"

"What in the forest is she wearing?"

"Feathers. That squirrel is wearing feathers."

And there she is—

Gillian, striking a pageant pose in a green feathered gown big enough to lead the turkey day parade.

She saunters forward, hips swinging, tail swishing, blowing exaggerated kisses into the crowd.

And then she stops—just to catch the light.

From head to shoulders, individual strands of shimmering glowstones dangle like a beaded curtain, framing her furry face.

Three teardrop-shaped emeralds rest against her forehead—one long in the center, two slightly shorter on either side.

With every kiss she blows to the crowd, the crystalline curtain sways gently, side to side, giving the illusion that this luminous veil simply hovers around her.

A glowstone headpiece.

Identical in every way—

to the one Kathra is wearing—

RIGHT

NOW.

Kathra doesn't move.

Even the air around her seems to freeze.

Her wings tighten. Her pupils shrink.

And just when she's about to lose it—

Mikki chimes in. "Kathra! It's time."

Kathra snaps her head toward Mikki—

Then whips it back to Gillian.

Gillian sails straight through the crowd, making a beeline for Jon.

Flirting shamelessly. Paws all over him. Laughing loud enough to turn heads.

"Kathra, did you hear me?" Mikki says, sharper now. "The cake! It's here!"

She tugs Kathra's wing, then hurries off toward the center of the refreshments display.

✦

On the stage, the horn section bursts into a triumphant roar.

Mikki's voice follows, bright and commanding.

"Everyone! Everyone!"

Clap Clap

"Please gather round!"

Guests begin drifting toward the refreshments display, curiosity pulling them in.

William stumbles through The Arch, spots Gillian in full-on flirt mode, and heads straight for his brother. "Tell me that's not happening."

JackRabbitt takes it in with a groan, but before he can do anything about it—

A heavy *thud* startles the crowd as the cake cart rumbles through The Arch, carrying a towering display draped in lush green velvet and cinched with a thick gold tassel.

Zeena Aromalotti and her team of caterers steer the mysterious showpiece carefully toward the center of the refreshments display.

"Careful now. Be very careful," she says in a tight voice.

But then—a jolt.

A wheel catches on the stone.

The whole structure begins to wobble.

A server drops a tray of glass.

It *shatters!*

But Zeena lifts a calming paw.

"Steady. Steady."

The cart settles.

Crisis averted.

Mikki lets out a sigh of relief and rushes forward to unhook the velvet ropes.

The cart rolls perfectly into place.

Mikki returns to Kathra's side, her paw barely brushing the underside of her wing.

She closes her eyes and takes a breath. Just one moment of silent pride.

The Meadow holds its breath too.

All eyes locked.

Watching. Waiting.

Zeena pauses, claws hovering over the gold tassel, waiting for Mikki's signal.

Mikki nods.

And with a quick pull of the cord—

The cake is revealed.

The crowd gasps.

Monocles drop.

Mikki and Kathra exchange confused looks.

It's... unbelievable!

Beneath the fallen curtain sit—

Two enormous walnuts, sculpted in cake.

Two glistening brown shells.

Heavy and round.

Nestled side-by-side in frosting.

Cradled by the base of the cake stand.

And swaying gently beneath the cake nuts—

Is an electric sign that reads:

Let's Go Nuts!

For a moment, The Meadow holds still.

Mikki blinks. Then blinks again.

"There must be some mistake."

Zeena flips through the order slip.

Kathra shouts, "Well, check it again."

Zeena checks and double-checks.

"It's correct. How can that be?"

And then—

From somewhere in the crowd—

One voice rises above the rest.

Laughing. Snorting. Cackling with delight.

Mikki shakes her head in disbelief.

"It's impossible."

Kathra's expression darkens.

"No. It's Gillian."

Her eyes flick back to the cake.

"*She* did this."

Mikki frowns. "What? I don't understand."

Kathra gestures at the cake, wings flapping wildly.

"Gillian sabotaged the cake!"

Mikki follows her gaze.

She takes one look at Gillian laughing—headpiece swaying.

And she knows... It's true.

IT WAS Gillian.

Mikki goes cold.

Her smile vanishes.

The light drains from her eyes.

"That bitch."

✦

Suddenly—

The stage lights dim, swallowing the crowd in momentary darkness.

Ashlyn appears at Jon's side. "Come on!"

He glances once toward Gillian.

"Just—trust me," she says, peeling him away.

Commotion fades to silence as the spotlight flashes—

and Tanny takes center stage.

Under the lights, his feathers are prismatic, painting the platform in cockatiel colors of silver, yellow, and the vivid splash of orange that beams from his cheeks. He is a star. Undeniably electric. But right now, he's not here to take the stage. He's here to give it.

"We have a special treat for you tonight. She doesn't need the spotlight. But it found her anyway. Everybody, give it up for Macy Abbitt."

Tanny steps back.

Jon and Ashlyn exchange stunned looks.

JackRabbitt and William snap to attention.

All eyes pulled toward the spotlight—

as Macy takes center stage.

She can feel the heat of the stage lights.

The weight of the microphone in her grip.

The thrill of possibility.

This is it.

The band kicks in—a slow, pounding piano rhythm, delicate and haunting.

She lifts the mic,

draws a breath,

closes her eyes,

and sings.

Lost in the plot of a storyline.
Bold and beautiful souls align.

As the world turns slow.
Passions we used to know.

Jon whispers to Ashlyn, "Isn't she a beauty?"

Ashlyn nods. "She always has been."

Macy steps back, and Tanny picks up the verse.

Another world where dreams still shine.
Waiting for you right on time.

All the days of our lives.
One life to live, guiding light.

The string section shivers to life, bows gliding in unison.

The brass section erupts with golden instruments flashing like fire in the light.

The music swells, carrying the song even higher than before,

As Macy and Tanny fall into harmony.

Oh, we can all be bright,
In the daytime or the night.
Watchin' them love and fight.

Through generations all the same.
Through the pleasure and pain.
A young and restless heart remains.

And as the music fills the stage...

Kathra breaks her silent rage.

✦

With one swift beat, she explodes into flight—

Nothing but fury and feathers, slicing through the air… straight toward Gillian.

"Take it off," she demands.

"Excuse me?" Gillian gasps, recoiling.

But Kathra doesn't wait.

She goes straight for the jewels.

She swoops high and plunges down—sinking her talons into Gillian's hair.

Gillian scrambles to keep the crown, but her squirrel arms are too short. She can't reach!

Kathra yanks once—hard.

Then again—harder.

On the third pull—

She tears it free, and lifts off in a burst of feathers.

She lands on the stone floor.

Wings flared wide.

Beak held high.

The headpiece clutched in her talons—tangled with a clump of Gillian's hair.

Then, with a flick of her foot, she kicks the crown into the air,

catches it with the curve of her wing,

lets it spin once,

and throws it down like a gauntlet.

For a split second, Gillian doesn't move.

She just stands there—breathless and heaving.

Slowly, her paw drifts upward, pressing against the fresh bald spot between her ears.

Her eyes go wide. Her mouth drops open.

And then—she shrieks.

A piercing, earsplitting wail.

She lunges at Kathra, spinning them both into a cyclone of fur and feathers.

"You overripe owl!" Gillian grunts, dodging a wing.

Kathra snaps her beak. "You gold-digging tree-hopper!"

The elegant crowd stands locked in place—unsure if they should intervene or start placing bets.

Gillian shouldn't stand a chance.

Not with her size. Not with those little squirrel arms.

But her bald rage makes her unstoppable.

She knocks Kathra to the ground, straddling her, pinning her wings just enough to keep her grounded.

Her paws clamp around Kathra's throat, trembling with fury.

William moves to break up the fight.

But JackRabbitt stops him.

"This is working well."

Kathra gasps—eyes wide, wings twitching.

"Help!"

JackRabbitt glances at William.

"Too well."

They both rush forward—

Just as Gillian releases.

Gillian and Kathra lock eyes.

Gillian still on top.

Kathra still pinned beneath her.

Kathra coughs—

But just long enough to make it believable.

Then slowly...

She smiles.

With a powerful shove, Kathra launches Gillian into the air—limbs splayed like a backward flying squirrel.

She lands on her feet, barely, then stumbles backward into the cake table.

She reaches back blindly to steady herself—her paw brushing against the frosting.

Then, she freezes.

Slowly, she turns, casting a dangerous glance over her shoulder.

Without hesitation, Gillian plunges her paw into the cake and rips out a fistful of nuts and frosting.

Kathra rises from the ground, calmly dusting herself off.

She gives Gillian a smug smile.

"You wouldn't dare."

Gillian laughs, looking her dead in the eye.

"Oh, yes I would."

She whips the sugary chunk straight at Kathra's head—

but Kathra ducks.

A nearby toad takes the hit, blinking slowly as the frosting drips down his snout.

Gillian doesn't stop.

She hurls another chunk—this one hitting Kathra square in the chest.

Kathra's beak clacks open, as she watches the thick brown frosting slide down the front of her gown.

Gillian bursts into laughter, bent nearly in half.

"Oh, Kathra," she wheezes. "I've been to some nutty parties, but this one takes the cake."

The frosting drips.

The crowd stares.

Kathra's eyes flash.

Then—

The lights go out.

The music swells.

And Macy and Tanny sing through the darkness.

Oh, we can all be bright,

Kathra CHARGES.

In the daytime or the night.

Gillian LEAPS.

Watchin' them love and fight.

Through—

The crowd GASPS.

Generations all the same.

The walnuts TREMBLE.

Through the pleasure and pain.

In SLOW MOTION

A young and restless heart remains.

They SMASH into the cake.

The nuts CRACK open.

The floor FLOODS with frosting.

And when the music stops—

The crowd erupts!

Half in shock. Half in cheers. Half unable to calculate.

Kathra and Gillian freeze—mid-brawl, mid-cake, mid-shame.

And just when it can't get any worse—

Lee Ann Lovely scrambles over the slippery scene.

"Oh, ladies! You're gonna want to remember this."

She leans in with her camera.

"Say nutcake!"

Click. Click.

✦

Amid the chaos, Mikki stands motionless—watching as a glob of frosting splats onto her golden heels.

Then slowly, one eye begins to twitch.

She inhales. Deeply.

She exhales. Deeply.

AND THEN SHE SNAPS.

"Stop it! Stop it! This is a fundraiser—not a food fight!!!"

But no one can hear her.

The toads are croaking.

The beavers are slapping their tails.

The deer are waving their wallets in the air.

The drama *is* the entertainment.

They know it's ridiculous.

They know it's impossible.

And they'll keep tuning in for more.

Because everyone loves a good show.

SPONSORSHIP PROVIDED BY...

ANNOUNCER

"Light as air. Soft as silk. A bath unlike any other."

CUT TO: A cozy woodland cottage.

A badger peeks into a steaming tub, watching as the shimmering bubbles rise.

A gentle swirl of rose petals floats across the surface.

ANNOUNCER

"Infused with pure rose extract and morning dew, *Bubbly Bath* transforms every soak into a dream."

CUT TO: A close-up of luxurious foam cascading over the edge of a porcelain tub.

Tiny iridescent bubbles catch the light, floating upward like whispers of mist.

ANNOUNCER

"Every creature deserves a little luxury."

CUT TO: The product lineup—glass bottles glowing with pink herbal infusions, labeled in elegant script.

ANNOUNCER

"*Bubbly Bath* by Shabó Cosmetics. Pure magic in every bubble."

FADE OUT.

Chapter Thirty-Three

The Beginning

Grace sits at her dressing table.

The gentle creak of her chair breaks the stillness of her childhood bedroom.

Of course, the room has changed over the years, but remnants of its history remain: the quilted bedspread her mother spent an entire winter sewing, the wooden chest her father carved as a gift for her thirteenth birthday, and the violin she bought with her first month's pay from working at the grocery store.

Tonight is her last night in Southbrook, but it's also her first date with Victor. It's her first real date, period. He's promised a romantic evening, and she wants to look and feel deserving of his attention.

Rarely have there been times in her life when she had reason to dress up. She doesn't need makeup for work or for church on Sunday. Still, her mother taught her the small rituals of beauty a long time ago—the little things that make her feel put together, even if no one else notices.

But tonight is different. Tonight is special.

Her fingers trace over the familiar items on her dressing table: the brush, the comb, the jar of cold cream, the wooden box that holds her few ribbons and barrettes.

She pauses as she touches the new item that Victor has left for her: a woven basket, its texture coarse and sturdy under her fingertips. Intrigued, she carefully brings it closer to explore its contents and inspect the items one by one.

Her fingers skim over unfamiliar shapes and materials: cool glass bottles and jars, a velvety pouch, and something soft and springy.

Cosmetics are new and exciting.

A thrill of curiosity dances through her as she picks up a bottle with a pump.

She presses it.

Poof!

A delicate, floral scent bursts into the air, soft and powdery with a hint of sweetness.

"*Furfume,*" she murmurs with a smile. The scent is nothing like the sharp, synthetic fragrances she has sampled at the grocery store. This feels decadent and expensive.

Next, she unscrews the cap of an oblong glass bottle. The scent of rose wafts up, rich and heady. Her fingertips dab into the liquid, finding it slick and smooth. This must be the *Bubbly Bath* Victor had mentioned.

How indulgent!

Bath time is usually a fast process for her. She has rarely allowed herself the luxury of a long relaxing soak.

She excitedly carries the bottle to the bathroom, where the clawfoot tub waits beneath a window. The hum of the coal-fired furnace resonates faintly, a steady undertone as it heats the water. Turning on the faucet, the sound of rushing water echoes through the tiled space.

Pouring in a generous amount of the rose-scented liquid, she hesitates, unsure of how much to use. When she steps into the steaming water, the bubbles greet her in an effervescent embrace, tickling her fur as they expand around her. The room fills with the scent of roses, softening the air. She lets herself sink into the warmth, her body relaxing in a way it hasn't in years.

The bubbles cling to her fur. She laughs softly when some find their way to her mouth.

When the water cools and the bubbles fade, she towels herself dry and wraps her body in her usual aqua robe.

Back at the dressing table, she sits and smooths a silky cream from her face to her neck. The new lotion feels luxurious, a step above her usual routine.

As she reaches for her comb, her paw accidentally bumps into a carved wooden figurine. She picks it up, tracing its familiar shape—a tiny clock face with delicate etched hands, whittled by her father when she was just a girl. A smile tugs at her lips as she remembers how she used to carry it everywhere. It was a source of comfort when the world felt too big.

She finds her comb and smooths its teeth through her wet fur, letting the motion soothe her. Each pass of the comb makes her feel lighter, as if shedding the weight of the past. She experiments with styles, carefully parting her ivory fur this way and that. Usually, she lets her bangs fall in front of her face, but tonight, she combs them back.

Her fingers find a small canister in the basket. She shakes it gently, and the faint rattling inside gives her a clue. "Furspray," she decides, pressing the nozzle cautiously. A fine mist settles over her hair, holding it in place with a delicate, floral scent.

Her paw returns to the basket, where she feels something small and cool nestled inside a soft pouch. She opens it and finds a pair of delicate earrings and a thin bracelet. She runs her fingers over the smooth metal and tiny embedded stones, feeling their subtle details.

Slipping the bracelet onto her wrist, she secures it carefully, listening to the faint *clink* as it settles against her fur. The earrings are next. Her paws are steady as she fastens them into place. A quiet thrill runs through her. She may not see them, but she can feel their elegance.

Satisfied, she moves to her bed and runs her fingers over the fabric of a new gown Victor has laid out for her. The material feels like liquid silk, flowing beneath her touch. A beaded purse sits beside it, its surface textured with tiny, looping patterns that shift subtly under her fingertips.

She lifts the gown carefully, slipping it over her head. The fabric cascades over her body, settling into place effortlessly. She smooths it down with her paws, adjusting the fit, ensuring it sits just right over her slim frame. The neckline is soft, and the hem brushes gently against her ankles. She runs her fingers along the beading at the waist, appreciating the fine craftsmanship.

A breath escapes her, slow and content.

She walks toward the door, where her luggage is packed and waiting. Her paw rests on the handle of her suitcase, ready to leave.

Then, just as she takes a step, a realization tugs at her.

She dashes back to the dressing table and grabs the tiny wooden clock figurine once more.

She clutches it to her chest.

Although she is leaving, there are some memories she isn't quite ready to leave behind.

Tonight is an ending, but it's also a beginning.

She returns to the door and picks up her suitcase.

Without hesitation, she steps forward...

and closes the bedroom door behind her.

Chapter Thirty-Four

The Dance

Victor stands beneath the pavilion, dressed in a sharp black tuxedo, waiting for Grace to join him.

He runs a paw across the side of his hair in one slick motion. His chestnut brown fur is shining, his mouse 'stache is waxed to perfection, and the well-worn work boots he's spent months in are gone—abandoned like a season that has run its course.

He glances around, barely recognizing the place where he once played Chessnuts with Barney and took countless water breaks with the Pumpkin Acres crew.

Tonight, the pavilion has been transformed by Grace's Southbrook friends. Garlands of wildflowers dangle from the rafters, meticulously woven and hung by the neighborhood Avian Club. The picnic tables are gone, replaced with a single round dining table built by the beaver crew.

Old Ruth, Lila, and Willow from the grocery store have dressed the table in an elegant cloth and a floral centerpiece bursting with bluebells. Two regal place settings await, crystal glasses gleaming beside a bottle of champagne freshly chilled in the river.

At the grill, Diggert stands poised and ready, his white apron tied tight. Overhead, the local tribe of fireflies lights the sky with a warm, golden shimmer.

This evening would not be possible without the efforts of Grace's friends, who eagerly lent their skills to help Victor as a heartfelt thank-you—a way to honor her kindness and contributions. Their participation is a testament to how deeply she is cherished. They know she deserves this... and more.

Victor flips his pocket watch open, the antique brass catching the light of the active fleet of fireflies. As he snaps it shut, the sound of tapping reaches his ears.

Grace's cane *clicks* gently against the stone path. The rhythm quickens his heart.

He lifts his gaze and sees her emerging from the shadows, her silhouette framed by the glow of the pavilion.

She is wearing the gown he chose. It's perfect, flowing around her like the river.

Red is a color he's never seen her wear before—and it takes his breath away.

Her fur is gleaming—and her hair is styled in a new way.

For a moment, he almost doesn't recognize her.

Grace steps into the pavilion, gliding directly into his arms.

"You look breathtaking," he says, voice filled with quiet awe.

He eases her back a step, eyes sweeping over her, taking in the full view.

"This dress!" he murmurs.

She smooths the fabric self-consciously. "Do you like it?"

"Do I like it?" He chuckles. "You've gotta be kidding me!"

He reaches for her paws and kisses them.

She blushes, then steps away to give the gown a playful twirl.

The scarlet fabric flares like a flame.

He enjoys the show... very much.

Laughing, she throws her arms around him again.

He breathes her in, catching the soft scent of her fur.

"Roses," he says softly, his smile fading just a bit.

She can't notice.

"Yes! Oh, Victor. The cosmetics basket was incredible. You spoil me."

He clears his throat, quiet but firm. "There's... something else."

He steps to the side and retrieves a velvet box from the table. He guides it into her grasp, and she takes it, running her fingers over its plush exterior.

"What is it?"

"Well, you'll just have to open it and find out." He grins, tipping back on heels, then forward again.

She gently lifts the top of the box, meaning to do it slowly.

But—

Snap!

The hinge springs open quicker than she expected.

She fumbles, now a little embarrassed.

He reaches out to hold it still.

Her paw hesitates at the edge before sliding her fingertips over a smooth, rounded shape on a delicate chain.

"A necklace?" she says, voice slightly raspy.

"Glowstone," he replies smoothly. "May I help you put it on?"

"Of course."

She turns around, gathering her hair, grinning girlishly.

He fastens the necklace around her neck.

She brings her paws up to feel the stone as he turns her back around. "I feel like a princess!"

"You're an *queen*," he replies, "and I intend to treat you as such. Come with me," he says, leading her to the dining table. "Tell me, have you tried champagne?"

"No, but I've heard of it."

He pulls out her chair, waiting as she carefully takes her seat.

She runs her paws over the tablecloth, the chilled champagne bucket, and the elegant place setting. Her fingers linger on the smooth covered platter and cool cutlery.

She can hear him rustling the bottle of champagne from the ice, followed by the *pop* of the cork. She startles slightly, laughing as the table rattles. He pours the bubbling liquid into their glasses, the fizzing sound filling the air.

Just then—

A cool breeze drifts through the pavilion, stirring the garlands of wildflowers and carrying the faintest chill.

Grace rubs her arms absently. "Feels cooler tonight."

Victor watches the wildflowers dance in the shifting air.

A single golden leaf drifts lazily from the trees, landing beside his plate. He picks it up, twirls it between his fingers, then reaches across the table, tucking it behind her ear.

"Summer is taking a bow," he says. "But at least it left you a gift.”

She chuckles, reaching up to touch the leaf in her hair.

Another breeze passes through, and she shivers this time. Victor rises from his seat, shrugs off his tuxedo jacket, and steps behind her. He drapes it gently over her shoulders, his paws lingering for just a moment.

“Better?” he asks, voice low.

Grace pulls the fabric closer, enveloped in the lingering warmth of him.

“Much better,” she says softly.

He returns to his seat.

“A toast,” he announces, placing a glass in her paw and raising his own.

“To Southbrook: The Glowstone of The Great River.”

Her fingers curl around the glowstone resting at her heart.

The soft red of her gown shimmers in its curved reflection.

She twirls the pendant once, then lifts her glass. “To Southbrook.”

Victor lightly taps his glass to hers, creating a *chime* that echoes through the pavilion.

She takes a tentative sip, the bubbles tickling her lips and tongue. A light, airy laugh escapes as a giddy feeling washes over her, as though she’s floating away on the bubbles.

Suddenly, she becomes aware of the sizzling grill. “What is that delicious smell?”

“Melt mushrooms,” he replies proudly as he lifts the lid of the silver platter in front of her. "I do keep my promises."

A look of delight spreads across her face as she inhales the scent of the mushrooms she's been dreaming of for months—deep, rich, and savory.

"We also have honey-glazed carrots, roasted chestnuts, and a salad of wild greens... Hold the tongs!"

She laughs. "I'll never live that down."

"Hee hee hee!" he chuckles, touching the scar on his ear.

The soft *clink* of silverware mixes with Grace's sighs of satisfaction.

"This is incredible," she says between bites.

Victor watches her with amusement as the moon climbs higher in the sky. The champagne bottle sits nearly empty, beads of water dripping from its sides. One of the candles on the table flickers low, its wax pooled into a warm, golden puddle.

Grace begins to slow, pressing a paw lightly to her stomach. "I can't eat another bite."

Victor opens a covered pie dish on the side of the table. "Not even a bite of dessert?"

He lifts the pastry knife expectantly. "This is tangerose tart. It's sweet and tangy. I thought you might take it with a dollop of whipped cream."

Her mouth waters as she listens, anticipation building. "Well... maybe I can make room for that."

He slices into the tart and places a piece onto her plate.

As she takes her first bite, a sudden chorus of birdsong fills the air.

She pauses, tilting her ears toward the sound. The melodies are lively and harmonious, echoing all around into the night.

Victor smiles. "This music has been commissioned specially for the occasion."

"You thought of everything!"

"Your friends wanted to make this an extraordinary night for you, Grace. You are very loved."

"Am I?" she says, the fireflies seeming to flutter now in her stomach.

"But be glad I didn't commission the rooster," he jokes, scooting his chair back and away from the table.

He stands beside her, holding out his paw. "May I have this dance?"

"Victor, I don't know how to—"

"Just follow my lead."

She takes his paw, and he guides her into a slow dance.

She surrenders to his rhythm.

"Grace," he whispers, "You are the most beautiful doe in the world tonight."

"Why thank you... Mr. Miller," she replies coyly. "I *feel* like the most beautiful doe in the world tonight."

He twirls her under his arm, then catches her close—his breath brushing her ear.

"Time should stop just to watch you."

He sighs, as she clings to him—like the moment could easily slip away.

They continue dancing in silence, only the sounds of their breathing and the gentle symphony of birdsong between them.

"Oh, I wish we could stay this way forever," she whispers.

His grip tightens around her ever so slightly.

He slows their steps, his paw tracing along the curve of her back.

She tilts her face upward, excitement swelling.

She can feel his breath, warm against her fur.

She closes her eyes, lips reaching for his.

But just as she leans in—

He pulls away!

Sharp. Sudden.

Before she can process it—

He clasps his paws together, takes a deep breath, and whistles into the wilderness—one long note, followed by three sharp bursts.

Grace flinches, pressing her paw to her chest.

"Victor! You nearly scared me to death!"

"I'm sorry, my dear," he says, chuckling softly.

His eyes sweep the sky, then return to her.

For a moment, he studies her in silence... as if committing every detail to memory.

"I could stay here forever," he says, stepping in close.

"But we have a flight to catch."

Chapter Thirty-Five

Roses

Mikki bursts through the front door of The Ranch like a gust of wind. The chandelier shivers with the motion, its crystals rattling like applause.

"Best worst night ever," she quips, tossing her gold-sequined purse onto the foyer console.

She can still hear the gasps of the crowd—and the complaints from the crew about the cleanup.

But she can also hear the laughter.

A win and a loss, all at once.

She chuckles, thinking of Kathra and Gillian, covered in cake, being escorted off the property.

It's bittersweet. Like most things.

One by one, she kicks her shoes into the growing pile of forgotten footwear on the foyer floor.

She pauses for a moment, letting the silence settle.

She moves into the main room, her gold-sequined gown still sparkling. She reaches the pink chaise—her usual perch of mourning—and collapses onto it, arms spread wide.

A deep, satisfied sigh escapes her.

The evening replays in her mind like a movie: the twinkling lights, the sensational music, the raucous cheers when the final auction item closed.

Fifty thousand scraps raised for The Forest ReLeaf Fund... in just one night.

Her voice breaks the stillness. "Imagine what I could do over the course of a year!"

She grins to herself, energized by the thought.

Her paws sweep across her jewelry, unfastening each piece, tossing them onto the table beside her.

Her rings *clink* against the glass.

The bracelet lands with a soft *thud*.

The earrings follow with a faint metallic *tink*.

And then—

Her paw drifts to the glowstone pendant resting heavy at her heart.

She reaches for the clasp… but stops.

A memory rises.

Her final night with Victor.

Dinner. Dancing.

He was wearing a handsome tuxedo jacket.

And I was wearing red.

She clutches the glowstone tighter.

He'd fastened the necklace around her neck and whispered in a way that reached all the way through her:

"*Time should stop just to watch you.*"

She presses the stone flat to her chest.

That was the moment she knew.

She wasn't just another one—she was the *only* one.

She was his queen.

And still is.

Now and forever.

Her chest tightens.

The feeling that carried her home begins to falter.

She rises slowly, her paws brushing over the cluttered coffee table as she makes her way to the wet bar.

The crystal decanter glimmers in the low light, calling to her like an old friend.

Her fingers curl around the bottle.

It feels... familiar. Comforting. Dangerous.

She lifts it halfway.

But then—

The voice of a real friend cuts through the haze.

Kathra's words echo in her mind:

It's time for a fresh start. You owe it to Victor. You owe it to yourself.

Her grip loosens, and the bottle meets the counter with a quiet *clink*.

Her ears swivel as she looks around the room, truly seeing it for the first time in months—

Truly seeing the pile of crumpled tissues and empty bonbon

boxes surrounding the pink chaise.

Truly seeing the once-pristine white carpet, now dulled and speckled with dust and crumbs.

She catches her reflection in the bar's mirrored backsplash.

At The Gala, she felt like herself again.

But right now, she barely recognizes the mouse staring back at her.

Her paw drifts to the necklace still hanging around her neck.

She closes her eyes and whispers Kathra's words aloud.

"It's time for a fresh start. You owe it to Victor. You owe it to yourself."

The words swirl around her, filling the room like a spell.

Suddenly, a surge of determination courses through her body.

She can feel the electricity in her fingertips.

She grabs a bottle and marches to the sink, pouring its contents down the drain.

The sharp smell rises up, filling her nose with temptation... but she doesn't flinch.

One by one, every bottle in the bar meets the same fate, each drop vanishing like an old ghost.

She gathers the empty bottles into her arms and tosses them into the trash with a satisfying *crash*.

That felt good. Really good.

So, she doesn't stop there.

She moves to the pink chaise, scooping up tissues and empty boxes, stuffing them into a garbage bag—clearing away a summer of neglect.

Like magic, the white carpet begins to reappear, and with it, a sense of awakening.

Each sweep of her paw feels like sweeping away the cobwebs in her mind.

She straightens stacks of magazines, dusts the mantle, wipes the mirror.

It's cathartic. Almost euphoric.

With each task, her breath comes easier, her shoulders lift higher.

She hums softly to herself—Tanny and Macy still singing *Restless Heart* in her head.

She floats toward the foyer, finding partners for strewn shoes and sweeping long-dead funeral arrangements into the trash.

Then, she notices a fresh floral arrangement. Roses. Delivered. In a vase. Lush and bold.

She hadn't ordered these. She has a garden full of them. Who would want to give her something she already has?

She lifts the card nestled between the blooms, curiosity flickering.

The camera will love you.

"Oh, JackRabbitt," she mutters, equal parts charmed and exasperated.

He's been persistent about her taking the Shabó modeling job. At first, the idea seemed impossible, but now... it doesn't seem so far-fetched.

JackRabbitt is a good friend. She respects the Abbitt family. She's always loved their lip stains and powders. Practically half her dressing room is filled with their products.

She tosses the card back onto the console and returns to her cleaning tasks, filled with hope for the future.

Her eyes fall onto a box tucked behind the table.

It's marked with bold letters: *Newmouse Enterprises*.

She stops breathing for a moment.

Her heart pounds as she drags the box into the center of the foyer.

The tape gives way easily under her polished claws, and she opens it carefully.

Inside are mementos from Victor's office. The sight of them brings a mix of warmth and sorrow.

She pulls out the hourglass they had bought together on their trip to Quaylem, its white sand still gleaming.

Next, she finds the honorary feather awarded to Victor by The Black Knight Counsel. He took such care of it—its sleek black quill unmarred by time.

Then, the heavy mouse head statue. Victor outbid the museum for it all those years ago.

And oh! The portrait of Prince Obsidian, still as regal and imposing as she remembers. It was one of Victor's most prized possessions.

At the bottom of the box lies an envelope stamped with the Anony-mouse Courier logo. It's marked: *Urgent*.

She suddenly feels uneasy.

She picks it up and carefully opens it, sliding out its contents.

Photographs.

Of her.

And JackRabbitt.

In the rose garden.

Arms entwined?

Faces close?

Kissing?

"No," she whispers, shaking her head.

"This didn't happen!"

She and JackRabbitt had shared laughter and hugs—but not this. Not kisses!

She flips through the photos one by horrifying one, searching for something, anything, to explain them.

The timestamps.

Dated just days before Victor's death.

"Victor must have seen these!

Is that why he left town?

Who would do this?

Who would plan this?

Lee Ann Lovely thrives on scandal, but not like this.

Who?

Who would want to do this to Victor?

To me?"

Suddenly, a memory stirs—carrying a truth too loud to ignore.

A phone call.

"*Mikki, we need to talk*," he had said.

"*There's been a terrible accident*," he had said.

"*I'll help you by taking the reins at Newmouse Enterprises.*"

And then—

Kathra's voice at the spa.

"*Are you sure you can trust him?*"

"*Kathra, of course I trust him.*"

The photos blur at the edges as fury sharpens everything else.

JackRabbitt was the one who suggested a walk in the rose garden that day.

She looks again to the photos, but the tears cloud her vision.

Yet, they are not tears of sorrow.

They are tears of white-hot,

all-consuming,

100% pure, justified rage—

burning away any lingering fog of self-doubt or grief.

The photos slip from her grip, scattering across the floor.

Her eyes flash to the vase of roses sitting on the console.

The sight of them—those symbols of new beginnings and moving on—makes her stomach turn.

The camera will love you.

"What a cruel joke!"

She lifts the vase—then hurls it.

SMASH.

Water streaks down the wall.

Glass shatters like trust.

Roses scatter like lies.

Then, suddenly, the floorboard creaks.

She looks up—

Victoria.

She falls to the floor—

Chest heaving,

dripping with fury

and fire

and clarity.

There is only one way to make this right.

And I will make this right.

I owe it to Victor.

And I owe it to myself.

Chapter Thirty-Six

Resurrection

The pen hovers midair, balanced in a trembling paw.

One wrong flick, one hesitation, and the entire illusion collapses.

JackRabbitt steadies his grip.

Behind him, William leans against The Grandfather Clock—legs crossed, paws in pockets.

Supervising.

"Come on, JackRabbitt. Clock's ticking. It's Friday. I got two yachts and a reputation to uphold."

JackRabbitt sighs. "Noted."

William shakes his head, impatient. "No, no. If you're gonna fake it, at least fake it right. Victor had a heavy paw. Press into the page like you mean it."

JackRabbitt adjusts his angle without looking up, then adds the final stroke.

He drops the pen on the table with a sharp *clack*.

"Done." He leans back, grinning. "Victor's ghost just authorized a stock sale."

William pushes off The Grandfather Clock and strides over, admiring the forged signature like it belongs in a museum.

"Abbitt Enterprises," he remarks, already getting ahead of himself. "It has a nice ring to it."

JackRabbitt flicks his wavy fur bangs from his eyes.

"And the best part?"

He looks up to the portrait on the wall.

"Victor's dead. There's no one around to contest it."

He puts his paws behind his head, cool and calm, already picturing the board's reaction when the news hits their desks.

But then—

A faint *creak* echoes from the far end of the chamber.

The Grandfather Clock ticks once. Then again. Almost noon.

A shadow spills across the glass.

Long. Flickering.

JackRabbitt freezes.

William straightens.

The double doors explode open—

And in walks Bonnie, the executive assistant—leading Mikki and Victoria into the room.

"Wait here," Mikki tells them, marching forward, envelope clutched tight in her paw. "I want to handle *this* piece of business personally."

JackRabbitt slips the forged document under a folder.

"Mikki?" He stands. "What are you—"

Smack.

No hesitation.

She slaps him.

Hard and loud.

His ears whip sideways from the blow.

"*You* did this!" she shouts.

"Mikki," he shakes his head, trying to catch up.

"You're gonna have to be more specific."

She flings the envelope. It hits his chest and bursts open, spilling the photos at his feet.

The room stills, filled only by the *flutter* and *slap* of prints hitting the floor.

Even William goes quiet.

Then—

Mikki's voice slices through the silence.

"You manipulated me."

Slowly, her tail begins to curl—

"You let me grieve him."

It coils, tight as a fist—

"You stood beside me like a friend."

Then it *springs* loose.

"I trusted you, JackRabbitt!"

He doesn't move. He can't. He tries to force a smile, tries to charm his way out... but his voice is too smooth, too late.

"Mikki, I—"

"You made me doubt myself."

She's shaking now.

"You made me think *I* was the one who hurt him."

Her eyes are wet and knowing.

He tries again.

"I didn't—"

But the guilt is already written on his face.

And she sees it.

There's nothing he can say. So... he says nothing.

She lets out a dry laugh.

"What was the plan—huh? To replace him with yourself?

In every way?"

He winces.

"Answer me!"

William clears his throat—just a subtle sound.

JackRabbitt glances over his shoulder, already knowing what it means.

His brother is about to take the fall.

Mikki could hate William forever, and it wouldn't matter. After all, William *is* the one who took the photos...

But William *is not* the one who should pay.

JackRabbitt lifts a paw. A silent stop. Then he turns back to Mikki.

"You're right. I arranged the photos."

William swallows, then slowly steps forward to take his place beside his brother—because that's the only thing he can do right now.

"Why?" Mikki's voice is barely a whisper. "Why would you do this?"

"Because..." JackRabbitt's ears droop forward, too heavy to hold upright.

"Because I knew that if Victor saw those photos...

That if he thought for even one moment you would choose me over him—"

He looks down at his perfect plan scattered across the floor.

"Well. I knew that was the one thing he would *never* forgive you for."

His eyes lock onto hers—and this time, he doesn't look away.

"So, I made sure of it."

The life drains from Mikki's face. Her jaw drops open, but no sound comes out. She backs toward the door without realizing it.

"You're sick."

She turns to leave—

"You disgust me!"

And she almost walks away.

But the rage drags her back.

She lunges at him—

Slamming both fists into his chest.

"Did you kill him too?

Did you arrange *that* too?"

He stumbles back but doesn't resist.

She shoves him again—harder.

"Did you, JackRabbitt?

DID YOU KILL HIM?!"

His gut clenches—ulcer flaring, truth rising.

Time is running out.

And then—

The wooden door of the clock creaks open.

Bong.

"Yes! I made sure he was gone—"

Bong.

"But I didn't kill him—"

Bong.

"I swear to you, Mikki.

I DID NOT KILL—"

Bong.

Mikki gasps.

She staggers back.

Her paws fly to her mouth.

"Victor!"

JackRabbitt spins around.

"Victor?!"

William stares.

Eyes wide.

Dead still.

"Hickory... dickory... dock."

Bong.

The final chime echoes through the room—

And Victor steps out of The Grandfather Clock.

"That's right, old boy. The mouse came down the clock.

AND NOW YOUR TIME... IS UP!"

He straightens his suit jacket, then turns, extending a paw behind him.

Grace emerges from the clock passageway, her ivory fur radiant against the steel-blue of her suit.

Gone are the days of worn sundresses with faded bluebells.

Her transformation is breathtaking.

The cane she once relied on is gone—abandoned with their luggage on the rooftop.

Mikki stifles a sob, her paws trembling.

Victoria rushes to her mother, clinging to her side.

JackRabbitt stares straight ahead, eyes dry from not blinking.

The whole room blurs at the edges—and only Victor's face remains in focus.

Victor tilts his head, relishing his rival's stunned silence.

"Well now, this must come as quite a shock."

He chuckles darkly, then takes a step forward.

"Here's something that *won't* come as a shock—YOU'RE FIRED!"

JackRabbitt's lips part, but no words come out.

"Bonnie—alert the press."

Victor's mouse 'stache twitches.

"The news of my death has been greatly exaggerated."

He grins.

Bonnie doesn't hesitate. She rushes toward the exit, heels crunching over the scattered photos on the floor.

The sound draws Victor's attention.

"Oh!" he says with feigned surprise, gesturing to the evidence.

Then he lifts his voice toward the hall.

"...And be sure to call that Lee Ann Lovely.

Tell *her* all about how JackRabbitt staged these photos—so that he could steal my wife and my life!"

JackRabbitt watches helplessly as the scene unfolds. His body won't move. It's as if his feet are cemented to a floor that's dropping out beneath him.

Victor rises on his toes, closing the gap between them.

"That's right. I know all about your little plan.

You wanted to take over MY COMPANY—

The company that I built—

FROM THE GROUND UP!"

Victor drops back to his heels with a sharp *thud*.

"Ain't gonna happen!"

His fists tighten, his stance poised for a strike—but before he can make contact—

A gentle paw presses against his back.

Grace.

Rage shudders through his body, but her touch grounds him.

He runs his paw through the side of his hair.

"What the hell do *you* know about building anything? You were born with a silver spoon in your mouth. You needed *me* to be dead... just so *you* could pretend to matter."

He gives his jacket a sharp tug.

"Well, old boy. I'm alive.

Kathra revoked my death certificate this morning.

And therefore—

Any deals you made in my absence will be deemed...

Invalid.

Illegal.

A fraud.

Just like you."

He pivots, eyes landing on JackRabbitt's 3D model of the forest. His gaze flickers with amusement as he moves toward it.

"Oh, what's this?

A nice little presentation.

Outer Forest exports, is it?"

His lips curl into a smirk.

"That sounds like a fine idea. One that will make me a boatload of scraps."

At last, JackRabbitt finds his voice.

"Oh! *Now* you're interested in exports.

That's rich.

You shot down the plan when I pitched it to you a year ago."

A dry, humorless laugh escapes him as he shakes his head.

"Guess it wasn't the idea you hated.

Just the mouth it came from."

JackRabbitt turns, stalking toward the door.

But then—

Something inside him snaps.

He spins back around, eyes blazing.

"Let me tell you something, 'Victor Newmouse'—

That's what you're calling yourself these days, right?"

Grace flinches.

"I could hear the rattling of your tail on the day you slithered into this town."

His fists clench.

"And even after you used your scaly tactics to buy up the soap mining rights, I *tried* to approach you—

Like a professional.

Like my father wanted me to!"

JackRabbitt stands tall, ears rising high.

"I proposed a partnership.

I suggested we work *together* to export goods to The Outer Forest.

But you—

You scoundrel—

You scoffed in my face."

He inches closer, his shadow slowly swallowing Victor.

"So yeah—

I was gonna take over your company and make right what you STOLE.

I was gonna sell the soap rights to my family,

and sell the mushroom rights back to Morel Grounds,

and sell ALL the rights back—

to ALL the families!"

His ears flatten tight against his skull.

"And then I was going to banish your name into the dirt."

Victor interrupts, shouting,

"And I knew it then, didn't I?

Just like I know it now.

All you ever wanted was to take over my company.

I built this company!

From the ground up!"

JackRabbitt laughs.

"Yeah—

But that's where you're wrong, Victor."

He bends down deeper.

"I didn't just want to take over this company.

I wanted to *destroy* this company—

FROM THE TOP DOWN."

A dark, wicked smile plays on his lips.

"But you know what I realized?"

He licks his teeth, his sharp incisors gleaming behind a bitter snarl.

"I hate this company.

I hate this tree.

And I.

Hate.

You."

Slowly, he leans in.

Eye to eye.

Nose to nose.

"I wish you really were dead."

Then—

He pulls away, eyes locked with Victor's, and turns toward the exit.

But as he turns—

His attention turns—

To Grace.

There's something about her.

She's... unusual.

Distant.

Intriguing.

There's a quiet strength in her posture, a poise that holds him for a moment longer than it should.

Grace can feel the force of his focus on her.

Then, without thinking, he speaks.

"Hey. You look like a nice doe. Let me give you a piece of advice."

He gestures toward Victor.

"That mouse over there?

He's a snake.

Oh, he loves to pretend that he's a crow.

But make no mistake...

He's a snake.

And he will swallow you whole."

He leans in, voice low and cutting.

"*Don't* feed yourself to him."

Victor's face twists with rage.

"GET THE HELL OUT OF HERE!!!" he roars, wetness flying from his lips.

JackRabbitt smirks.

"With pleasure."

And with deliberate slowness, he presses a paw to his cheek, looks to Mikki, then walks out the door.

Grace stands motionless, her heart pounding in her chest.

Something in JackRabbitt's words rings true.

Not just his final words, but *all* of them.

And for the first time, Grace realizes—

She doesn't really know Victor at all.

Still standing where JackRabbitt left him, William gives a lazy stretch.

"Well, Victor, that was quite a twist.

But, if that's the final cliffhanger..."

He takes a quick peek inside the clock.

"I think I'll be going now."

He makes his way toward the door as if he has all the time in the world.

Victor jabs a finger upward and shouts—

"You want a cliffhanger? I'll give you a cliffhanger."

He swipes a photo from the floor and flicks it, hitting William in the back.

"Whose pawprints are all over these photos?"

Victor rocks back on his heels, slipping his paws into his pockets.

"What? Were you hiding in the bushes, Billy Boing?!"

William pauses and turns around, the faintest flicker of amusement passing over his face at the nickname:

Billy Boing.

He smirks.

"Victor, I've gotta give you credit—

That treequila you keep in your private liquor stash?"

Mwah!

He kisses his fingers.

"You do have great taste."

William grins, then slowly strides toward the door.

But then—

A face he doesn't recognize—

One with a presence impossible to ignore.

Waist-length, wavy dark brown hair,

Cascading over a curvy shape.

Almond eyes that burn with fury.

She is striking.

Sensual.

And—

Before he can process another thought—

She *spits* right in his face.

Warm. Wet. Thick.

"Rodent!" she hisses, her voice rich with disgust.

He jerks back, blinking hard as his brain scrambles to catch up.

He looks at her again, slower this time.

Up. And down.

Something electric buzzing behind his eyes.

And then, he sees it.

The watch.

Brass, scuffed, delicate—and chained to her wrist.

Undeniably the same one he picked up at The Club that night.

A jolt stops him cold.

Impossible.

He glances around the room, as if to double-check the cast list.

Victor's daughter?!

He wipes his cheek, glancing at his now-slick paw with

revulsion.

The corners of his mouth twitch.

He stumbles toward the drapery, grabs a pawful of curtain, and dramatically drags it across his face.

He turns around—

Slow. Seething.

Stalking toward her with a fire of his own.

"Rodent?"

He laughs.

"That's your species, not mine."

Then—it hits her.

The voice.

Low. Sharp. Edged with frustration.

She's heard it before.

The balcony. The courtyard. The restless murmur below.

It was him.

Heat rushes through her body, sudden and sizzling—a reaction too volatile to control. But whether it's fury, shock, or something else, she can't untangle it fast enough.

THUMP.

The deliberate stomp of his foot.

Hard enough to rattle her.

Hard enough to hold her.

She trembles.

He sees it...

And it delights him.

His smirk deepens.

"At least I know what I am.

Princess."

He gives her a wink.

Then he turns his back and swaggers out the door, slamming it hard behind him.

Victoria exhales, chest rising and falling as she stares at the door, still vibrating on its hinges.

It was him.

Victor watches his daughter's expression shift, seeing the embers of something unspoken.

His eyes darken.

Those damn rabbits.

Victoria's eyes drop to the watch on her wrist—and suddenly, it's not William she's thinking about anymore.

"Daddy!" her voice rings out as she launches herself into her father's arms.

Mikki follows close behind, barely able to contain the sob in her throat.

"Daddy, I can't believe it. Am I dreaming?" She clings to him, trembling. "Oh, I want to hold on and never let go!"

Victor gathers her close, pressing his muzzle against her hair. "Oh, my baby. My sweet Victoria. I will never let you go again."

Mikki's paws are on him next, gripping his shoulders, her wide eyes darting over his face, as if trying to match him to the ghost she's been carrying.

"Victor, where have you been? What happened?"

She pulls away briefly, then throws herself into his arms again.

"Oh, there are just so many questions!"

Victor's voice is steady and reassuring.

"And I will answer them all—in due time."

His eyes soften.

"But right now, just let me look at you."

He takes a step back, studying them both—Victoria, radiant despite the weight she's carried, and Mikki, her beauty dimmed only by the exhaustion in her eyes.

Then, unable to resist, he pulls them both close again.

"Mikki," he mutters.

"And my daughter."

He draws in a breath.

"And my son!"

His voice lifts with sudden urgency.

"Mickolas. Where is Mickolas?"

"He's at school—oh my goodness, Daddy, he needs to know!" Victoria exclaims, clutching his arms. "He needs to know that you're alive!"

Victor nods, his grip tightening. "Get word to him. Fast!"

"Yes, yes! I can't wait another second to tell him. I'll—I'll be back!" She pauses. "Just don't go anywhere."

"I swear to you—

I will never go anywhere again."

He holds her face in his paws, finding more forgiveness in her eyes than he deserves.

He abandoned her.

Just like *they* abandoned him.

She waited for him.

Just like he once waited for *them.*

For now—

She still looks at him like he never left.

But *only* for now.

Victoria dashes out, her energy electric, her feet barely touching the ground.

And the moment she's gone, Mikki turns fully to Victor.

She doesn't just embrace him—

She melts *into* him—

Burying her face against his chest.

Like her soul has finally found a place to rest.

She pulls away just as quickly, her paws skimming over his back, his arms, his face.

And then—

She gasps.

"Your ear!"

Her paw trembles as it hovers over his scar.

"What have they done to you?!"

Victor doesn't move.

Doesn't respond.

But somewhere behind them—

Grace begins to fade.

Like a bluebell lost in a garden of roses.

Mikki's paws cup his face now, her voice urgent, desperate.

"Victor, the photos—they're not true. I don't know how, but JackRabbitt must have set it up to look like something was happening between us.

I swear—I've always only ever wanted you.

Only *you*!"

She shakes her head, tears shimmering at the edges of her lashes.

"Oh, Victor, the one thing that never changed was how much I love you."

Victor meets her eyes.

And in them—he sees it.

The truth.

This was *their* story all along.

On pause.

Waiting for the writer to reveal it.

But the show is not over.

Bonnie bursts through the door, her voice slicing through the weight of the moment.

"Mr. Newmouse, the press has arrived."

Victor nods.

And the truth tucks itself back behind his eyes.

"I'll be back."

Then he pivots—

toward Grace.

His voice softens as he nears her, careful not to leave her in the dark.

"Just give me a few minutes," he says, his voice quieter now, meant just for her.

He gives her paw a gentle squeeze.

Light. Steady.

And then—he's gone.

Rushing out the door.

Leaving Mikki and Grace behind in the silence of the Sky Chamber.

Mikki wipes away the remnants of her tears and turns toward Grace with a bright, almost dizzying energy.

"I simply can't believe it. Victor's alive!"

Her thoughts rush forward like a flood.

"Oh, I have laid awake so many nights, wishing this could be true!"

She taps her foot lightly, too giddy to stand still.

"And it *is* true, isn't it? It's unbelievable."

She paces as she speaks, her heels scuffing softly across the polished floor.

"I'm just so grateful for this chance to reunite my family."

She presses a paw to her forehead, sweeping her hair back.

"Victor and I have been through everything. Dating and marriage. Two children. Building The Ranch together."

She gestures wildly, like her body is racing to keep up with her mind.

"Then, the divorce—but who cares about all that?!

He was dead, and now he's resurrected!

Oh, it's a miracle. An absolute miracle!"

Her laughter bursts loud, then hiccups into silence.

Grace swallows hard.

Mikki's voice, smooth as satin, spills effortlessly into the space between them.

She smells faintly of perfume and powder.

Her words—her unfiltered joy—paint a picture that Grace had never fully seen before.

Then it hits her, gently but completely:

She is standing inside Victor's kingdom—

But she is not his queen.

That role was filled long before she ever met him.

Mikki's perfume grows stronger as she moves—roses trailing behind every step.

"We started out as complete opposites, I tell you."

She giggles as the words tumble out, like she's told this story a hundred times.

"He was so romantic."

She rubs her temples, muttering half-formed thoughts between the words.

"And of course, I had no idea he was a billionaire."

Her breath catches mid-word, like she's speaking faster than she can think.

"And I didn't care because, well...

You know—

Love is blind."

Grace stiffens.

She presses a paw to the hidden heartbeat in her belly.

Yes.

It was.

NEXT TIME ON THE FAUNA AND THE FLORA...

FADE IN: A beautiful forest clearing.

Wedding music plays.

OFFICIANT

"You may now kiss the bride!"

CUT TO: A paw gripping an official document.

VICTOR

"I have a court order here granting me full custody of Victor Junior!"

CUT TO: Claws digging into the arms of a chair.

JACKRABBITT

"You want this chair?!"

SMASH CUT: Shattering glass.

JACKRABBITT

"Have a seat."

FADE TO BLACK.

JOIN US AGAIN FOR THE FAUNA AND THE FLORA...

STARRING...
(In Order of Appearance)

Victor Newmouse
COSMO RAINWRIGHT

Grace Atoms
MIRA GRAINSNAP

Colonel Austin Douglas
ROOK GOLDENBRANCH

Biff Milson
RUSSELL TREETUFT

JackRabbitt Abbitt
DASH HOPPERFIELD

Kathra Chansoar
SORREL SILVERWING

William "Billy Boing" Abbitt
JOEL PETEMOSS

Mikkole "Mikki" Reid Fester Manecroft Newmouse
MARIGOLD FIELDS

Victoria Newmouse
VIXEN NIBBLEWICK

Ashlyn Abbitt
LUX WILDERMERE

Jon Abbitt
OREN SPINWICK

Macy Abbitt
DAISY RABBINDALE

Gillian Abbitt
QUINN HOLLOWAY

Lee Ann Lovely
ALUNA NIGHTPLUME

Zeena Aromalotti
PETRA TANGLEWEAVE

Tanny Aromalotti
SKYLER CLOUDSTEP

Brack Squirrelton
BRAMLEY BLACKBARK

Laura Venmore
BRYNDA NUTFLICK

A PRODUCTION OF...

Newmouse Media

This is a work of fiction. Any resemblance to actual animals, persons, or events—real or televised—is purely coincidental.

Thank you for spending time with *The Fauna and the Flora*.

If this story moved you, please consider these simple ways to help support the book. What grows next depends on you.

Leave a Review on Amazon
Amazon welcomes reviews from all readers. Your words can help more travelers find the forest.

Visit RestlessForest.com
Join my email list to receive the latest Chenoa City news.

Spread the Word
You are the wind that carries this story forward.

Read it again
The Fauna and the Flora is a story that truly blooms on second read, when you know... what you know now.

But wait... The story isn't over.

If you loved *The Fauna and the Flora*, there's so much more waiting for you:

✦ Full audiobook, narrated by the author
✦ Original song *Restless Heart*, sung by the author
✦ Bonus e-book of gossip, fashion, and Book 2 spoilers, featuring:
— Lee Ann Lovely's post-Gala gossip column
— An apology letter from Zeena Aromalotti about the cake "mishap"
— The Meadow Security report with official statements from Kathra and Gillian
— A best-and worst-dressed list
— A sneak preview of Book 2's big event
— And more!
✦ Behind-the-scenes podcast with in-depth story and character discussion
✦ Signed paperback editions with an exclusive bookmark

All available now at RestlessForest.com

Author's Note

It's June of 1993. I'm 13 years old, home from school on summer break. The TV is on, and I flip to my very first soap.

I'm hooked.

The drama, the romance, the endless story—it pulls me in and never lets go.

Now, more than thirty years later, I've poured everything I know about classic soap storytelling into this fully independent work—written, narrated, and produced entirely with my own paws. I hope you feel the magic of soaps in the pages of this book, because life's drama belongs... in fiction.

Until next time,

Ali Cattail

Restless Heart

Lost in the plot of a storyline.
Bold and beautiful souls align.

As the world turns slow.
Passions we used to know.

Another world where dreams still shine.
Waiting for you right on time.

All the days of our lives.
One life to live, guiding light.

Oh, we can all be bright,
In the daytime or the night.
Watchin' them love and fight.

Through generations all the same.
Through the pleasure and pain.
A young and restless heart remains.

Discussion Questions

Q1: Which character was most compelling? Least? Why?

Q2: Victor and JackRabbitt enter as contrasts. How did your view of them evolve over time?

Q3: Grace grows reluctantly into a hero, while JackRabbitt insists on seeing himself as one at any cost. How do their contrasting journeys drive the story?

Q4: Macy experiences humiliation and triumph. How does her arc speak to identity, vulnerability, belonging, or courage?

Q5: Roses are tied to Mikki, while Grace is linked to bluebells. How do these symbols reflect their roles in the story?

Q6: How do family dynamics fuel the novel's conflicts over legacy, power, and control?

Q7: *The Fauna and the Flora* contains references to classic literature and nursery rhymes. How many did you notice, and what effect did they have?

Q8: What do you think happens after the ending?

Q9: If you could rewrite the ending, what would you change?

Q10: Looking ahead, what do you predict for Book Two? Which storylines feel most urgent to you?

Q11: How is F&F similar to the soap operas you know—and how is it different?

Q12: The novel blends soap-opera drama with classic literature and magical realism. How did this mix affect your experience?

Share answers in your book club, blog, video, Amazon review, or join my discussion on YouTube.

@RestlessForestBooks | #RestlessForest

The Fauna and the Flora

Book 1: Return To Chenoa City

Written by Ali Cattail.

Visual Design and Vocal Performance by Ali Cattail.

Produced and Published by Ali Cattail.

SCAN TO VISIT
RestlessForest.com